Family Stories for
Every Generation

Family Stories for Every Generation

Sylvia Rothchild

WAYNE STATE UNIVERSITY PRESS

DETROIT 1989

Copyright © 1989 by Wayne State University Press,
Detroit, Michigan 48202. All rights are reserved.
No part of this book may be reproduced without formal permission.
93   92   91   90   89   5   4   3   2   1

Library of Congress Cataloging-in-Publication Data

Rothchild, Sylvia, 1923-
   Family stories for every generation / Sylvia Rothchild.
      p. cm.
   ISBN 0-8143-2240-9
   1. Jews—United States—Fiction.   2. Family—United States—
Fiction.   I. Title.
PS3568.0859F36   1989   89-5561
813'.54—dc19   CIP

Remembering Elliot E. Cohen
who encouraged me in the beginning
and grateful to Seymour Rothchild
who encourages me still

A man strikes many coins from one die
and they are all alike. God strikes
every person from the die of the first
man, yet not one resembles the other.

The Rabbis

"You say less than human, more than human.
Tell me please, what is human?" . . .
He liked to think "human" meant accountable
in spite of many weaknesses.

From "The Victim" by
Saul Bellow

Contents

The Mothers

In the morning Kaminsky's candy store in East Flatbush was a sleepy place. Samuel Kaminsky silently handed his customers their newspapers through a small opening in his glass window without even a good-morning or a thank-you for the change.

The women who came down with hoover aprons over their nightgowns and curlers in their hair stepped cautiously on the freshly washed linoleum and left the price of a package of cigarettes on the counter quickly. Their slippers clattered on the pavement as they hurried back to their apartments before they were seen with pale, unwashed faces and eyes that were blank without mascara and eyebrow pencil.

The torpor, however, dispersed itself like a morning mist when the day wore on. By noon the street was filled with mothers pushing baby carriages and women staggering under the weight of bags of groceries and fruit. Mr. Kaminsky quickly wrapped piles of egg salad and salmon salad sandwiches in waxed paper for the luncheon trade and scowled at the children who bothered him for a penny lollypop.

At two o'clock, when I wanted to stop at the store for a sandwich and a milk shake before taking the subway uptown, it was necessary to squeeze past a row of parked carriages before I could open the heavy plate-glass door. The store was crowded and, like the street outside, seething with activity. Glasses and spoons were thrown about noisily and everyone shouted to be heard above the din of the jukebox. The atmosphere was tense and a calamity always seemed imminent. It might be a tray of dishes that would fall, a child to be spanked for spilling his ice-cream cone, or an argument about a look, a tone of voice, an accidental push.

One afternoon I climbed up on a revolving stool in front of the counter, which was covered with bright-blue plastic material, and looked around for Mr. Kaminsky. He was behind the cash register framed in chromium and fluorescent light, but scowling as usual. The openness of his ill humor alone made it bearable. It was no secret that Kaminsky had no love for the women and children who spent so much time in his store and they in turn had only jibes for him. But they came and he fed them as he had been doing for twenty years.

"What's yours?" he asked without looking at me.

I watched the customers reflected in the mirror that ran the length of the store, while he poured milk into the mixer. They were all women; some had little children with them. Every one of them was fat. They ate their sundaes and frappes carefully and washed them down with seltzer water. The deliberate way they savored each spoonful made me feel that whipped cream and nuts were among the pleasures of life that were not to be denied. If you die of diabetes, the devil with it!

They spoke in loud, belligerent voices that I couldn't help overhearing. It was as if they were too obsessed with their own anger to care that they were sharing their grievances with everyone around them. Someone directly behind me whom I couldn't see said, "I came home at four o'clock in the morning."

"What did Harry say?" her friend asked.

"Since when do I care what Harry says? It's none of his business when I come home."

"Oh, go on; how much did you lose?"

"Fifteen dollars less to give to the doctor. So what of it?"

I turned to see who was talking and found that she was fat like everyone else and looked as if she had been molded of foam rubber, with no skeleton to support it inside. Her face was made up as carefully as a mask. Pancake makeup filled the pores in her skin; the lashes were darkened with mascara, and her mouth was rouged in a shape that bore no resemblance to the tight, narrow lips underneath. Her hair had been set at the beauty parlor recently and she wore a beautiful spring coat of soft, yellow, velvety material.

Her friend was not so striking. She was plump too, but her face was lumpy and her features not well defined. Glasses gave her a softer look than the woman sitting opposite her and, though her hair was dyed the color of mahogany, she wore very little makeup. Her black loose-fitting coat worn over a purple-print dress was obviously not so expensive as her friend's.

"Why do you aggravate yourself?" I heard her say. "For what?"

Two booths behind them, a little boy, perhaps three years old, wearing long wool trousers and a printed bow tie, slid from the bench to the floor. His mother, whom I could see in the mirror that covered one wall of the store, screamed, "Look at your suit! Are you crazy? Get off the floor, stupid." She pulled him from under the table and tried to force him to sit up while he kicked and howled.

"Take me home, I'm all done," he wailed.

"Are you going to sit still for a minute or do I have to give it to you? For God's sake sit still a minute, do you hear, or I'll give it to you."

He half sat and half stood, as angry and stubborn as his mother. His back was arched stiffly so that his feet could touch the floor. "Then buy me a toy; I wanna toy," he whined.

"Shut up or I'll give you a toy in the head! I'm warning you Stevie, I'll murder you." Then his mother continued talking to someone in the booth with them.

The jukebox kept playing the same song over and over again. It was a familiar Jewish dance that I had heard countless times at family weddings, but when it came out of the big machine it was called "The South American Samba." I wondered how such a mistake could be made.

Mr. Kaminsky tossed a sandwich in my direction and reached for the milk shake when the talk in the store was silenced by the loud screech of brakes and a terrifying scream outside. I jumped off the stool and ran out with a few others to see what had happened.

There was a laundry truck with its front wheels up on the curb. In the street a little boy was crying while he dusted off his cowboy suit. His mother crouched beside him and kept him from chasing his wide-brimmed hat, which rolled over and over in the dirt near the curb on the other side of the street. The sidewalk was strewn with oranges and potatoes that the woman had dropped when she ran to the boy, and some people were already kicking them as they walked by. Others picked them up, only to put them down on the pavement again when they found that the bag was torn and there was no place to put them.

I stood with a few other people watching the woman, the boy and the driver of the truck. The driver opened the door slowly, his face bone-white and his hands shaking. He stood still, biting his lips and rubbing his hands together, not yet sure what had happened to him. When he saw that the woman and the boy were all right he leaned up against the front of the store and fumbled in his pockets for cigarettes.

"I saw it." said the man from the delicatessen next to Kaminsky's. "It wasn't your fault."

The driver shook his head and said, "Damn kids!"

The woman with the boy was short and slight. When she picked her son up, his feet dangled below her knees. She carried him to the sidewalk and put him down gently, as though he were a toddler. Then she bent down until her face reached his and without any warning slapped his face. "Here," she cried, "for running in the street!" She slapped him again and again and her fingers left red stripes across his cheeks. The boy stood with his legs wide apart and his mouth wide open, too stunned to cry.

"All right, that's enough," an old lady watching her said. "Enough, he won't do it any more." She grabbed her arms from behind to stop her, while she tried to reach the boy.

"It's none of your business," the mother shouted. "What's it to you? I never hit him before in his life. Yeah, he's five years old and I never hit him. So what does he do? He runs in front of a truck."

The delicatessen man lifted the little boy, who was now crying as hard as he could. He carried him into the candy store and sat him on a bench. Mr. Kaminsky put a dish of ice cream in front of him but he kept on screaming.

The older woman half led, half pushed the mother into a booth and brought her some coffee. But the more she tried to quiet her, the louder she shouted.

"I nursed that boy for a year and a half, while the other women were playing cards. I never hit him. He stood on my head, he pulled pieces from me and I didn't lift my hand. Do you know," she asked, "how much food I stuffed into this child? For what, so he should run under a truck like a lunatic?" She turned to the boy and seemed ready to slap him again.

Mr. Kaminsky stood in front of her booth, a disgusted look on his face. "Ssh," he said, "you're a lunatic yourself. Stop screaming. You'll drive everyone out of the store. What do you want from him? He's a child."

She looked up at him defiantly. "Shut up. What does a man know? Do you think he grew out of my head? What do you know? Did you ever carry a kicking child in you? Did you ever feed one?"

"Ssh, ssh," he pleaded.

"Don't shush me," she shouted. "I lost two children already. I know what I'm talking. You think it's nothing, five years can get smashed under a truck!"

The woman in the yellow coat smoked a cigarette and rolled the edge of a paper napkin nervously between her thumb and forefinger. She didn't look at the woman and boy.

Her friend, however, seemed almost sorry that she hadn't run out to see what had happened. She asked nobody in particular, "What happened? What's the matter with her?"

"Crazy," said Mr. Kaminsky, "just crazy. What's the matter, you never saw a lunatic before? Her one and only runs out in the street; and he could have gotten killed. So she wallops him good and screams and hollers as if somebody did something to her. Talk to a woman like that! You'll fall into her big mouth and never come out again."

The old lady beside the mother shook a threatening hand at Kaminsky and said, "Shah."

Kaminsky took her arm and asked, "Who is she? You know her?"

"How should I know who she is?" the old lady answered. "It's my business who she is?"

The little boy who had been screaming for a toy stood quietly in front of the crying youngster. He stood on tiptoe so that he could see over the table and looked the sobbing boy right in the face. "Why he's crying?" he asked the old lady.

"Come back here, Stevie!" his mother called when she heard his voice. "Come back here and mind your business, Stevie! Don't make me call you again. Stevie!"

Stevie went toward the door and his mother jumped up from the bench to chase him as he ran out when it was opened by a woman and a little girl coming in. She pulled him back and he collapsed and screamed as she dragged him. She paid Mr. Kaminsky while the boy thrashed in her arms like a fish and she called to her friend, "Don't forget to call me tonight."

"Will I give it to you Stevie," she muttered. "Just let me get you home. Can't I sit a minute? You can't let me live, can you?"

When I looked at the other mother and boy again, she was wiping her face with her handkerchief and sipping coffee. The older woman beside her stood up to leave and said, "Calm yourself now, and don't hit him like that any more. It's not good to hit a child like that. It's always better to go with good than with bad, remember."

The mother didn't answer her. The boy, watching his mother drink her coffee, began to eat his ice cream, which looked like creamed soup. Kaminsky lifted his eyes to the ceiling, while he watched the boy drip it all over himself, but his mother didn't say a word.

When the boy was finished she walked over to the counter. She took some money from her purse and put it in the glass dish near the cash register.

"Never mind," said Kaminsky.

"What do you mean, never mind? I pay for what I eat."

He took the money and waited until she and the boy were out of the store before he took mine.

"God protect us from women," he said petulantly. You can't get along with them and you can't get along without them."

The two women stood behind me. "So what have you got against women?" the eyeglassed one asked. "Some living you'd make without women, Kaminsky."

The one in the yellow coat prodded her, "Come on, let's go. We don't have all day."

But Kaminsky didn't hurry and I stood waiting for my change. "You know what should have happened to her?" he said. "The boy should have been hit. Yes sir, that's what she needed. A few bruises, a broken arm, a little something for a remembrance and she'd know when she's well off. Yeah," he said. "You don't believe me, but I'm telling you that would fix her. She'd be thanking God, not yelling like an idiot." He wiped his hands on his apron and shook his head despairingly, "A crazy woman."

I put my change away and the heavy door shut quietly behind me. Outside the sun still shone brightly on the carriages and strollers, and the women leading little children by the hand.

The Golden Years

If anyone had told Simon Halpern a year ago that he would soon spend every day sitting on a park bench instead of in front of a sewing machine, he would surely have laughed. "What will I do all day?" he asked when his wife suggested that he retire. "Do you want to make a rag out of me? What kind of person can sit with empty hands all day?"

"You don't earn any more than you would get if you stayed at home," she reminded him.

"So I don't earn as much as I used to, would you like me to go out and steal a little more?"

"We won't talk about it any more," his wife answered; "be well, and work as hard as you like."

Three days before his seventieth birthday, however, he came home from work early with the fingers of his right hand stiff and immovable. He insisted that it would be all right in a few days. But his hand did not improve. No one believed it would and after a few weeks, though he still assured everyone that he would be back at work soon, he too doubted that it would be possible.

Simon did not change his routine any more than was necessary. His wife knew that he could not. He awoke at five-thirty just as he had done for fifty years. Each morning he was surprised anew

Reprinted from *Commentary*, March 1952, by permission; all rights reserved.

to remember that he had no place to go, that the keys to the shop were returned to the boss, that the subway would grind out of the station without him. It was Sunday every day of the week but he refused to think about it. He washed and shaved carefully, brushed his thin iron-gray hair with the wispy, ivory-backed brush his wife had given him before his marriage. Then he took his false teeth from the glass where they were soaking all night, and put them in his mouth deliberately. They had never fit properly and his gums were always sore where they rubbed against them but he wore them stubbornly even though no one but his family would see him.

He took his prayer shawl and philacteries from their velvet cases, wrapped his prayer shawl around his shoulders, and wound his philacteries carefully around his left arm and again on his brow. Then he said the morning prayer. He loved the morning meeting with his God better than any other. Praying while the streets were empty and the houses still with sleep made him feel as though he alone in the world had the Lord's attention.

Though he relished the privacy of the morning, he didn't mind sharing it with his two-year-old grandson. Many mornings the little boy would climb out of his crib without waking his mother and run into the kitchen to see his grandfather. Simon would take a fresh diaper off the line that was strung across the bathroom and struggle with his stiff fingers until he changed the boy's pajamas. Then he would reach into the oven where his wife stored the cookies she baked each Friday and give the child one for each hand. He would help him up into a kitchen chair before he began his prayer, turning frequently to look at the soft round face still puffed with sleep. The boy couldn't sit still for long. He would jump down and pull his grandfather's trousers and the fringes of his shawl. Sometimes Simon prayed with the boy perched on his shoulder like a monkey. If the child moved or tried to turn the pages of the prayer book, Simon made a humming noise with his lips closed and didn't interrupt the prayer.

As soon as the boy had been dressed and given his breakfast, Simon would wheel him down to the park in his stroller. They didn't stop at the shelter where all the men gathered, but stayed in the sun where there were mothers and other little children. When the weather was warm, he would lie down on the grass and let the boy jump all over him. He would snatch him up in the middle of their play and kiss the nape of his neck, bite into his buttocks and pretend to devour him.

On rainy days they sat together at the bedroom window, watching the cars, or they squatted on the linoleum in the living room to build houses of blocks and dominoes. His daughter Evelyn came into the room every few minutes to say, "Watch yourself, Pa. You'll hurt your hand, Pa." Or she would call from the kitchen, "Why don't you leave him alone for a minute, Pa. Don't kiss him so much!" Simon often thought that if not for the baby the first months at home would have been unbearable. He kept hoping that he could make the little boy his; that with sheer love alone he could woo him to his way of life.

But they didn't let him have the boy long enough. Once he overheard his daughter telling a friend on the phone: "If we can only get Allan away from Pa. It drives me crazy. He gave the baby a glass of coffee this morning. Imagine! If he turns over in his crib, Pa is there to see what's the matter. It makes me so nervous." Three months later his son-in-law came home from Japan and resumed his civilian life and they went to California to live.

Simon was miserable, though people kept congratulating him on having his apartment to himself, on no longer having his sleep and meals disturbed. He and his wife found themselves in an endless, frightening silence. She suffered from arthritis and was in bed a good part of the day. She would lie down as soon as her work was done. He sat in the chair beside her bed reading the Yiddish newspapers he bought every day. Sometimes the whole afternoon would pass while she lay dozing in the bed and he sat at the window, listening to the bathroom faucet drip, the radiators knocking, and the footsteps of the people who lived above them.

One afternoon he offered to cook the supper, just to relieve the monotony of the day. He bought what was necessary at the corner grocery store and made a *mamelige,* a pudding of yellow corn meal, which they had not eaten since Evelyn came to stay with them. "How can you eat that? It's as heavy as lead," she would complain. He thought of her as he poured the melted butter over it and heaped little mounds of farmer's cheese and sour cream next to it. Then he broiled a herring on top of the stove, ignoring, as his wife could not do, the grease that splattered all over the stove and wall. "Gussie," he called, "it's ready." He blessed the bread and the two began to eat. They struggled with the portions he set for them. The *mamelige* was lumpy and the herring burned the blisters in his mouth. After four or five bites, he pushed the dish aside and his wife watching him did the same.

"It's good, Simon, it's very good, but I'm just not hungry. One doesn't get an appetite lying in bed."

"No," he said, "it's not your fault. It isn't good; it isn't good at all. Tell me why is it that in America nothing has any taste?"

"Why pick on America?" she asked. "Things have a taste here. It's we who have no taste. Who says food has to taste good to people who have no teeth, no hands, no feet? Don't pick on America. America has nothing to do with it."

Simon went back to the park the next day. He felt foolish going by himself just to sit but he found forty or fifty men there already. They sat on the benches under the shelter near the mall where the band played in the summertime. Some read newspapers; some played checkers or cards; some talked excitedly in little groups and others sat with blank pallid faces neither looking nor seeing. He found an empty bench and sat down to read his paper. When he was finished he got up and walked slowly around the walks with his hands locked behind his back, stooping forward as though he were looking for something on the ground. It was hard to make the morning pass just walking, and he finally returned to the shelter to find someone to talk to.

A plump, bearded man sat beside him and smiled. "You're a newcomer here, aren't you?" he asked Simon. "What are you on?"

"What do you mean 'on'?" Simon asked.

"On," said the man. "On old age, on pension, I mean where do you get money so you can sit in the park?"

Simon was embarrassed. It was not proper to ask a working-man what he earned; that was his own business. Why should a total stranger ask him such a question?

"Don't be ashamed," his bearded friend went on. "We're all

the same here. Take me for instance. I used to have a little grocery store, but now I'm on assistance for the blind. I can't complain; they're very nice to me."

But Simon couldn't bring himself to answer him. Instead he asked where the nearest telephone was and went home.

He was about to cross the wide avenue that ran along the park when a car pulled up in front of him. "Simon," his brother called, "what are you doing here in the middle of the day? Jump in. How are you feeling?"

Unwillingly, Simon settled himself in the car beside his brother. "I heard that you finally got smart and joined the loafers," he said with the cigar still in his mouth. "Shall I take you home?"

"Yes," said Simon, "I'm going home." They were in front of the house in two minutes.

"I can't stop now, but tell me, Simon, how are you doing? Do you need some money?"

"I'm doing fine. Everything I have is God's and mine. I don't owe anything and I don't want to owe. I'm satisfied."

"That's also doing? I probably give more away a week than you earn."

Simon fumbled with the door handle but could not open it. "If you had listened to me you wouldn't be a failure."

"You think every workingman is a failure. But there are lots of them in America and I'm there with the others. If I'm satisfied with my life, what do you want from me?"

His brother helped him open the door. "Give my regards to Gussie," he said.

"Who took you home?" his wife asked when he came in.

"Hymie," he said.

"In a new car?" she asked.

"I don't know. All cars look the same."

"It's a new car, Sarah told me. He bought her a new squirrel coat too."

"With all the fat on her she needs a fur coat to keep her warm?"

"It's not what you need but what you want," his wife said quietly.

"I'll tell you what Hymie wants. A little sense and understanding; a little appreciation of what is right and wrong; a few feelings that can't be bought for money. I wouldn't trade one week of my life for all of his, with his comforts."

"No one is asking you to," his wife said with a finality he could not break.

Simon avoided the bearded man the next day and sat down next to a drawn, sick-looking man wearing an old torn overcoat that was tied together with a safety pin. He greeted him with a nod but when Simon offered him part of his paper he did not answer. Simon decided that he must be deaf and sat down on a bench opposite him to read. He was almost finished when the bearded man came over and greeted him like an old friend. "Come with me," he said, "I want you to hear something. It's better than the theater when this bunch get together. It's something to hear." Simon folded his paper and stuffed it into his pocket and followed him along the walk until they stopped in front of two men who were shouting at each other. One was short and heavy with a thick shock of white hair. He waved his hands wildly as he spoke to a tall, thin man wearing a new hat and coat, well-creased trousers, and polished shoes.

"Tell me one thing." the short man shouted. "Tell me, do you believe Abraham was the father of his people, tell me do you believe it?"

"All right, so I believe it," the man answered.

"Then agree that today Abraham would be thrown into jail in no time. For what was he? He was the first troublemaker; he was the first revolutionary. He didn't listen to his father; he smashed the idols; he couldn't be satisfied with what he had. Today, you'd holler, Communist. What I'm saying is that Jews aren't supposed to be satisfied. They're supposed to complain. They're supposed to make the world better."

"With your ideas you'll make the world better? I could live without it being so much better," he said, putting his hands into his coat pockets.

A short bald man who was on the outside of the circle, listening, pushed himself forward and in a hoarse, raucous voice called out, "The world will never change and you Communists won't make it any better. Cain killed Abel and since then there's always been fighting and struggling. I'm eighty years old and I've seen something in my time."

The tall man answered first, "You're calling me a Communist? Why don't you listen to what goes on and see who the Communist is here?"

The short man spat on the grass. "What a repulsive bunch you are. You're dead already and you don't know it. Everyone's dead in America. Even my own sons. In my house the father is the revolutionary and the sons are the reactionaries. Is that normal? In my house the television is the Bible and the ball-players are the prophets. For that I say, 'Thank you, America.'"

The circle broke up and someone murmured, "It's a pity he can't afford a ticket right back to his home town. There he would really lick off a good bone; America isn't good enough for him, the big shot."

"Nu," said the bearded man to Simon, "didn't I tell you? What do you think?"

"I don't like Communists," said Simon, "but I like to listen. It's like being back in the market."

"You haven't heard anything till you hear Grossman."

"Who is Grossman?"

"Grossman, you don't know Grossman, he used to be a millionaire. He owned all the Osman furniture stores; even now he's still worth ten thousand. But such a *nudnik* you have to go far to find."

"So what is there to hear if he's such a *nudnik?*"

"Nobody lets him alone, that's the thing. For instance, yesterday after you went away, we were holding our sides laughing. Grossman came along and starts with his story. Grossman has only one story, about his store from the rag business, the apartment on Riverside Drive, summers in Atlantic City and winters in Florida; anything to make us drool. Sometimes he even tells it in English. That's how it was yesterday. He went on and on about the same old thing when Klonsky, he's the one with the white hair you just heard talking, Klonsky asks him, 'Mister,' he says, as if he doesn't know his name. 'What's the matter you can't speak Yiddish so everyone can understand you?' Grossman doesn't flicker an eyelash. He just starts the whole thing over in Yiddish, right from the beginning. I thought Klonsky was going to pull all the hair out of his head. 'Enough!' he shouts at him. 'We just heard the whole thing; once, twice, ten times, fifty times is surely enough.' Then he rubs a little salt on, 'Don't forget,' he tells Grossman, 'millionaires are a dime a dozen in America. All you need is a newspaper stand, a dry-goods store, even a wagon that sells knishes or sweet potatoes and you're all set.' I'm telling you this is the life."

The man in the torn overcoat sat on the bench opposite Simon every day but they never spoke to each other. One morning Simon was surprised to find him with his face red and swollen as though he had been crying. He couldn't help but glance up from his paper every few minutes to look wonderingly at the unhappy face opposite him. Then he saw that there were tears streaming down the man's face though he made no sound and the expression on his face was unchanged. Simon got up and sat down beside him. "What is the matter?" he asked quietly, not expecting an answer.

"They're sending me away," he said in a whisper. "This is my last day here. Tomorrow they pack me up, and away." The tears then came too quickly and he stopped talking.

"Where?" asked Simon. "Who is doing this?"

He tried to swallow his sobs that emerged like belches. "My own children want to bury me alive. They're sending me to a home." And the tears streamed again.

Simon put his hand on his shoulder. "Don't be foolish," he said. "That's not burying alive. Hundreds and thousands of people are in homes and they live until they die. What's so terrible? Stop crying. It's not such a terrible thing. You may even like it there."

"No," said the man. "No one will come to see me. I'll be as lonely as a stone, all the days and nights. My children won't come and who else do I have? I was the youngest in the family, all, all gone." He almost choked as he pressed the sobs down.

"I'll come," said Simon. "I'll find a few other men here and we'll come to see you. Stop crying." The man moved to the end of the bench to make room for a few other people who had stopped to talk and he huddled there, taking deep breaths to control his tears.

Before Simon left the park, he took out his address book. "What's your name?" he asked the stranger.

"Ziskind," he answered, "Abraham Ziskind."

"And to what home are you going?"

"To Carole Street, near the market," he answered.

"Oh, I know," said Simon. I've never been there, but I know."

Two weeks later Simon persuaded his friend to go to the home with him. He didn't know the man's name, but when talking to his wife he called him "the Beard." They walked together through the most crowded streets in the neighborhood, past pushcarts, and trucks, down a street where there were not even alleyways between the apartment houses and the street was a gully flanked by two walls. The home was an apartment house like all the others. There were the two marble steps, the same grillwork on the doors and only a small sign saying *Moshav Zekanim* to distinguish it from the houses next to it and opposite it.

"So this is the place," Simon said. "Every year a collector comes and I give him two dollars and I never knew where it went."

They pushed the heavy door open and in the small lobby where the other houses had doorbells and letter boxes there was a hole in the wall, about a foot square. A woman stuck her head out and asked, "What do you want?"

"We came to see Mr. Ziskind," Simon said.

"In Room Fourteen," she answered, and her head disappeared from view.

They stood on the threshold looking for someone who would know where Fourteen was. It was quiet except for the noise of pans rattling and water running somewhere in a kitchen and for a moment neither Simon nor the Beard realized that there were several people in the hallway. Under the steps at the back, where there was a door leading to the basement, a shriveled, toothless old lady with a kerchief on her head sat on an apple box. On folding chairs, on both sides men and women sat staring into space like wax figures.

A voice at Simon's right called out, *"Vehmen zicht ihr?"* [Who are you looking for?] and the Beard answered.

"Ziskind, Room Fourteen."

"Upstairs, the second floor," was the answer.

When they turned to see where the voice was coming from they saw the entrance to a small synagogue, where several men were sitting.

They took the steps slowly. The Beard held the banister on the right and Simon held on to the wall. The wall was rough where the paper was torn off in large strips and the steps were worn into shallow bowls. At the turning point on the staircase they left the smells of the first floor—strong odors of disinfectant, food, garbage, and the musty smell of old books from the synagogue—for the dusty smells of carpeting, old sweaty clothes, and improperly washed bathrooms. The Beard held his nose and said, *"Pfui."*

"Never mind," said Simon. "Smell your share and go along."

There was no one in the first room they passed. The next was so crowded with furniture that they had to look carefully before they saw Ziskind sitting with his hands folded and his head down. He wore a skullcap on his head and a dirty tweed jacket over uncreased rayon trousers. He looked as if he had not shaved since he had come to the home. Only a little gray light came down the shaft from the skylight into his room. There was a wall only two feet from his window so that there was nothing to look out upon.

"Hello, how are you?" Simon asked with forced cheerfulness.

Ziskind looked at them for a minute as if wondering whether to answer. "I am just as you see me, just as I look, that's how I am."

Simon and the Beard looked at each other significantly. He looked dreadful, as if he were not much longer for this world. They stayed with him for half an hour. Simon talked all the time and Ziskind seemed apathetic. When they stood to leave, however, he jumped up and seized Simon's right hand in both of his own and said, "I thank you for coming. I didn't think anyone would ever come. God will repay you. Please come again, I beg you."

Simon and his friend didn't talk about the home to the other men but it was on their minds for many days. The Beard, seemingly out of the blue, would ask him, "What kind of slop do you suppose they give them to eat there?"

"How should I know?" Simon would ask irritably, annoyed that he was forced to think about it.

When his wife asked how it was, he said, "How should it be, a lot of old people, that's all."

It rained for a week after they had gone and then Simon's hand became very painful. A month passed before he and the Beard went to see Ziskind again. They found the entrance hall crowded with women and for a moment they thought they had come to the wrong building. Then they noticed the old folks, dressed in good clothes. *"Oi, it must be a funeral,"* was the Beard's decision. They went upstairs and found Ziskind just where they had left him.

"What's going on? Somebody went away? Who are all the women?"

"It's nothing; some kind of party. They're charity ladies," said Ziskind.

"So what are you doing here alone when there's a party?" the Beard asked.

"If they want me, they can come and call me," Ziskind answered petulantly.

"Don't be foolish," said the Beard. "If it's a party, maybe there's some schnapps or wine, and lots of pretty young women are there already. Don't be an old fool. Let's go down."

They pulled Ziskind, still unshaven, in dirty, crumpled clothes, down the stairs. The old people were already in the dining room and the women were carrying teacups, glasses, and plates.

"Here are some more," one of the women called as she ran to greet them. "Come, come, come," she said, holding Simon by the arm. "Now don't worry, we saved some cake for you, you're not too late." Simon tried to shake her hand off, but she held him tightly as if he were a little child that might run away. She led them to one of the long tables that were used for meals and pulled the chairs out for them. Another woman in a large feathered hat stood at the head of the room. "My dear friends," she said slowly as though she didn't expect to be understood. "We have come to celebrate some birthdays with you. We want you to know that even in your golden older years you can still have happy birthdays. Let us all rise and sing happy birthday to Mrs. Bella Gold, Mr. Abraham Selkin, Mrs. Celia Kroll, and Mrs. Molly Greenstein." Some of the people stood up, but only the guests sang. Then a large cake was brought in and pieces were carried to everyone, with glasses of tea. One of the guests played the piano while the tea and cake were devoured.

"Aren't you eating your cake?" the Beard asked Simon.

"It'll stick in my throat. What kind of foolishness is this? Let's go."

"Wait another minute," said the Beard and proceeded to drink Simon's tea and eat his cake.

"Mr. Goldman," announced the woman at the piano; "will now play for you on his violin."

Mr. Goldman, one of the members of the home, shuffled forward with his violin. He scratched at it for a few minutes and then sat down. Then a tiny woman sang a long song in a thin wavering voice. She had scarcely finished when a man stood up and told an obscene story. Simon got up to leave but the Beard kept motioning for him to sit down.

"What's your hurry, we can stay another minute," he begged.

Ziskind still sipped his tea, looking around at the guests as if they had descended from Mars. Behind him, four women were filling little brown paper bags with candy, nuts, and tangerines. Simon remembered filling such bags himself for his grandson's birthday party a few months before.

The people laughed at the story-teller and he was so encouraged that he did a *kazatska* and then sang a *double-entendre* song called "But I Don't Know How" in a flat, tuneless voice. Simon felt himself quivering with exasperation and shame. He squirmed out of the narrow place behind the chairs and went toward the door. He had almost reached it when he heard a woman's voice call him, "Mister, wait!" He didn't turn and she ran all the way out to the lobby with a little paper bag in her hand. She caught his sleeve breathlessly, and said, "You didn't get your candy, here it is."

"Let me alone," he waved his hand at her; "I don't need any candy." Then he let the door slam behind him.

When he stopped for a traffic light he looked back and saw

the Beard hurrying after him as fast as his fat legs would take him.

"What's your hurry?" he asked breathlessly. "You could have waited another minute. We came together, let's go home together."

"I can't stand to see old people get up and make fools of themselves like children. It makes me want to sink into the ground."

"Don't take it to heart, it was just a party. Nothing would be better? At least it shows the women have some respect."

"That's also respect, to make fools of people?"

"Is it their fault if the people are fools? Beggars can't afford to be so proud."

"But when a beggar loses his pride, what is he? A common beggar; it's the beggar that can't afford to lose his pride. And without pride, there's no respect."

"Take that up with Klonsky, I'm not a debater," said the Beard.

When Simon stopped at the bakery on the corner of his street, the Beard continued on to his house. Simon bought a pumpernickel and some rolls and hurried down the block and into the hallway, feeling a little guilty because he had been away longer than usual. He didn't notice the ambulance in front of the house. He climbed the steps to the first floor, pulled his key out of his pocket and pushed it into the lock. It didn't turn properly and he put the bag under his arm and tried to use both hands. Then he realized that he had been closing it instead of opening it. He wondered why his wife had left the door open. He had only opened it a crack when he knew that something was wrong. He heard no voices but he sensed at once that there were people in the house.

He walked through the long foyer quickly but not until he reached the entrance to the kitchen did he see the woman from the apartment next to his standing with her hand on the sink. Opposite her a blond young man in a white coat sat in Simon's chair at the kitchen table.

"What are you doing here? What's the matter? Where's my wife?" Simon felt his voice as one does in a nightmare.

"I'm sorry, Mister, but your wife had a heart attack an hour and a half ago. There was nothing we could do when we came. I'm sorry."

"Nothing is the matter with my wife's heart. She has arthritis."

"Sorry, Mister."

"But I was only gone a little while. See, I have the rolls. I was only gone a little while."

Simon stood at the door of their bedroom, his face twisting as if he were struggling to catch his breath.

"Look, Mister, I'm sorry to bother you but would you please sign this form. I've been here an hour already. It'll just take a minute."

Simon sat down to sign. When he finished, the doctor folded the paper and put it into his breast pocket. He put his hand on Simon's shoulder and went out quietly on rubber-soled shoes.

The neighbor still stood near the sink. "She got scared and knocked on my door. I called the emergency. Is there anything I can do?"

"No," said Simon; but then added, "Please send telegrams to my daughters." He hunted in his little book for an address in Washington and another in California. "Please call the synagogue for me, too." The woman took the slips of paper and hurried out. She seemed relieved to have reason to go.

When she left, Simon sat down on the edge of his bed. He reached over across the narrow aisle between the beds and uncovered his wife's pale peaceful face.

"So you are the lucky one," he said. "You found favor in His eyes. Oh that I too could be there safely beside you."

Then he covered his face with his hands to hide the tears, *"Mamele, Mamele,* what will I do now?"

My Mrs. Schnitzer

I was standing next to the kitchen stove, peering into the array of pots, basking in the warmth and abundance of home. I sampled a chicken wing from the soup, then a piece of stuffed fish, and a few strands of noodle pudding. My mother watched me approvingly, certain that I had starved all of the long year spent at college so far from home.

"Better than cafeterias?"

"A hundred times better," I said.

I thought for a moment that she would begin again the long discussion about my going away from home. "Why," she asked over and over again, "when there are so many schools in New York is it necessary for you to go to Chicago?"

I couldn't tell her, but it was necessary, and I hoped she wouldn't ask.

She didn't. I was grateful. Instead she told me the family gossip, the births, the deaths, and the weddings.

"Did Papa write that your Mrs. Schnitzer passed away?" she asked, not turning from the sink where she was washing pots.

The noodles seemed to turn to clay in my mouth, and I had to return some to a napkin before I asked, "When?"

"When? About two months ago, maybe three, Mrs. Miller told me. I met her in Klein's."

Reprinted from *Commentary*, May 1952, by permission; all rights reserved.

"What did she die of?" I asked casually, impersonally, as if it made no difference to me.

"She had a stroke. What would you expect? The way she carried on, it's a miracle that she didn't have an attack ten years ago."

"What about Hershel?"

"Who knows, they probably put him away."

I thought of my Mrs. Schnitzer the rest of the day, the week at home, and even on the train going back to school. Fat, noisy Mrs. Schnitzer would never have another fight with her neighbors, never slap her tall son and scream, "Why should you be such a fool, Hershel?" and never again feed me crisp, cheese-filled cakes and chick peas when my mother wasn't looking. There was a secret understanding between the two of us that I had never been able to explain to my family.

She had lived next door to us in the first house I remember, a tenement in Williamsburg in Brooklyn. We had identical apartments beginning with a thirty-foot-long entrance hall, filled with boxes of clothing, dishes, an ice box, brooms, boxes of soda water, everything that couldn't fit into the three crowded rooms beyond it. But there the similarity ended. Our family was brought up to love quiet, gentleness, and self-control. Shouting, display of temper, the briefest lapse from politeness in even the smallest thing was sternly forbidden. If in a harmless discussion, my sisters or I raised a voice my father was quick to ask, "Why are you fighting?"

"But we're not fighting, we're just talking," we protested.

"There is no one deaf here. If you are just talking, then speak softly. You will be heard."

We learned to speak softly. There were times when the house was electric with tension, but it was as if padded, insulated with silence.

Right next door, behind a wall that seemed to be made of paper, Mrs. Schnitzer shouted and cursed. "What devil brought you home?" she greeted her husband at ten o'clock at night. "Is this a time for a man to come from work? Or didn't you go to work? Why didn't you drop dead on the way?"

This we heard as plainly as if there were no wall between us. Papa would clap his hands over his ears and shut his eyes. "A shame," he would say trembling. "A woman with no embarrassment, no feelings." In his eyes she came to be the epitome of vulgarity and coarseness, and he could hardly bear to look at her. He avoided her as Mama avoided the mice that scurried across the kitchen floor when night came. If he heard her footsteps in her long hallway when he was leaving our apartment, he would wait until she was safely down the steps and out the front door before he ventured out of our door.

Mama did greet Mrs. Schnitzer, but I doubt that they ever said more than good morning or good afternoon to each other. Mama, however, had no more to do with the other people in the house. She had lived there since she had married and watched it lose its newness and elegance and become shabby and poor. Her neighbors had never been her friends. She never visited them or joined them in front of the house where most of them spent their afternoons. When her work was done she sat at the kitchen window or in the rocker near the dining room window. She sat by the hour watching the people come and go and I often wondered what she thought while she sat so still, her chin in her hands. Papa and Mama sat outdoors only on the hottest Sundays in summer. Then they walked to the bridge plaza and looked for an empty bench under the sickly trees that grew there out of the pavement. They sat there quietly, among strangers, reading their papers.

It was impossible for me to be so still. As soon as I could, I made friends out of sight of our house, where I could play stoop ball and potsy without being called from the window. I played running games around the corner in the middle of the street and climbed the iron fences that surrounded the brownstone houses. I found that the freedom was worth the inevitable scoldings when I cam home dirty and torn. Though I was often filled with remorse because my mother seemed so dissatisfied with me, the need to run away was too strong to deny, even to please her.

I made friends with Mrs. Schnitzer quite accidentally, though I let our friendship grow out of a kind of spitefulness, knowing that Mama and Papa thought her so dreadful.

It began harmlessly one Friday afternoon. Mrs. Schnitzer walked into the entrance hall of our house behind me and picked up a spelling test paper that I had dropped. I heard her call "Rayzel,

Rayzel," her voice echoing in the empty hallway; but I didn't stop. Everyone called my Rosalyn since I entered school and I had forgotten that I was Rayzel too. I took the steps two at a time, but she caught up with me, waving the yellow paper in her hand. "You dropped your paper," she said, looking at it as she handed it to me. "Such a beautiful paper! Your mother should hang it up so that everyone can see it." I took it from her, thanked her, and continued up the steps. She came up beside me.

I was about to hurry ahead of her when she said, "What would I give to have my son bring such a paper home? Do you know my Hershel?" I shook my head. I saw him often near our house and also among the motley lot of children in the ungraded class at school. I had never spoken to him, but I had never laughed at him or the others in his class. Their stupid, empty faces filled me with a feeling of horror that was akin to fear.

"Tell me, Rayzel," she asked, "what does your mother do with the papers you bring home?"

"Nothing," I answered.

"She doesn't even give you a nickel for a paper like this? Tell me the truth."

"I don't even show them to her," I told her. No one made any fuss about test papers at our house. It was expected that we would get A's.

"I like to look at such nice papers," she said. "Save them, Rayzel, and show them to me."

I never brought any papers to show her, but each Friday I found her standing in the doorway of the house. She always asked whether I had taken any tests and I showed her the papers. There were always A's and once even an "Excellent" that she asked to keep if I was going to throw it away.

Mrs. Schnitzer now had something for me to taste whenever she met me. She unrolled a paper napkin or a piece of waxed paper and offered me some honey cake, cookies filled with cinnamon and raisins, or a handful of hot chick peas. "Is it good?" she asked, as if I were a judge of fine baking. I wolfed the delicacies while going up the steps, always making sure to be finished when I reached our door.

My mother saw us talking to each other one afternoon and asked, "What does your friend Schnitzer want?"

I couldn't answer her. When Mama called someone my friend it meant that she held no good opinion of them. She insisted that my friends were to blame for all of my real and imaginary faults and for my lapses of good judgment that seemed to increase as I grew older. Still I couldn't give up Mrs. Schnitzer and the praise she lavished on me.

Our friendship grew in little snatches of conversation stolen in the hallway or on the steps of the house where everyone sat in the summertime. On warm nights when I was not permitted to go away from the house, my friends came to see me. We sat on the steps and played Ghost, took turns telling stories, or singing popular songs. When it was my turn to sing, Mrs. Schnitzer applauded loudly. I was embarrassed and pleased at the same time. One night Hershel sat down on the steps beside us. At first we sat and squirmed, uncomfortably quiet, not knowing what to say. Then the other girls began to tease him. I begged them to stop and for many weeks I listened to choruses of "Rosalyn loves Hershel, Hershel, mershel, loony-head."

One evening Hershel left his house after supper and at midnight had still not returned. Mrs. Schnitzer, after waiting all evening at her window, stood in front of the house, a heavy carving knife in her hand. "I'll cut him into pieces, the idiot," she shouted to some women who were still sitting outdoors. "I'll break all his bones. I'll fix him so that he stays out all night. He won't live to go out of the house again." They watched her silently, knowing that she was frightened out of her wits, but no one took it upon herself to comfort her. I stayed awake, too warm and disturbed to sleep, tossing and turning until nearly one o'clock, when I heard someone say, "Here he comes."

From my bed near the window I heard Mrs. Schnitzer beating her fists on Hershel as if she were pounding a drum. "Murderer, fool, where have you been?" she shouted as she pulled him into the house with her.

We moved away from Williamsburg when I was fifteen to a small two-family house near Sheepshead Bay where there were not as many people on the whole street as there were in the apartment house we left behind. Neither my father nor mother ever went back to it, but I came to visit my friends on the street once or twice a month. Whenever I passed the house I found Mrs. Schnitzer sitting on her folding chair outside. One Saturday afternoon she asked me to come in with her. I felt like a conspirator as I followed her into the familiar hallway, already uglier and smaller than I remembered.

We sat at the kitchen table and I munched some cookies and sipped milk. Hershel wasn't there and I was glad, because he still frightened me and I didn't know what to say to him. "How is Hershel?" I asked.

"Hershel," she said, "is Hersheling." Then very slowly, as if she found it hard to say, she added, "You know, Rayzel, you're a smart girl, and you understand many things. Can you understand then, that I know that Hershel will never be any different than he is. He will never grow into a normal human being. I know that my husband too will never be a man like other men. He will never have any understanding or consideration for anyone. It's his nature. I'm not a foolish woman, Rayzel; I know these things. My trouble is that I can't believe them. How can I believe every day that the Lord chose me, me out of the whole world for His personal fool, His favorite scapegoat?"

What could I say to her? I sat holding my cookie, not eating it, wondering what my mother would say if she heard her talking like this, instead of shouting wild, meaningless curses.

"Look, Rayzel," she spoke loudly as if to wake me up and make me listen. "I believe that everyone should have a little misfortune to give them compassion for those who know nothing else but misfortune, and to teach them that the world was not made for pleasure. But a little, a measure with justice. It's not necessary to pour salt on the wounds for a whole life."

Then she looked up at the ceiling and said, "Excuse me, my dear sweet God in heaven. Excuse me, I made a mistake. I married a gambler and a fool whose parents died in an insane asylum. But I didn't know these things when I was seventeen years old. Why didn't You tell me? And why couldn't You at least have given me some decent children to brighten my life? Couldn't I have had something, something without fighting, something for free because I was lucky?"

Then she looked down at me and laughed, making her face look young and quite pleasant. "I waste my time, Rayzel. He's too busy. He doesn't hear. It's a big lively world He takes care of." Then she lowered the pitch of her voice which had become so high it was almost a falsetto and asked, "What is happening to you, Rayzel? Do you have any friends at the new house? Do you like it where it's so quiet?"

I didn't like to talk about myself or the new house to her. It sounded as if I were boasting and it called attention to the wide gulf that was dividing us more and more each day.

Almost a year after we moved, I stopped visiting my old friends and Mrs. Schnitzer, too. The thought of her put a hollow feeling of guilt in my middle, but I didn't come and I didn't write, though I meant to. It wasn't until the first summer after I was in college that I saw her again.

I had a part-time job in an office in the old World building, opposite the City Hall. I was through for the day at three o'clock and I was walking across the park to the Park Square station when I saw a woman wearing a white rayon dress splashed with blue and red flowers and an ancient black felt hat on her head. I couldn't help laughing at the sight, her movements were so like caricatures of the pigeons' that waddled all around her. Her bosom came first and the back of her wiggled and strained to catch up with it. She walked toward Nassau Street, stopped and turned to Broadway, took a few steps and turned again. She was obviously lost. I had come halfway across the square when I recognized her and hurried to catch up with her.

"Mrs. Schnitzer," I called. "Wait a minute."

She stared at me as if I were a ghost. "Rayzel," she grabbed me and hugged me. "I've been wandering here like a lost dog. I look and look for a face I can ask a question of and who do I find? I could eat you up, I'm so happy to see you."

"What are you doing here?" I asked her.

"What am I doing here? God knows. I'm in a wilderness. As soon as I got on the train at Fourteenth Street, I knew it wasn't right, but the doors closed so quickly. I asked a man if it goes downtown and he says yes. Then suddenly he grabs my arm and says, 'Get off; we're almost in Brooklyn.' I got off and here I am. How far is to Delancey Street?"

"You'll need a trolley," I said. She looked so confused and worried that I offered to take her. "I don't have anything special to do. Come, let's go."

I took her arm when we crossed Nassau Street and the fear and tightness seemed to leave her. We walked past the construction crews who were fixing a new entrance to the Brooklyn Bridge and stopped next to a noisy driller to wait for a trolley that would take us along the Bowery to Delancey Street.

"How is the house?" I asked, shouting above the din.

"The house is the same but the people are changing. The old-timers are moving away; Italians, Spanish, and Negroes are moving in. Not in our house, but all around."

I shook my head to show that I was listening. "How are you and Hershel?"

"Everything is the same as it was. Only that the people in your apartment are very cheap, common, and dirty. I don't even look at them. The children run in the hallway, all day long, filthy, without shoes on. Hershel isn't in school any more, so I have more time to worry where he is and what he does. He tried a few times to do some work, but he knocks things over, he hurts himself, he forgets where he's going. So it isn't any good. Then there are times when he shuts himself in the bedroom and won't come out and other times he goes off I don't know where and my eyes creep out of my head until he comes back. What's there to tell?"

All this she shouted above the noise of the drill, while she held my arm tightly. There was a great crowd waiting for the trolley and when it came we were among the last to squeeze into it. I was glad that I had come with her, because she would never have got on without me behind her. She held my arm when the car lurched and she looked questioningly out at the Bowery.

"Some fancy neighborhood, Rayzel. It makes Williamsburg look like paradise."

I smiled my answer. The desire to talk was gone, now that we were wedged knee to knee. The trolley moved slowly and noisily, almost reluctantly, as if it were impeded as much by the damp and the heat of the day as the heavy load it pulled. The passengers were still, as if it were too great an effort to contest the noise of the wheels.

Then Mrs. Schnitzer's voice broke the silence. "Who's pinching there?" she asked.

Behind her, so close he was almost on top of her, was an unshaven, poorly dressed man. His face was shrimp-colored and expressionless. His pale blue eyes had no light of recognition or understanding. His breath was foul, and his clothes dirty and perspired. He looked out the window and didn't turn his head.

"I'm talking to you, mister. Are you deaf? Who do you think you're fingering?"

Her voice fell on the silence like a stone in water and laughter rippled out in waves all around us.

"Don't stand watching birds fly. I'm talking to you. Do I have to box your ears to make you listen?"

He didn't move a muscle. "Let him alone, Mrs. Schnitzer," I begged. "He doesn't know any better. Ignore him."

"No," she said loud enough for everyone to hear. "I'm not a little girl that stands on one foot and then the other, making herself small. I don't make believe nothing is happening because I don't know what to do. I'm not afraid of anything, not of anyone, not even of myself."

She looked right into his face, but he didn't move.

"Don't think because you're a tramp, I'm a tramp. Nobody pinches Bella Schnitzer, do you understand?"

A man in the back called out, "Throw him off, lady."

Someone else with laughter in his voice added, "Push him through the window."

Bella grabbed his sleeve and pushed him toward the center door. The people in the way tried to make a path for him. It was hard to push him, like moving a heavy recalcitrant animal. He muttered something I couldn't understand but moved very slowly. At the next corner, the conductor, a heavy young man who could have been a wrestler, made his way through the car, took the man by the arm and in a voice that brooked no argument said, "Get off."

The man stumbled down the stepway and wavered in the street while the trolley pulled away without him. The passengers in the back saw him sit down on the curb.

The trolley moved along more quickly as if the driver was trying to make up for lost time. Few people rang the bell to get off and the dreary streets we passed had no passengers waiting for us. We were at Delancey Street in a few minutes and the trolley emptied.

We stood on the street corner and Mrs. Schnitzer looked as though she hated to leave me.

"Where are you going?" I asked.

"To the loan society on Essex Street," she said. "It's a wonderful place. I don't know what I would do without it. One week the ring goes in and the watch comes out. Then the ring comes out and the pearls go in. Sometimes everything is in. Still we live. I'll pay my bills and take the car over the bridge home. I know my way here."

She held both my hands in hers. "How can I tell you how wonderful it is to see you? I know you're busy, but if you have a chance, don't forget Bella Schnitzer. Have a good time, Rayzel, and be smart. Don't let anyone fool you. Do what you want and don't try to please everyone. Remember it's a hurrying life and why and for what? No one tells you, just rush, rush, rush, and quick before you turn around they want to turn out the light and pack you up in a box."

"Take care of yourself," she said, kissed my hands and left me there.

The Soldier and His Girl

The ringing woke Estelle at ten o'clock on Sunday morning. She stumbled half-asleep to the door but found no one there. The ringing continued and she hurried to the phone that was hidden under a heap of bills and old newspapers in the kitchen cupboard. Before the receiver had reached her ear she heard Sid say, "Hi, did I wake you?"

Estelle pulled a kitchen chair over to the phone and said, "Good morning."

"Look, I'm in the army," he said. "I came in from Camp Dix late last night. Thought I'd see you today, but I have to stay home with the family. You wouldn't want to come here, would you?"

She said, "Sure," feeling that he had wanted her to say no. "Why didn't you write to me?" she asked. "I didn't know what happened to you."

"I don't write," he said. "Wait a minute, will you?" She looked at her fingernails, which were bitten down to half moons, while she waited for him to come back to the phone.

"If you're coming here, you better come to dinner. Around two o'clock. We're on Eastern Parkway, near Utica Avenue." She wrote the number he gave her on the edge of a piece of newspaper.

When he hung up, she sat down on the edge of her bed and

put her hair up in pin curls. She heard her mother at the door before she was done and opened it for her. Her mother's arms were laden with paper bags. The odor of fresh rolls filled the kitchen.

"I'm going out this afternoon," she said as if talking to herself.

"Where?" asked her mother.

"To Sid's house. I'm having dinner with his family."

"Thank God," said her mother.

"It doesn't mean anything."

"Did I say it means anything?" her mother answered. "But did you have to cry all week? Who is he that you should cry for him?"

"All right Ma, all right."

"But I'm asking, do you know yet what he does for a living?"

"He's a bookkeeper."

"Where?"

"I don't know where. What difference does it make, where?"

"I don't know, Estelle. I don't see how a boy can come into a house three times a week half a year and never say a word to anyone. What are we, wild animals that will bite him?"

Estelle's mother poured some coffee for her and watched while she took nibbles out of a sweet bun and turned the pages of the Sunday paper. When Estelle was finished she carried the dishes to the sink and took out a nail file and some polish. She painted her fingernails and toenails carefully and then sat waiting for them to dry.

When she went back to her bedroom her mother was making the bed. Estelle took some clothes out of her closet and held them against herself critically. She tried on first a blue suit and then a brown checked one. "Which is better, Ma?" she asked.

"They're both nice," her mother said. Estelle looked at them for another minute and decided on the blue one. She washed slowly, and left a trail of powdery footsteps in the bathroom and the hall-way. The scent of toilet water and face powder followed her wherever she went.

Her mother looked her over when she had finished dressing. "You look nice. Don't worry how you look." Her lips brushed Estelle's forehead quickly, "For good luck." She followed Estelle out into the hallway. "When do you think you'll be home?"

"Maybe late. We may go out in the evening from his house."

"Be careful, Estelle," she said solicitously, but her daughtr stopped her with an outraged "Ma," and she could not tell whether it was the anger of acquiescence or defiance.

"I'm not a baby, Ma. I'm twenty years old."

Estelle took the subway for the three stations. The ride was shorter than she expected. When she came out of the train, it was only half past one. She stopped to look in the mirrors of all the gum-vending machines she passed, wondering at each one whether she should have worn a hat. It looked so formal, she was tempted to carry it. But she left it on. The sun was warm outside, and the air glistened so that she blinked when she came out of the darkness. The trees on Eastern Parkway were covered with tiny leaves, still bright green and waxy. She walked a few blocks in the opposite direction and turned in time to come to his house at five minutes to two.

Estelle rang the bell in the outer hall and walked noisily across the tiled floor to the self-service elevator. When she came out on the third floor, Sid was waiting for her. He put his arms around her and they stood close together until they heard a doorknob turning somewhere in the hall. No door opened but they moved apart and Sid opened the door to his family's apartment. He took her hat and pocketbook and she looked at him carefully. She thought he looked younger in his army shirt, even thinner than usual, but less serious.

Sid's two older sisters and their husbands were in the living room. Sally and Marian both looked like Sid, narrow-boned, dark-haired, with sharp-featured intense faces. Estelle was confused by the brothers-in-law. They were introduced so quickly that she didn't know which was Morty and which was Sam. They sat together on the couch, sharing the sports section of the paper, and said "Hi" without getting up. Sid's father and mother came out of the kitchen together and Sid introduced Estelle.

"What do you think of Sid going in the army?" Marian, the younger sister, asked Estelle. "Some surprise."

Estelle nodded.

"Come in. Sit down," Sally said. Estelle sat down in the chair closest to her.

"Show your girl your uniform Sid," Sally said. "She'll never know you with the broad shoulders. Go on, take your jacket out."

Sid left the room and came back quickly wearing a visored cap that reached almost to his eyebrows and a jacket much too large for him. He came in stiffly, bowed low, pulled the jacket in back to make it fit, and shouted, "Hut, two, three, four, hut, two three four."

"Not so loud, Michael's sleeping," Sally warned, but he marched on his heels all the way through the living room, to the foyer, and back through the dining alcove. He stopped in the middle of the living room, pretended to drop his rifle and pick it up. He bent forward at a precarious angle and leaned on the imaginary rifle with his mouth hanging open and his eyes crossed. His sisters and their husbands bent over and shook with laughter. Estelle, not knowing what else to do, laughed with them. Their laughter made him sillier and sillier and his faces were more dreadful each minute. When he stopped and stood with his hand on the piano, waiting for the others to stop laughing, they only laughed harder. Then Estelle saw his mother standing behind him in the doorway that led to the kitchen. Tears rolled down her cheeks and she said, "Look, look what they're sending to war."

Sid's father took her arm from behind and said almost sternly, "Not now Annie, not now. This is not the time." He pulled her into the kitchen and a few minutes later, when the others in the living room were still gasping with laughter, he called out, "Come and get it, everybody."

The table in the alcove next to the kitchen was laden with food. The napkins were buried under the plates and the silverware hung over the edge of the cloth. They took each other's glasses and silverware and didn't know the difference. There was chopped herring and chopped liver and chicken soup and stuffed fish and olives and pickles, even grapefruit that Estelle discovered after the dishes were taken away to make room for the tea. Long after they had all had enough to eat, there was roast chicken, potato and noodle puddings, *kashe* with gravy, and finally applesauce and sponge cake. Sid's father pressed wine, beer, and soda water on everyone all through the meal. "Have something," he begged. "This is on Sid.

Have a little more, it will give you an appetite."

Estelle sat next to Sid, her knee touching his, wondering how the others would move from the table after consuming so much food. "I'm going to burst," said one of the brothers-in-law. "Why did you make so much, Ma?"

"No one forced you. You didn't have to eat so much," she said drily.

"Now there's a girl for you," said Sid's father pointing to Estelle. "She'll make a good wife. She doesn't eat anything. Someone will save a lot of money on her some day."

The daughters helped carry the dishes to the sink and Estelle moved to help them but Sid's father took her arm and gently pushed her toward the living room. "Company doesn't wash dishes," he said. "Sit down."

The two brothers-in-law left the house. "They're going over to our apartment to watch the ball game on television," Sally said. Sid went to answer the phone and came back to say, "I have to run down the street for a minute. I'll be right back." He squeezed Estelle's hand and hurried to the door.

"Where's he going?" his mother asked. She came into the living room with her apron on and her hands wet. A few strands of hair were loose from the bun she wore at the nape of her neck.

"Why didn't you ask him?" her husband asked.

She shrugged her shoulders and raised her brows as if to say, who can ask Sid anything.

"Sit down Annie. You worked enough already. You have plenty of helpers in there. Take off your apron and fix your hair."

She took her apron off and dried her hands on it. Then she made a vain effort to tuck the straying hairs back with the others. She sat down on the edge of the chair, gingerly, as if she were not accustomed to sitting. After a long silent minute she turned to Estelle and asked, "Do you know where Sid is stationed?"

"At Camp Dix," Estelle said. "Didn't you know?"

"Camp Dix?" she said slowly. "Where is Camp Dix?"

"In New Jersey."

"New Jersey isn't far away," she said as if she were asking a question.

"No, it's not far," said Estelle. "Why didn't Sid tell you?"

"Sid is a funny boy. He doesn't talk. We never know where he goes, what he does. He doesn't tell us and it's hard to ask him. If he wants, he answers us but he doesn't tell us anything. Do you know what I mean?"

Estelle nodded.

"Do you think he even told us he was going in the army? A week and a half ago he says I'm going. Doesn't say where. Oh how much aggravation he gives us."

"What are you complaining to her for?" Sid's father asked. "It's her fault?"

"I'm not complaining. I'm just talking."

She touched Estelle's shoulder and said, "I'm very glad to see you Estelle. I'm glad you came."

Sid's father left the room, and as if she had been waiting for him to go, she stood up quickly and took a photograph album, almost four inches thick, from the top of the piano. "Do you want to look?" she asked.

She put the open book half on Estelle's lap, half on her own. It was heavy, even with the weight divided. At the beginning there were pictures of herself and her family. They wore bathing suits or wedding dresses, long formal suits with fur pieces and plumed hats, dresses covered with beads. They posed in Monticello, at Sharon Springs, leaning on a gate at a farm, at Coney Island, in front of an apartment house in Manhattan. It was exactly like the album Estelle had at home, even the few foreign pictures from Poland, with plain, sad faces, funny haircuts, and sack-like homemade clothes. Estelle looked at the pictures but was listening all the time for the door to open. When they came to Sid's pictures, she paid more attention. She looked thoughtfully at the fat naked child that smiled from each page. First in his mother's arms, then on his father's shoulder, his sister's lap. He was lying on a leopard skin, grinning broadly, and then the baby pictures ended. It was as if he had not existed for the next ten years. Then there was a Boy Scout picture with Sid's face circled, and his Bar Mitzvah pictures. He stood alone in one, with the same face he still had, serious except for the mouth that looked as if it had swallowed a smile. The prayer shawl hung smoothly without creases and the prayer book was closed in his hand. Opposite this was a picture of Sid standing between his grandparents. His grandmother had the same full mouth and black brows that his mother had but she wore a wig and a long-sleeved dress with the skirt down to her ankles. She was a head shorter than Sid. His grandfather was almost as tall as he. The old man with the short pointed beard and the young boy resembled each other. Estelle first looked at the picture to be polite but she kept staring at it, trying to see what features they had in common. Sid's mother seemed pleased at her interest.

"My mother died only two months later," she said. "My father passed away seven years ago. Sid was the apple of his eye," she said, her eyes filling. "I wonder what he would say to his going in the army. And Sid is so pleased to go. It's a joke to him. If only he weren't so anxious to go, it wouldn't hurt me so much. It's as if he wanted to run away from us all."

"I can't get over it, somehow," she continued. "In the old country, my father moved heaven and earth to keep out of the army. My husband came to America and *my* son goes."

"What are you telling the girl, Mama?" Sid's father asked from the foyer door. "This isn't Russia or Poland or Austria. In America you go to the army if they call you. What's the matter with you?"

"I know," she said humbly.

"If you know, then what do you want? Why are you so foolish? Your son went to school here; we make a living here; we have a nice house and all the food we can eat. We have the best, the best of everything, and if you have to go to war, you go."

"And if you don't want to go?"

"If you don't want to go, then you sit in jail, so stop the woman's talk."

Sid's mother moved to get up and Estelle helped her put the opened album on the couch. She went to the window and waited there until she saw Sid coming into the house. She went to the door to meet him. It opened as she came to the foyer and the two brothers-in-law came in, laughing and jostling each other. Estelle had decided which was Morty and which was Sam at the dinner table, but she forgot again, they looked so much alike, both heavy and tall, with round pink faces and eyeglasses. They passed Estelle and went into the living room. She opened the door for Sid. They stood close together in the foyer while he took his jacket off. She thought she could feel her heart beating and her face flushing.

"We won't stay long," he whispered. "I just made some plans for tonight."

Sid noticed the open album as soon as he came into the room. "Why do you have to take that thing out for, Ma? Can't a man have any privacy?"

"What's so private about an album?" she asked innocently. "We were just looking at your Bar Mitzvah pictures and I couldn't help wonder what your *zaydeh* would think about your going to the army."

"What he would think? What can he think?" her husband said. "The world is different than he left it. Why do you have to repeat the same thing over and over. It's time to be still about it already."

"What are you screaming at her for, Pa?" one of the sisters called from the kitchen.

"Look Ma," Sid said. "You wanted me to stay home today. I'm home. But if you're going to spend the afternoon crying over me, I'll never stay home again."

"Don't do me any favors," his mother said. "I just want to tell your father one thing. A war is still shooting and killing. It's not a pleasure trip for summer. And it's not a joke for a boy to go away."

One of the sons-in-law, who had been sitting, staring blankly into space, suddenly came to life. "What are you talking? You know what you're talking?"

They all turned to look at him.

"I spent three years in the army, remember? Maybe I wasn't such a marvelous soldier, but I was there. Let me tell you. I had a friend, a kid maybe twenty-two years old, left a pregnant wife some place in Iowa, Idaho, some place, God knows."

"So," his wife asked, her voice rising and falling with the single word.

"Let me talk a minute. You can't start a story in the middle," he answered. She made a wry face and fidgeted in her chair. He continued.

"Anyway at the beginning, this guy, I can't even remember his name, he wasn't any more of a shooter than I was. We both were always running and hiding, scared out of our pants. Then one day I see he's shooting and a little later, he's not only shooting, he's enjoying himself."

"OK, so come to the point," his wife prodded.

"The point is, you get used to it, like anything else."

"Tell me, Morty, you got used to it too?" his mother-in-law asked.

"Sure," he said. "Sure I got used to it. I'll tell you another thing. One day at the very end, we were some place in Germany, this same fellow and I. I don't remember if we were on patrol or just wasting time, when we saw some enemy soldiers. They were far away but not too far. This guy shoots and I shoot after him. It was no different than shooting ducks on the boardwalk at Coney Island. It's just like anything else, like I said, after a while you get used to it." His wife buried her face in a copy of *Life* magazine and nobody answered him.

"But the funny thing," Mort went on, "is that later we found that the war was over and we didn't even have to shoot them. But it didn't bother us much."

Sid sat next to Estelle on the couch, curling her hair with his finger. Waves of love and sleepiness flowed over her.

"But what was the good of it then?" Sid asked. Estelle was surprised to hear him. She thought he wasn't even listening.

"It's not a question of the good of it. It's how it is. That's what I'm telling you."

"Sure Mort," his wife said. "We know you get used to it." She kicked her foot rhythmically to some music singing itself in her head. "You can get used to anything. Who knows better than I?"

"Well," said Sid's mother. "Your grandfather was nobody's fool but he didn't believe in fighting."

"What do you mean, didn't believe in fighting? He was probably scared," Morty said belligerently.

"My father wasn't scared, Morty," Sid's mother said quietly. "If you were half as brave as he, you would have nothing to worry about. I can remember as if it were yesterday, and it was almost fifty years ago, that someone broke into our house. My father filled his hands with sand and threw it in the man's face. He was twice my father's size, but my father beat him with a stick, with a stick mind you, not a gun, until he nearly killed him. I and my brothers and sisters looked out from the corners where we were hiding with our mouths open. Even then we knew that for him, fighting was the worst thing in the world. He couldn't even spank his own children. If a fly came into the house, he would open the door and chase it our rather than kill it."

"Are you talking about *zaydeh,* the little old guy?" Sam asked.

"Yes, that's who I mean. He came to your wedding, remember?"

"And you, Pa? Were you ever in the army?" Morty asked Sid's father.

"Me? I was in Rumania. Why should I go in the army? For the two cents a day they paid? For the black coffee and hard bread they gave the soldiers? You think it's today? They chased us from one place to another. We never had a decent place to lay our heads. My father's house was one room with a dirt floor. Ten children in one room. What can you understand? I'm proud to have my son fight for America. How can you appreciate anything when you don't know how it was?"

"And you can't appreciate without sending young men out to kill each other? To send them away in their best years?" Sid's mother asked. "What do you get for such appreciation? A nice thank you, from whom?"

"I'm ashamed to listen to you," her husband said, and left the room.

"Don't take it so seriously, Ma. The world isn't coming to an end," the older daughter said.

"What shall I do then? Shall I laugh with you? Laugh! I'll laugh too when you explain what is accomplished every few years with the fighting. Their minds are all changed, all those in the cemeteries?"

"What are you worrying for? It's not time yet to worry. Sid will probably spend all his army days behind a desk anyway," the younger sister said.

"And if not Sid, who are the others, they're not mothers' sons?"

"See children, how good your mother is?" Sid's father said,

standing in the doorway. "Her own children aren't enough to worry about. She worries about everyone, everywhere. The whole world is her problem."

Estelle thought that Sid's mother was going to cry, but she stood up slowly and took a box of chocolates from the top of the piano. She carried it around the room, offering it, "My Mother's Day candy," she said to Estelle.

Estelle and Sid left soon afterward. The sisters and their husbands remained. Sid had borrowed a car from a friend and they drove out of the city to a place he knew of for dancing. It took almost two hours to get there, because he wasn't sure of the way. When they finally found the night club, it was crowded. Their table was far from the orchestra and not close enough to the windows to enjoy the cool air. They ordered sandwiches and rum cokes and left their table to dance. The music was slow, but they cut the time in half, taking careful, measured steps around the other dancers. Estelle felt as if she were floating, hardly touching the floor at all. Sid stared at her while they danced, meeting her eyes again and again until she hid her face in his shoulder.

They danced until the music stopped before the entertainment began. From their table they saw only the heads of the Spanish dancers and nothing at all of the comedian and the juggler. But they remained until the dance music began again. They came out into the cool moist air a little before midnight. Sid drove slowly, still uncertain of the way. They stopped for a while to look at the moonlight shining on the Hudson and then they continued home, stopping frequently to ask for directions.

Estelle was home at half past two. Sid kissed her quickly in the hallway and hurried out to the car. When she opened the door she heard her mother turning in bed and knew she had been waiting up for her. The morning seemed like a week ago. She felt so tired that she wondered how she had remained awake so long. She took her clothes off quickly and fell asleep without even washing her face.

At seven o'clock Estelle turned the alarm off and pushed her face deeper into the pillow. She awoke at noon, with her mouth dry and her hair in snarls. Her mother looked at her coldly as she came into the kitchen. "What do you want for breakfast?" she asked. "Or are you still full from yesterday?"

"Fried eggs," said Estelle.

"I don't mean to mix in your affairs," her mother said without looking at her. "But tell me what kind of girl comes home nearly three o'clock in the morning when she has to go to work the next day?"

"Sid's in the army. He only had one day off."

"He's in the army so you can't go to work; is there at least a ring in the proposition?"

"I told you yesterday there wasn't. He's in the army. I don't even know when I'll see him again. Look Ma, please let me alone."

"That makes it better? Now he goes away, without promises, nothing. I hope you had a good time."

"I did," said Estelle. "The best time I ever had."

When Estelle was dressed and ready to leave for work, her mother asked, "What kind of family does he have? Did they make you feel welcome at least?"

Estelle stopped at the door and shrugged her shoulders, "A family, like anybody else."

The Story of Josef Neuberger
Autobiography of a First-Generation American
My Grandfather

While searching for some old books in our attic, one afternoon, I found a crumbling prayer book, loosely wrapped in brown paper. A mouse had nibbled at the wrappings and I opened it, planning to wrap it more securely. In the middle of the book I found a small notebook, its pages yellow, the ink faded a pale green. In the middle of the first page was written, *"Dos Bashreibung Fun Mein Yugent,"* [A Memoir from My Youth]. Underneath it was the signature "Josef Neuberger." In smaller letters at the very bottom of the page was written, "Blessed is the Name, Adonoi is God." The pages of the notebook were densely covered with tiny Hebrew letters. The words were a mixture of Hebrew, Yiddish, and German. It took several weeks before I could understand the writing. The *gimel* that made the *g* sound, the *mem* that made the *m,* were written identically. The *zayin* and *ches* were indistinguishable. Words and whole sentences were abbreviated. The Hebrew, of course, was written without vowels, and consonants stretched frighteningly along line after line. It was however, written for his grandchildren and I could not put it aside until I had rewritten it in my own hand and translated it into English.

I am one of Josef Neuberger's twenty grandchildren and I knew him until I was almost thirteen. We were good friends, as close as an old man and a young girl can be.

I still have a box filled with the presents he gave me, not ordinary presents, real treasures. There is a little porcelain bird, a dinner bell with a painted parrot seated on a perch, a paper weight shaped like a lion. In many folds of tissue paper lies a shell necklace, with a mother-of-pearl heart in the center, too heavy to wear. Beside the pink satin handkerchief, a souvenir from Rachel's tomb, lies the last present he gave me. It is a bottle, shaped and painted like a fish, with a cork protruding from the mouth. He gave it to me on my twelfth birthday. It was filled with wine and he cautioned me to save it for the two of us to drink on my wedding day. He found such treasures on pushcarts on Hester Street and Rivington Street, painted them, took them apart if it was possible, so that when given, they were unmistakably his.

Josef Neuberger was always spoken of as a remarkable man, not great, not brilliant, not, God forbid, successful, but nevertheless a giant among men. If I had not my own memories, I might have thought, like others who had not known him, that his family had made him larger than life; that they had conjured up a giant out of worn old memories because they needed a strong man to lean upon. He was, actually, an impressive figure. When most grandfathers were small, bent, shriveled people, he was tall, taller than his children. He held his head high. His reddish beard was brushed and neatly parted in the center, his clothes were always clean and pressed, and his calfskin shoes gleamed. He carried an ebony walking stick which he flourished when he talked. The gilt dog's head on the top of the cane jumped like a puppet in his hand.

He came to the graduation exercises of my junior high school and my teacher was delighted with him. She shook his hand up and down while he smiled and said, *"zehr fein, zehr fein,"* [very nice, very nice]. He couldn't speak a word of English and seemed so unconcerned about it that people usually apologized to him because they couldn't speak Yiddish.

"Now there's an aristocrat for you," I heard Miss Maguire say to another teacher. "Such distinguished bearing! You just don't see people like that nowadays." Miss Maquire put her arm around me when we said goodbye and she congratulated me on having such an elegant grandfather.

When I was very young, all the Biblical heroes had my grandfather's face. When he wore a flowing white robe and jeweled skullcap on Passover, he looked to me like a smaller version of the Almighty Himself. In spite of his imposing mien, however, he rarely seemed solemn or forbidding. He rode his grandchildren up and down on his boot, and playfully pinched their bottoms. He enjoyed throwing babies in the air, while their mothers squealed with fear. He was proud of his strength and once showed us that he could lift a chair high in the air, holding only one of the legs. He told stories to anyone that would listen and after his dinner on Saturday, he sang *Z'miros* until it was time for his afternoon nap. My cousins and I fought for the privilege of brushing his beard and untying the laces of his shoes.

As I grew older, I separated my grandfather from the vision of the Almighty that I carried and gave him instead the role of the Lord's watchman. It was he who must not know of the ride taken on the Sabbath, of the forbidden food tasted, of all the numerous transgressions that tempted us on all sides. When we were uncertain of some course of action, he told us what the Lord would accept and what was repugnant to Him. With the "thou shalt not" so plainly in view, even small sins brought us more fear and discomfort than pleasure. If his children and grandchildren strayed from the path he set for them while he was there to lead them, it was not because they opposed him but because they were not strong enough to oppose the society in which they lived. Again and again, I heard my aunts and uncles say, "I try to live like Mama and Papa. I do the best I can," their voices showing plainly that they did not think they were succeeding.

My grandfather presided over the celebration of festivals and holy days like a king over his court. On Passover he conducted a Seder, and led the family in singing until the small hours of the morning. The neighbors sat in the hallway to listen until we went home. On Purim, he watched while all the grandchildren, and some of the children too, masqueraded and performed for him. He gave

the Chanukah money to the children and received the first fruits
of his daughters' ovens on Succoth and Shavuoth. They all came
with delicacies to tempt him and watched jealously to see whose
he would taste first. On the High Holy Days he wore a tall silk hat
to the synagogue and sat up on the platform facing the congregation. After the services were over, my cousins and I walked home
with him. We all lived in Williamsburg then and the walk was from
the synagogue on South Fourth Street and Marcy Avenue to Division
Street. Broadway was crowded with the traffic hurrying to the Williamsburg Bridge and there was neither a traffic light nor a police-
man where Broadway and Marcy Avenue intersected. My grandfather
did not stop for traffic. He held his cane high and, single file, like
a family of ducks, we crossed behind him, while cars screeched to
a stop all around us.

All of his waking hours not spent in prayer or study were
passed at a crude wooden table near his bedroom window where
his paints, brushes, and drawing materials lay always ready for use.
My grandfather painted signs, pictures, bottles, coconuts, and trays.
The signs were in Hebrew, in German, or in Gothic script. The
pictures were a strange collection of primitive work. He had never
studied art or even visited a museum. There were many peacocks,
painted on black velvet, blue eyes with silver-spotted tails, red with
gold, some all the colors of the rainbow. There were many country
scenes painted on white oilcloth in lieu of canvas. In his tenement
apartment on Avenue C in lower Manhattan and again on Division
Street in Brooklyn, he painted a distant world of barns, ponds,
ducks, chickens, deer in the forest. He seemed more concerned
with the design of the whole picture than with the problems of
perspective. I remember a farmer's wife standing next to a house,
her head reaching the chimney, her waist higher than the door.
Ducks that waddled next to chickens were sometimes ten times
their size. The water in his ponds was wet though the sun shone
like a flat gold piece in the sky. In his dining room there was a
large picture of the sacrifice of Isaac. A huge angel perched on a
dwarf apple tree, his wings drooping to the ground. The apples
were made of tinsel paper, from chocolate-covered cherries that we
saved for him. He glued them on in glittering circles that shim-

mered in the candlelight on Friday night. Some of the pictures were flat almost like Egyptian drawings, or the illustrations in the old Passover Haggadahs; others were realistic scenes of snow heaped high in the fields, lambs in pasture, and deer with gentle eyes. There were recognizable portraits of his favorite rabbis, with the intricate detail of the beards, the fur of the *shtreimel* and the folds in the caftan caught with pen and black india ink. Every few years he found a new medium. Bottles were irresistible. Nothing that could hold wine or water escaped his brush. For a while he covered two-foot squares of oilcloth with apples, grapes, and pineapples. He framed them as pictures and then added two handles so that they could also serve as trays. When he tired of the trays he busied himself with coconuts. He painted hideous faces on the rough, edible part, cut a small circle on the top of the head, with a knob on it so that it could be lifted easily. The coconuts were natural collectors of old jewelry, hairpins, paper clips, and rubber bands. There was a Dutch shelf two feet lower than the ceiling in the dining room, where I slept, on which the coconuts stood in a row leering at me.

I spent many pleasant hours with my grandfather while he taught me to copy his ducks, his dogs, houses, and figures. While I covered the pages as he showed me to, he told stories of his childhood. I listened carefully, but I remembered only isolated incidents, never gleaning enough to reconstruct a way of life that I could visualize. My parents did not talk of their early days. It was as if they had purposely forgotten the details. I often wondered about my grandfather. What were his beginnings? What was the source of his dignity, so nicely balanced with humor and gentleness? I looked into his memoir eagerly, hoping to find the spring from which his complicated spirit flowed; the patience, the desire for beauty and perfection, the individualism and faith, all bathed in innocence that was not cloaked in foolishness.

After many months with three dictionaries at my side, this is what I found:

Josef Neuberger's Story

The time has come to set down the story of my joys and

troubles, but I sit staring out of the window, asking myself why I try to do this. I awakened from my nap only half an hour ago, and my eyes are still heavy, but not as heavy as my feet. Each day as I life one leg and then the other to pull on my boots, I marvel at what a burden they have become. These same feet took me barefoot in the mountain snow, barefoot while I held my boots in my hands, loath to spoil them on the wet ground, and now I can scarcely lift them to tie my boots.

When I came into the kitchen to wash, Eltse was sorting *kashe*. It was in a little mound on the porcelain table and she shoveled it into a dish with her fingers, carefully pulling out the black specks. She had been ironing while I slept and the kitchen smelled of steam and starch. The two hot flatirons were still cooling on the stove.

I have spent more time looking out the window than writing. From the fifth floor, I can, thank God, see the sky as well as the rooftops. It is well worth climbing five stories for that piece of sky. It must surely seem like a prison down in the dark lower stories, especially for those who have no windows in the front. Strange that I have never become accustomed to the ugly flat rooftops. I see them as fresh each time as the first, fifteen years ago, when I thought that the city had been devastated by fire and that the roofs had been burnt off. I can see the people, the wagons, and the cars below, scurrying like so many insects. With the fire-escape bars between them and me, they are on exhibit, like animals in a zoo.

In our comfortable room with the mirrored oak buffet, a china closet filled with glass and silver, and a round table on thick carved legs, the words I prepare to write seem like strangers to me. I am a stranger to myself. Yet how can one help but wonder at the many lives a person can lead, so many and so different that it is a miracle that one knows who he is. That alone is reason to write, to look again at all the lives I have known, at all the roads He has spread out for me. I ask myself whether I write this for my children and in truth, I think not. What can I tell them now that I haven't told them already? What that is new can they learn now that they have little ones of their own to teach? They are in His hands now, not mine. Perhaps, however, those little ones will read this some day and learn that a life doesn't hang ripe, like a fruit waiting to be picked, but that each of them will have to make his own. Each one must plant his seed, tend it carefully as it grows and for each moment of carelessness or foolishness, pay and pay. Of course, whether things go one way or another depends upon one's *mazel*. Should they ever wonder what I mean by mazel, let me explain that to be *mazeldik,* that is, to have mazel, supposes three things: first, that all doors one comes to should be found open and welcoming; second, that whatever work a person finds to do should appear easy for him; and third, that he and his work should find favor in the eyes of all who behold them. Every man, naturally, has such mazel as He has ordained, sometimes good and sometimes bad, however it pleases Him. And I? Some doors have shut angrily in my face, many things that I have tried to take in my hands to do have fallen apart before I could even begin, but for reasons I cannot know I have still found favor in the eyes of those around me. The pleasure I have found among family and friends has made it impossible for me to argue with the Lord of the world, strange as His ways can be.

Now I will begin the story of my youth and my early life with my family. It is a tale of wandering from village to village, from city to city, a search for a simple livelihood that did not end until a brief while ago, a search that used up the strength of a family as the years ran by.

I was fifteen years old when my father chose a bride for me. We went to see her during the week of Passover. It took us three hours on horseback to travel from Ferescul to Gebirge, where she lived with her father and her grandmother. Her mother had died when she was very little and her father had an inn very much like our own. Eltse was small and so shy that she didn't say a single word to me all the time I was there. But she was very pleasant to look at, with a wealth of brown hair on her head and skin the color of cream. She moved very quickly, but her face was serene and her voice soft, not shrill like some women's. I remember my pleasure at her tiny ankles. The women in my family had ankles like tree stumps. Her father gave me a beautiful silver watch worth ten *gilden,* the finest present I had ever received. My father, may he rest in peace, left the bride forty gilden. We stayed with them from

Friday until Sunday morning and then went home, not to return or
write to each other for four years.

At home there was no talk of a livelihood for me. It was understood that when the time came I would find some small business
that would earn us our bread. I spent the four years studying at the
synagogue, occasionally helping my father in the inn or my uncle
in the forest, where he employed many men to fell the trees.

Even when it was time for the wedding and my new clothes
were prepared, when the pantry was filling with the baked goods
and meats that we would take to the wedding, I had no idea of how
I would support my bride. Our family traveled to the wedding
together with the wagon of *strudel, lekach,* and *fluden,* with herring,
wine, and brandy besides. There was my trunk of new clothes, with
new boots half a yard tall, and a new fox-lined coat that was my
great joy.

It was May, and the wedding was outdoors. The trees were
covered with blossoms and it seemed that only good things were
possible. There was dancing and feasting for a week and then the
guests went home and my little wife went back to her tasks and I
looked for things to do, during the three months *kest.* There was
nothing in her village to keep us there when the three months were
over and we decided to return to Ferescul, where my parents lived.
I had heard that there was a mill there for sale and we prepared
to buy it. We packed our clothes, the pots, pans, and linens that
were part of the dowry, and arranged to travel on a *splaf,* a flat raft
made of thirty or forty logs tied together. The splaf traveled on the
man-made waterway between Kanyateh and Vishnitz. We were traveling only five of the ten miles. The splaf was used in warm weather,
when the water tumbled noisily over the dam, carrying with it
whatever came in its way. The water was full of large stones, roots,
and branches and it took a strong and skillful man to manage a
splaf safely. In the winter-time, the water was a thin sheet of ice and
horses with cleats on their shoes pulled sleds along the frozen way.

The morning of our departure, the grandmother decided that
she would come along and visit my parents for a few days. We were
all busy packing and finally I loaded our possessions on the splaf,
the trunk of clothes, the bedding, and household goods. I wrapped

rags around the trunk and tied the smaller packages to the logs so that I need not worry that they would fall into the water. When I was ready, I helped Eltse on and sat her on top of the trunk and then went back for the grandmother. "Is it safe?" she asked me, pointing to a deep crack between two of the logs. She was really frightened and clung to the railing of the dock until some of the other passengers mocked her. "The crack was there when you were young and beautiful, old one," someone said. I pulled her away from the rail and put her on top of the trunk, next to my wife. Eltse comforted her and gossiped with her to distract her from her fear and I watched the driver, marveling how he maneuvered the splaf through the boulders and stumps in the water. The sun was warm and the water sparkling. There were willows along both banks bent into the water like girls washing their hair. We passed some wild ducks, some fisherman on the shore. People waved to us, little children hooted, and we heard halloos from the wagons that passed on the road along the water's edge. Then with no warning, without a chance to catch a breath, the peace and quiet was broken by a tearing sound and my feet parted of themselves beneath me as the splaf began to break in two. By the time I regained my footing and turned to my dear one, the logs had broken apart, pouring the people and trunks into the water. I hurried to my wife, who was struggling to keep the old lady afloat. The water reached to their necks, but the current was strong and they were so frightened that their fear alone could have drowned them. I held on to the two of them and together we made our way to the shore, our clothes heavy weights about our legs, our shoes deep in the mud that tried to suck us into the earth. When I saw my charges safe on the ground, I returned into the water to see what I could find of our possessions. Those that were tied to the logs had already gone downstream. The heavy trunk was deep in the mud, entangled in branches, sopping with water. I reached down again and again. It was impossible to lift it. Finally I opened it. The water had already seeped into it anyway and everything was ruined. I came back to shore with a small handful of wet clothes and linens, all I could carry, and we sat together on the shore as dumb and bewildered as the other survivors. Next to us lay the bodies of two who had lost more than their possessions. The driver was one of them. We all looked out on the water on which there was no vestige of accident. The sun still shone brightly and the leaves shimmered on the trees. It was hard to thank Him for our lives, sitting there wet with all our possessions in the mud. My dear one sat biting her lips, silently, not crying for all of the years of work that she had lost, though when I thought of my new fox-lined coat that I had never worn and would never even see, my lips trembled. The old one wailed and sobbed and we could say nothing to comfort her because she said again and again, "I knew and I knew and no one listened to me."

We went in a wagon the rest of the journey and came home to my father's house empty-handed. But we bought the mill anyway. My uncle lent me the money and we had nothing else we could do. Did I say we bought the mill? It was the mill with the two stones and the hard dirt floor that bought us. Not only did it buy us but it was ready to devour us alive. It was a silent mill, with few customers bringing grain to grind. It earned us the water for our kashe, but the kashe we had to earn for ourselves. After a few hungry months, when we had imposed too long upon my father, who had other children to provide for, I left my wife at the mill and went to work in the forest for my uncle. His land was a day's journey away. My job was to supervise the thirty young men who cut the trees, to keep them at their work, to stop their fighting, to make sure they made a full profit for Uncle David. The forest, however, is a proper place for animals and when human beings go into it to live it treats them just as it treats the bears and the wolves. We slept on the hard, bare ground, winter and summer. We ate *mamelige* and *brinze* for breakfast, dinner, and supper. On the Sabbath, for a change I ate the mamelige cold instead of warm. Meanwhile my wife struggled with the mill alone.

When I finally came home after three months, I came with a cow that I had bought with eighty precious gilden. The cow was as big as a deer, but the milk poured out of her just as well as out of a cow for a hundred gilden. This visit, however, was so unsuccessful, that to this day the month in which it occurred gives me a feeling of anxiety. The second day that I was home I had a visitor, an envoy from no one less than His Majesty Franz Joseph himself. He knocked loudly on the door and walked in. His clothes were as bright as a bird's, but his expression as dark as the blackest year. He came to remind me that I was twenty years old and that I had not served in the army, I, without whom they could hardly get along.

I did not sleep that night. Here we were in debt, with a mill that we could not keep, and though it could not keep us either, we could not part with it because no one else wanted it. Our first child was stirring in his mother and the prospect of four years in His Majesty's service seemed too much to bear. One could always buy one's freedom, but what would I use for money? Early in the morning, before the birds were up, I went out on the doorstep, rolled a cigarette, lit it as if I were going to enjoy a smoke, and then after taking a few puffs, I pressed it against the sole of my bare right foot. First one burnt hole and then another. They sweat poured down the sides of my face, mixed with tears. The I rubbed some dirt into the sores and waited for them to fester. The next day I made a crutch so that I could walk and when the officer came again I told him that I had tried to extinguish a fire by stamping on it and had burnt my feet.

He trusted me just as I trusted him. When I told him jokingly that it was better to lose a bargain with a clever man than win with a fool, he did not laugh. "You'll serve," he said angrily. "You can pay the hospital bill for the cure and then you'll come and serve."

Well, I did not serve. I paid the hospital for its services and myself for the pain, but I kept irritating the wound with all kinds of caustic substances, and it did not heal. Four times they called me and each time I still limped. The swelling that went down on Monday came up on Thursday until they grew tired of looking at me, almost as tired as I was of them. Meanwhile, my wife, though happy to have me at home, worried about the outcome of the foolishness. She enjoyed the cow and we both reveled in the butter and the cheese that filled our empty larder. In my absence she had been baking rolls and cakes that she sold to the inns and wealthy homes, and the broken ones, the misshapen ones that she could not sell, gave us a feast every day now that we had a glass of buttermilk and a piece of cheese in addition.

Just as we began to take our little cow for granted and to love her as a useful member of the family, she was taken away from us. How? How can a cow be taken away? Not stolen, not shot by a hunter accidentally, not suddenly afflicted with a sickness. She stood blithely in the meadow, this cow of ours, in my Cousin Samson Meyer's meadow, that is. We didn't have a place to pasture her. A summer shower, out of the ordinary in October, began to fall out of the sky. A small clap of thunder, a larger clap, a streak of lightning cracked the heavens in two and the rain poured not only down, but sidewards also and even leaped up from the ground as if to go back into the sky again. And a bolt of lightning, with the whole earth beneath it, with forests and fields, with empty roads and rivers, chose my little cow for its target and killed her instantly. That night I sold the meat to a Gentile for five gilden. Should he ever remember to pay me, I will gladly take out my little book and inscribe the date.

I was tired, tired of calamity, tired of threats about the army, tired of the forest and the *mamelige* and *brinze* and even more than weary of the useless mill. Without telling my wife what I proposed to do, I traveled to Vishnitz, to learn a trade. I put my pride aside and apprenticed myself to a painter for fifty *greitzer* a day. After three months, I received a pleading letter from my wife, who had heard that instead of hunting for a business I was wielding a brush and staining my beard with paint. She begged me not to shame her by turning to a laborer's work, only to come home and together we would find a way to keep from starving. Not too sadly, I parted from my painter boss. Just as I was leaving Vishnitz, however, I met an uncle of mine, David Sherf. I told him, when he asked how it was with me, that I was without a livelihood, my wife with child and a mill I could only sell to an enemy my only business. He seemed really sorry for me.

He had with him two horses and a wagon that he was taking to market. He expected to get as much as a hundred gilden for them, but listening to my story, he recalled that with two horses and a wagon one could earn ten gilden a day easily, without lifting a hand, by buying salt in the mines in Kose and carrying them to Yablentz. That was all there was to it, he said. I would get it on the wagon in Kose, take it off at Yablentz, and bring home ten gilden a day. Since I had not seen ten gilden in a week since my marriage, except of course in the forest, it seemed an irresistible proposition. But where could I get two horses, I who a short while ago had lost a cow? But everything was easy for my uncle. He offered me the two horses for only eighty gilden and said that I could pay him at my convenience. For the moment it seemed that all my problems were solved. He gave me the horses there in the market place and I went directly to Kose for the salt. The air was cold and biting; the blades on the wagon-sled slid quickly over the ice and made the journey easily while I counted how many weeks it would take to pay for the horses, how much money I could save by Pesach, what a wonderful *bris* we could have on sixty gilden a week. Finally I put the load of salt on the wagon, paid for it and turned around to Yablentz and home. I turned, but the horses stood where they were. What was the matter? Nothing was the matter. These horses just did not like to pull a load. They took two steps and sat down for a while as stubborn as donkeys. It seemed that I pulled the horses and the wagon together. The journey home, which was to take me two days, took me and my fine horses five days. When we came to Stebnitz at the foot of the hill, they stopped completely. They wouldn't move an inch. They stood waiting for me to pull the wagon. I pleaded with them, they didn't move. I beat them, they didn't stir. It was twilight and I thought surely that I would remain there and freeze to death with my masters. Finally I sat down and wept and begged, "Dear God in heaven, help me for my wife and child's sake if not my own. What have I done to deserve such a thing? Why should a man have to die of cold and hunger because two horses are lazy? Nothing stirred on the snow. I saw not a soul, just sky, water, and a mountain, and me in the middle. Then as I sat despairing, I hear a shout from the other side of the water "Halloo!" someone called. "Take you over the hill for twenty greitzer." "Yah!" I called "Come and I'll pay you." Twenty greitzer, if he had asked fifty, could I stay there all night? He came from across the water with two half-dead horses. He tied them before my own, called out, *"Veyoh!"* and in no time we were at the top of the hill. When I stopped at the inn on the other side I was like one rescued from the grave. But I was not to be much more comfortable than before. Cold, hungry, frozen as I was, I did not dare sleep in a warm bed. If I slept, what would become of the salt that had already cost me so dearly. It was so cold that birds fell dead and frozen with the snow, but I slept in the barn, at the foot of the wagon.

I brought the salt to Yablentz Friday before sundown, only a small vestige of the load I had bought, and then I had to unload the frozen pieces, without losing even more. But what is the use of telling anything further? Any of the young Gentiles who carried salt from Kose to Yablentz earned if not ten then surely five or six gilden a day, and I the great businessman who deals in horses could scarcely eke out three gilden. Why? Because my aristocratic horses did not like to work for a living. I should have sent them to the Yeshiva and let them spend their days in study. In study and eating, for they ate up whatever little they earned. Finally, only a few days before my son was born I was so steeped in hatred for them, for all the misfortune they had brought me, that half in earnest, half in jest, I said, "A little miracle, dear God, put an end to these horses before they make an end of me." And He heard me so quickly that I could scarcely stand the shock. I came into the stall the next morning to feed the noble beasts and one of them was lying with his legs in the air. It appeared that he had fallen and his good companion had trod on him. The standing horse looked at him without regret, as though he had accomplished something out of the ordinary, a helper to the Lord of the Universe, an executor of miracles.

Where was I now? In search of a livelihood for a change. Mine had blown away as the summer blows away, leaving the whole world naked and bare. My son was born, and we made merry at the *bris* and the *pidyon ha-ben* but we sang more than we ate. My wife could make a fine repast out a handful of sawdust, but she was not well and who else could make something out of the air. Many times we would find on Fridays and holidays that a basket of food had been left at our door. We never knew where they came from until my Aunt Miriam died and the baskets came no longer. She was a rare woman indeed, almost too good for this world. I am sorry that my children could not know her.

My uncle came running to see me when he heard about the horse. He had almost despaired of ever getting his eighty gilden. He took the good horse, so good it should have been drowned before it was born, and left me the other, which was almost, but not quite dead. In fact there was still a large spark of life in him. A peasant offered me thirty gilden for the horse, he was sure that he could cure him. But Samson Meyer, my cousin, who heard him make his offer, said, "Don't be a fool. If he can cure it, so can I." Then you can get fifty gilden for him in the spring. He was so sure and so insistent. He even offered to take the horse back with him and feed him. "Whatever my cow leaves, he can have," he promised. Finally I let him persuade me. He persuaded me, but He was persuaded otherwise. On the way to Samson's house the horse laid himself down on the ground and died and took with him to the other world my thirty gilden. My cousin tried to comfort me, "I'll make it up to you. It's my fault. I'll pay you thirty gilden for my mistake." But he didn't say when and I never found out.

Twenty years later, when my wife and children were ready to leave for America, my uncle collected the payment for his horse. When he came to bid them goodbye he took back with him a bundle of pillows that they had wrapped to take to the boat with them. The debt was finally paid and my aunt could add to the collection of pillows and blankets heaped in the middle of each bed which already reached halfway to the ceiling.

The next dream? Everyone said, "Josef, you need an inn, not horses. A man who can talk to people, who has some learning behind him, and many friends as you do, has no right to confine himself to dumb animals. With your reputation for good fellowship, with your family and friends alone, you fortune will be made." I told myself that if three men look at you and say that you're drunk, it is surely time to lie down and go to sleep. Now how many had told me about an inn? Enough to convince me. On the road between Kose and Yablentz, not far from the hill, I built a house with my own two hands. And with God's help I finished it and opened it for business. We served meals and drinks and provided a few beds for overnight guests. All kinds of people stopped with us. The family, however, did not always understand that they were to pay for our services, and other guests did not come often enough. I remember well the night our second son was born. There was a storm outside that drenched the whole world and shook the houses and trees as if they were made of paper. We had four guests that night. The inn, however was only one large room and my wife needed it for herself that night. I apologized to the guests and begged them to find another place to sleep. I can still see them going out into the rain, grumbling, angry at the child that wanted to come into the world. The son was born, a beautiful boy, and some of our lodgers remained long enough to come to the *bris*.

The inn brought us no prosperity. It was not as bad as the mill, but still not enough to keep us fed. The only other thing I could do was go back into the woods for my uncle, mamelige and brinze, and an animal's life. Reluctant as I was, I went. It was not easy to leave a woman alone at an inn with little ones of her own to care for. The peasants who came to drink would never leave until they were drunk. Once drunk, they would try their best to kill each other. Once one took another's eye out with his gun. They would tell my wife, while they still could talk, "If we fight don't be frightened, we won't hurt you. Take your children and hide yourselves on the stove until we are finished." They never did touch her or harm her, but the fear and the worry were harm enough. I would lie night after night on the hard ground and think of how she fared there alone. Once I came home unexpectedly, to find I could not leave her there alone any longer. Eight young hooligans spent the afternoon at the house. They departed so full of drink that they could hardly stand, but when they came out of the house, they thought of a lively thing to do. They picked up handfuls of rocks and threw them at the house. Eltse and the children were on top of the stove, feeling the house shake all around them, fearful for their lives. I heard the commotion long before I reached the house. When I came in sight of the devils I was so angry that I could have killed them. One at a time, I picked them up, beat them, and threw them down on the road. Those beatings earned me the title of *"hazak"* an honor not often given to a Jew. But it was safer with the peasants to be feared than loved. This, however, was the end. I knew I could no longer leave my family alone. I wrote my uncle, thanked him for treating me so well and helping make my life so easy and pleasant. I told him that it was time that I brought my family to a city, or my children would only know of the brawling life in a tavern and never be able to talk to people. I decided to sell the inn and finally found a buyer who paid me five hundred gilden for it. Then we set out for Lenkovitz, near Zernovitz. Lenkovitz was not really a large city, but after living in the woods so long it seemed like a metropolis to us.

I bought a lumber yard in Lenkovitz. It seemed like a good business. It had earned its owners kashe and wheat, fish on Friday, and meat for the Sabbath. Like the others before me, I went to Yablentz to buy wood. My uncle was pleased to hear that I too was dealing in wood, and he even gave me a present of some lumber, almost enough to build a house for ourselves. I took that as a hopeful sign, never before had my uncle given me anything for a present. I brought the wood back to Lenkovitz, an investment of two hundred gilden, ready to open my business and build a house for us to live in. Temporarily, I had set up a rough shack, no larger than a *succah,* with a good brick oven for cooking. We planned to live there until I could obtain a permit to put up our house.

What does the Almighty do? He brings a flood to Lenkovitz that floats the whole town away. Our little shack was high up on a hill and from our window we could see the water rising and rising, houses swimming on the water, people in boats where forests and fields once were. The lumber yard was at the bottom of the hill and we saw that swim away as if we had not paid for it. The water came up to our doorstep and began to recede. My lumber yard was left unrecognizable and not until six weeks later did the water recede sufficiently so that I could see if I could find anything of my investment of two hundred gilden. I found very little, salvaging only enough to build a house, with little to sell, though there would have been plenty of customers had I had some lumber to sell.

It was necessary to have a building permit in order to build a house in Lenkovitz. Jews did not get permits without great sums of money. I, of course, had no money. The peasants in the neighborhood came to see me as soon as I had bought the land and told me quite plainly that if I should try to put up a house without a permit, they would promptly burn it down. They said, however, that with a permit I could do as I pleased.

I thought about the matter for a while and then went to the mayor of the town, and brought along a present for him, a bottle of very fine schnapps. "What do you want?" he asked me. "Nothing," I said. "Only that you taste what I brought you." He did me a great favor and tasted a little. I let the taste speak for me. After all, how can one know a stranger? One who bears good gifts must surely be good himself. Meanwhile he took one taste and another and called to the kitchen that potatoes should be put on to bake. It didn't take long before he became quite gay and exchanged all manner of familiarities with me, jokes about the town, about the flood, about women and such things. The cautiously, but firmly, I told him that I had a small request to make, one that he must not refuse. He leaned back in his chair and said that for his part all things were possible. I told him then that I wanted to build a small house but was afraid that my neighbors would not let me if I did not have a permit. I showed him my receipt for payment for the land and then took out the paper requesting a permit, already filled in, and gave it to him to sign. He called his wife and asked for the seal. She moistened it carefully and pasted it on the paper. "Here you are," he said. I left the schnapps and hurried home. I immediately began to build. The next morning a crowd of people came to inquire about my permit. There was no friendship in their faces, but when I showed them the seal they turned themselves toward town to see the mayor. The mayor had slept well, and when he awoke he had forgotten about me, about the seal, and my house. When the villagers were done with him, they gave him reason to forget the taste of the schnapps too. But I built my house with neither the approval nor the friendship of my neighbors. We lived in Lenkovitz for eight years, never earning a proper living. I decided again to sell my house and my business and go to a large city either to work or find a business. We came then to Lemberg [or Luov].

Lemberg was a large city with much business, much work, and many, many poor people. Here, I said, if I am miserable I will be no worse than the others. I sold the house in Lenkovitz and took my children, who by this time numbered seven, and traveled to Lemberg.

We searched until we found a place to live. The only thing we could pay for was a tailor's shop. It was one large room. The tailor worked there all day with his assistant and we had the room all night. The rent was six gilden a month, a terrible price for so little. But my wife, my children, and I, and two boarders, besides, lived there for several years. My children were able to find work in the city, though I walked the streets from early morning till late at night, and found nothing to employ me. Once in a while I found something for a few days but the wages were no more than seven gilden a week. Still, if it had lasted a week I would have felt myself lucky. If it weren't for the children's earnings we could have starved. Itzik, my eldest son, earned eight gilden a week, of which he gave me five. Chantze earned sixty cents, Brantze two gilden and, Rachel fifty cents. The others earned nothing.

We lived on old bread and herring, and it was a sad Sabbath that did not find even that on the table. I remember such a Sabbath, when I wanted to borrow a gilden. I came to a man who could lend one, offering my *tallis* as collateral. But the value of *Talleisim* was small in Lemberg and I had to return home for my coat. I borrowed the gilden and we had more than enough to eat.

When the children grew older and earned more we took other rooms, and paid as much as twelve gilden a month. But in all the time in Lemberg we always lived from hand to mouth and there were many times when the hand went to the mouth empty. One evening the children came home from work and found nothing to eat for supper. I asked them to pretend that it was Yom Kippur, to go to bed without complaining, and in the morning there would surely be something for them. But God brought the morning and forgot the breakfast. Again I promised them, go to work, when you come home there will surely be something for you.

Such days and nights were not infrequent in Lemberg. Our dear God gave us the strength and patience to bear it. Not only to bear it, but not to bow our heads before it. Of all of us, my good wife was the strongest. At a time when we went hungry every other day she found a wallet with a hundred gilden that the landlady had lost. A hundred gilden was a fortune for us, but she returned it. I don't know what I or my children would have done. But in returning it she made me richer than by keeping it. For the moment, it seemed that we could afford to return it. Each day I ask for her only strength and health, that she may yet be happy with the children for whom she suffered and struggled so much. Many times, during the lean years, I thought that our children were fortunate indeed that their own mother, and not a strange woman, had borne them.

The time came when we could not bear the bleak future of Lemberg any longer. My parents had married off their youngest child and gone to Palestine to die. My older sons were soon to be threatened with service in the army. The hope of the world was in America and we, who had nothing to leave behind, were ready to go. I went first with my two eldest children, and as soon as we had saved enough for passage for the others my wife came with them.

Earning a living in America was a different problem. Here there was no shame, except for a lazy man. One put oneself in harness and worked. It was not possible to grow rich, but I was no longer concerned with riches. It was more important that we were in no danger any longer of being hungry or homeless. My sons and I were all painters. We painted tenements and stores, synagogues, covered with murals, wedding halls, and endless apartments. I thanked Him every day for the chance to work.

The work, the hard work, is done now. My sons and daughters look out for me. Our needs are not great. I have no complaints against the Lord of the Universe. I wish for my children and my children's children an easier life than my own, but when they reach my years may they not be less satisfied than I. Let them remember too that more important than an easy life is the strength to withstand whatever life He gives.

Postscript

There it ended. I was thirteen years old when he died. I

remember watching in awe while all the adults I knew, and many I had never seen before, crowded his house, the hallways, and the street outside. Many wept loudly and wrung their hands. I had loved him, but I couldn't cry, though my knees were weak and the ground shifted beneath my feet. It was much later that I knew that they wept not only for him, they wept because fathers die; they wept for innocence and certainty; for an old order that was dying, that they could not keep and could not bear to throw away. Surely some wept because the Lord's watchman was gone and they were not sure that they could commune with Him alone.

A Family of Four

Martha and Joe Shur walked along the bay for an hour before they decided to take the apartment. They had seen so many and decided against so many that it was hard to be sure any more. It was always the older Mrs. Shur who found the flaws. The ceilings were too low or the foyer was too small. The tiles might be broken in the bathroom or the walls might have cracks. "It isn't as if you didn't have a place to stay," she would remind them. Sunday after Sunday they would come home with nothing accomplished. It was easier to decide without her. They paid their deposit and signed the agreement. Then for a while they walked around the flat field, overgrown with tall sweet-smelling weeds and swamp grass, where the new apartments were to be built.

Joe's mother had hoped all along that they would include her in their plans. For weeks they had wavered back and forth, undecided, and then they had decided that she could live with them, but as soon as they talked about it Martha knew that it would be unbearable and she had cried so much about it that Joe had given in. Meanwhile the older Mrs. Shur did not know what they thought or planned. She waited nervously for them to decide.

She did not hide her disappointment when they told her. "It won't make any difference," she said. "We'll see each other a few times a week anyway. You can't get rid of a mother so easy. But you'll be sorry when you have a little one that I'm not closer. And it's a terrible waste of money to pay two rents. But do what you want, don't let me tell you."

They watched their house go up as eagerly as those in the suburbs watched their bungalows take form. They came back week after week to see what the bulldozers and derricks had accomplished even after the weeds were dry and dead and they could see the garbage, empty bottles, and old tires strewn all over the lots. They knew which windows were theirs.

The last few months together were difficult for Martha and her mother-in-law. The tensions that had been hidden for two years suddenly could be borne no longer. They quarreled about the lights and the dishes and the housework and then made up with tears and kisses. "You worked all day, go sit down and take a rest," Mrs. Shur urged Martha when she offered to help in the evening. But as soon as the girl did sit down the woman showed resentment.

The evenings were quiet. "When you're eating, eat," Mrs. Shur would say. "Later you'll talk." But when they were done Joe would nap on the living room couch, his mother would do the dishes alone, and Martha would cut pictures of furniture and recipes from the magazines she bought.

The baby was to arrive a month after they moved in. The days moved slowly, anxiety, excitement, and anticipation each taking its turn. But time passed and the furniture was bought, the clothes accumulated in a frenzy of buying, and Mrs. Shur supervised the purchases. She knew about the quality of the fabric and the finish of the wood just as she knew how a suit should be made and how a dress should be finished inside. Martha could not argue. She was not permitted any mistakes. If she hesitated her mother-in-law would insist on buying for her whatever she must have. Martha waited.

Four months later she woke in her own bed with a crib beside it. Joe called her from the kitchen. She heard him but she buried her face deep in the pillow. Then the baby cried and she jumped to pick him up. The door of the refrigerator slammed shut. Martha blinked when she came into the kitchen. The baby was on her shoulder, its moist young head wobbling as she walked. She carried a diaper and a bottle in her free hand.

"There's nothing for breakfast," Joe said.

"What do you want?" she asked.

She looked at her reflection in the mirror over the telephone table. Her hair was tangled around her face, her eyes puffed.

"What do you want?" she asked again.

"Some breakfast."

"There's eggs in the refrigerator. The cereal's in the closet. There's bread on the table."

"I don't want any eggs."

"The appetizing store was closed yesterday. It's closed Wednesdays."

"Then you should have gone on Tuesday," he said. He fixed his tie and ran a comb through his hair. His cheeks were pink from shaving. He looked young and handsome. He stood holding the doorknob, looking at her crumpled nightgown that hung loosely beneath her cotton housecoat.

"Aren't you going to kiss me goodbye?"

"Kiss the baby," he said sharply. "He takes all your time anyway."

The door shut behind him. The baby began to cry. Martha went to the refrigerator for a bottle but found they were all gone. She left him to scream in his crib and began to gather together the milk, corn syrup, and water for the formula. She read the directions carefully. She read them every single time and wondered why she could not remember from one time to the next. Then she thought the infant was holding his breath and she ran to the crib to get him. Then she couldn't remember which of the ingredients she had put in the bowl and whether she had measured them properly. The bottles steamed in the sterilizer and the nipples were disintegrating while she hunted for the tongs that she had dropped behind the stove. "Shut up!" she shouted at the baby and she realized that she was crying too. Finally she held him while she poured the milk into the bottles. He sucked on her shoulder hungrily and fell asleep before the bottles were ready.

Martha had a work schedule posted in the kitchen. She had

copied it from a magazine. It told her when to make the beds and sweep and cook the supper. At three o'clock she had finished her chores. The apartment was dusted and swept, the baby's clothes were washed, the supper prepared, and the kitchen in order. Stephen slept on his stomach in his carriage, ready to go outdoors. Martha brushed her hair. It hung to her shoulders. She pulled her jacket down. It was tight and she couldn't button the top of her skirt, but she didn't look very different from the girl in the tinted wedding photograph that hung over the living room couch. She put the last blanket in the carriage and turned it so that she could get it out of the door.

The buzzer rang and Martha opened the little metal peephole to see who it was.

"It's me! Open up, it's me!" said Mrs. Shur.

Her arms were full of brown paper bags. "How are you and how's my little boy? How's my darling little boy?" she put the bags on the kitchen table and went to the carriage.

"I was just taking him out," Martha said.

"Now, three o'clock you're taking him out? The sun is gone. He should be out twelve o'clock, not now. What's the good of dragging him out now?"

"I wasn't ready at twelve o'clock," Martha said. "I just got finished. I have to go to the store. Do you want to wait here or do you want to come with me?"

"You're taking him out like this? What's the matter, you're out of your head? This isn't July. Where's the woolen hat I bought him? I didn't buy it, it should lay in a drawer. You call that a hat, it's no thicker than a handkerchief."

"It's seventy-five degrees outside. I'm just wearing a thin suit. He doesn't need a woolen hat."

"What's the degrees? It's April. It's changeable outside. In a minute it's bitter cold. Listen to me. I raised a child already."

"Look, I'll be back in a minute. Why don't you just relax? I'll be back before it's bitter cold."

"Go then, but leave the baby with me."

"No, I want to take him. It took me an hour to fix the carriage and dress him. It's just for a few minutes."

"What are you going to buy?"

"Whatever I need."

"Why are you such a stubborn child? You don't need anything. Whatever you need, I brought you. Come, look here. For supper tonight I brought you a chicken soup with barley like Joe likes and the chicken naturally and for tomorrow there's pot roast with vegetables. All you have to do is heat it up. And here's some chopped herring and an apple pie. I even found a piece of belly lox, white and fat as butter. You can't buy such quality here. The stores are too fancy. And a pumpernickel and some onion rolls for breakfast. So what do you have to buy? I even brought a jar of chicken fat."

Martha stood at the carriage and watched her mother-in-law spread the bags over the table and chairs. "Why do you bring so much?" she asked. "You don't have to bring all this stuff. I made supper already. We don't need it. Why do you bring things all the time? I don't ask you to."

"Look, Miss Independence, I'm a mother. You don't have to ask me to bring. I don't come here with empty hands. Tell me what did you cook for supper?" She did not wait to be told. She lifted the covered dish on the stove, sniffed, and asked, "What is this? You could throw it away and never miss it."

Martha's head throbbed. She bit the inside of her cheek till it bled. "It's a salmon-noodle casserole."

"And that's a supper?"

"There's fruit-jello salad and antipasto in the refrigerator." She had suspended the fruit in lime jello. Each cherry was fixed. The peaches formed a star.

"Look darling, you can learn now that you can't nourish a man on salmon noodles and jello. That you can eat for lunch tomorrow. My son needs a rich soup, a thick piece of meat. No wonder he looks like he does. I'll be glad to bring it, if you can't make it. And it won't hurt the little one either. In another month a few spoons of soup is a hundred per cent better than all the cans in the store."

"I'm going out," Martha said. "I'll be back soon."

"I talk and you don't listen. You can't take a baby out like that. You're fit to be a mother like I'm fit to be President. You're a baby yourself."

Martha took her hand off the doorknob. The baby stirred in the carriage. "I don't need you to tell me what do to," she said shrilly. "Just leave me alone. Keep your stuff and leave me alone."

"That's a fine thank-you. For this I was at the butcher at eight o'clock in the morning. For this I traveled an hour on buses to come here. I didn't expect such a thank-you."

"Look, please stop. I don't want to hurt your feelings."

"You please stop," she shouted. "Stop being such a baby and grow up. What have I done to you you're so bitter against me? I did you some harm? I came to see your baby? I brought you good things to eat? For this, you say please stop?"

"All I want to do is go out for a few minutes. I haven't been out for two days. I didn't know you were coming. I didn't expect you. I'll be right back."

"You didn't expect me. I need a formal invitation. At least I should have the privilege to sit in the chairs I bought you. Or is that too much to ask?"

"Mother, what you gave us is ours now. You didn't take a mortgage out on me," Martha said desperately and then added lamely, "You could call me up. It would only take a minute to say you're coming."

"I know you're home. Where would you go with a little baby? For the price of a call I'm on a bus and I'm here, even if you're not so anxious to see me."

"Please understand me. I want to do things for myself. I want to learn how to cook and how to keep house. I was working until six months ago. Why can't you give me a chance?"

"I don't give you a chance? My only pleasure is to help you. What have I but Joey and you and the baby? What are my pleasures? You're my only pleasure. For what do I live but to see you happy? And for this I get 'take your stuff and leave me alone ... don't mortgage me.' Is this words to give a mother? Is that what you want to hear from Stephen? You can take my word that however you treat me, so exactly he will treat you. Remember that."

The baby squirmed in the carriage and began to cry. "Oh my little bird, my sweet little bird," the older woman crooned. She pulled the covers back and touched his diaper. "Wet," she said, "wet as a cat," and still crooning she said. "Don't cry, little heart, your mama will take off her suit and put on an apron and take care of my best love." She opened the cotton hat and unbuttoned the soft blue sweater.

Martha hurried to the bathroom. She shut the door behind her and stood in front of the mirror, panting as if she had been chased. She blew her nose and threw cold water on her face. When she came out the baby was half naked. His grandmother had powdered him. He kicked his heels and grinned. His face was bland and unconcerned. He looked just like his father.

"You're still wearing your jacket?" her mother-in-law asked. "Oh my, look what you did to it." There were dark semi-circles under the armpits. "Why don't you wear shields? Why should you sweat so much, it's not so hot today?"

Martha didn't answer her. She replaced the baby's diaper and said, "All right, you take care of him. I'll be back soon."

"It's a pleasure," sang the grandmother. "It's a pleasure to play with my little love."

Martha waited impatiently for the elevator. She jumped in quickly when it stopped, wary of the unpredictable door. She read the scribblings carved into the mahogany paneling and shrugged her shoulders. It was a brand new house. Some parts of it weren't even finished yet and already somebody had scribbled. Outside she walked carefully between the carriages, tricycles, and wagons. The steet was full of children. The mothers knitted, gossiped, and read, seated all along the house and the play area behind it. She didn't see anyone she knew. She looked in the bakery window, but remembered the pumpernickel and apple pie. She stopped in front of the drygoods store and looked at the blouses and gloves and the baby clothes. She hesitated a moment and went in. Martha watched a woman who wanted a pink over-the-shoulder bag for bottles. The storekeeper had taken out a large variety, blue, black, and green, but the woman waited for a pink one. "It's not practical," the salesgirl said.

"Look, I asked for pink, do you have it? I want something different, something different and pretty. These are very ordinary. If you don't have it, say so."

The salesgirl gathered the bags together. "You want a diaper and bottle bag. What could be so different about a bottle bag? You can't expect a Paris creation for four dollars."

"Never mind," the young woman said petulantly. "I'll look around a little more."

Martha tried to attract the salesgirl's attention but she began to wait on a young woman with a little boy in a carriage. The young woman's mother came into the store and said, "You're still here?"

"I want some sleepers with the feet for a two-year-old boy," the young woman said.

"A size four should be all right. Is that the baby?" the salesgirl asked pointing to the boy.

The mother nodded and the boy strained at the harness.

"Take a six," the grandmother said.

The salesgirl held up the pajamas so that the young mother could see. She hesitated, not so much because the decision was so difficult, but rather as if she was in the habit of hesitating. "I need two," she said. "I think a blue and a green."

"The fours?" the salesgirl asked again.

"Take a six," the grandmother persisted. "He'll outgrow."

"Four," the young woman said. "A four will be all right."

The older woman tapped her daughter's elbow, "Listen to me," she said. "Take my advice."

The daughter turned to Martha. "Listen to her. Did you ever hear anything like it? Why don't I take a size twenty, maybe a forty-two would be good too? For Godsakes, if he outgrows it I'll throw it away and get another. Do you understand? All my life I didn't own a thing my size because of her. Nothing was ever bought for now. What do you want from him?"

"I only said he's growing fast. Before you know, he'll outgrow." She said it meekly but stubbornly.

"Take a four and a six," the salesgirl said. "You can bring it back if it isn't good."

The older woman sighed. The younger shook her head angrily.

Martha bought some stockings and followed the quarreling mother and daughter out of the store. They bickered and fought all the way home, not for any new reasons but to punish each other for old grievances. Listening to them somehow made Martha feel better.

Before she came into the house she decided what she must do. I won't pay any attention, she told herself. I just won't pay any attention to her.

When she opened the door she found her mother-in-law sprawled on the couch with the baby. He pulled her glasses and held a clump of her hair in his hand. He kicked his feet and squealed with delight.

Joe came in at six. The soup was simmering on the stove. His mother fed the baby a bottle. He kissed Martha in the kitchen. "I'm sorry about this morning," he said sheepishly. "I brought you a sample sweater." He hung up his jacket and squeezed her again. "Were you sore at me all day?" He shrugged his shoulders to show that he didn't plan to talk about it any more. "When did Mother come?" he asked.

"She brought a lot of stuff for supper and she came at three o'clock," Martha said. "I already cooked some. What do you want?"

"Gee, I don't care," he said. "I meant to tell you we had a big party today for the bookkeeper who's getting married and I don't want any supper. A cheese sandwich'll be enough."

When the baby was asleep they sat down together. Mrs. Shur had the soup she had brought, Joe his sandwich, and Martha the salmon she had prepared.

"Joey, eat something," his mother begged. "I didn't carry it here for myself."

"Tomorrow, Ma," he said. "Tomorrow's another day. Did you see the sweater I brought Martha? It's a fifteen-dollar sweater. It's a sample."

"If you're eating, eat," she said. "You'll talk later."

Martha carried the first forkful to her mouth and the baby began to cry.

"How they know," the grandmother said. "Just sit down to eat and they know already. I'll go hold him," she said. "You eat, Martha."

But Martha jumped up before her. "Your soup'll get cold," she said. She came back in a minute with the infant on her shoulder. She propped him up high and held him with her ear and her left hand.

"That's the way I used to eat when you were little," the grandmother said to her son. "How the sight reminds me." She crumpled some crackers into her soup and said, "Well, here we are, the four of us all together. The soup is good, Joey. You should try some."

They ate silently. The baby snored vaguely. The milk he regurgitated trickled down the back of Martha's dress and he was warm and wet where his blanket touched her breast.

End of a Year

The trees were ablaze. The water was on fire. Anna Cooperman spent her days sitting on the bank of the Charles River or the pond in Fenway Park, unmoved by the glories of a New England autumn. Rain or fog would have suited her mood much better. Her daughters worried about her. She seemed always on the brink of tears.

On Saturday her eldest daughter Georgia came to take her for a drive. Georgia waited two hours while her mother dressed. Anna could not hurry. She was always afraid that she would forget something of importance and be humiliated. Brown shoes with a black dress, a crooked seam, soiled gloves, or unpolished nails would ruin her afternoon. She was very careful and managed to achieve a kind of perfection in brown gabardine, mink scarf, and the velvet hat she had bought on Boylston Street. She could have passed for fifty-five instead of seventy-one. It pleased her to hear people tell her that.

"And after waiting for her all that time, we did not drive two blocks before she fell asleep," Georgia told her sister on the telephone. "I drove out toward Canton, the way Pa liked to take us, but she wouldn't even get out of the car at Blue Hills."

"Poor thing," Martha said. "I'll have her to dinner tomorrow. She hasn't been here since Larry had the measles."

The Salvation Army band woke Anna Cooperman early on Sunday. At eleven o'clock she and her friends sat on a bench at the edge of the Charles River and watched the parade of carriages and dogs. Mrs. Baum stroked her Bassett hound dreamily. Mrs. Hess watched a couple lying on the grass. She turned from them to look at her watch every few minutes. They were to lunch at Howard Johnson's at ten minutes to twelve. Then they would play cards until it was time for tea. They napped after tea.

"Where will you drag us to tonight, Anna?" Elizabeth Hess asked.

Anna sulked. "You can sleep in your bed tonight," she said curtly.

Her companions laughed and nudged each other. "No lectures, no concerts tonight," Hilda Baum said. "I can take off my shoes and watch Milton Berle."

Anna loathed the women sitting with her. They were her neighbors, not her friends. She was ashamed to sit with them. She had taken them to Symphony on Saturday night and they were like two bad children. Elizabeth slept with her mouth open and Hilda remained in the ladies' room after the intermission. "The squeaking grates on my nerves," she said. "I can't bear it."

It was not the first time and Anna had no reason to be surprised, but she took their reactions personally. "My dear husband loved these things so," she assured them after she had coaxed them into coming to a lecture at the Ford Hall Forum, or chamber music at the Gardner Museum or Jordan Hall. She admitted that she could not understand much more than they could, but she wanted respect, the only thing they could not give.

"They all mumble so nowadays," Anna complained at the forum. "They used to speak up much better."

"They should take more nourishment," Mrs. Baum suggested. "If they ate more, they might have more strength to talk."

Anna Cooperman could not explain that she did not come for the speaker or the music. It was enough to enter Symphony or Jordan Hall and smell the seats and see the stage. Being there established her identity. She even met people who recognized her and hurried over to take her hand. "How good to see you, Mrs.

Cooperman! How well you look!" She did not know their names and had no memory for faces, but her friends envied her those moments. They proved that she had actually been the wife of a prominent man, a politician with many friends, a philanthropist who knew how to share.

Yet she spent most of her time with two women who happened to live on the same floor of the Marlboro Arms Hotel. She did not approve of Hilda Baum, who had been divorced three times and did not even have a child to show for her trouble. Anna could not understand Elizabeth Hess, a doctor's widow with children in England and South Africa. The Hesses had run from Germany because of Jewish grandparents they scarcely knew. Elizabeth had been baptized as a child and had lived as a Christian. She had never recovered from her bewilderment.

At one o'clock Anna set up the chairs for cards and put chocolates and cookies in a dish. She shifted the chairs so that she could sit under her husband's portrait. Neither Baum nor Hess seemed worthy of the honor.

The phone startled her. It rang so seldom. She sat down on the bed as she lifted the receiver.

"How are you, Annie? This is Esther Schwartz."

"Fine," she answered, as she hunted in the barren labyrinth of her mind for the face of Esther Schwartz.

"Forgive me for calling so late, but we just happened to speak of you and Morris was furious to hear that I hadn't seen you all these months. The new grandchildren keep me busy as a cockroach. But here I am to wish you a happy, healthy New Year, free from all sorrow."

Anna strained to remember and finally saw not only the face of Esther Schwartz, but the length and breadth, the full two hundred pounds, of her. Morris Schwartz and Samuel Cooperman had shared the same office in their early days. She could remember the names on the glass door and she could remember the dinners at the Schwartzes' house where there was always too much to eat and drink, too much conversation, too much effusiveness. They embarrassed her and she insisted that she could not understand their Yiddish jokes. She sat smiling vacantly while her husband explained that she had grown up in Switzerland and spoke French and German beautifully, but no Yiddish. But at the Schwartzes' house she met people who watched her grope for a word and tried to help her by speaking Yiddish.

"So, Annie dear, if you are alone tonight, give us the honor of having you to dinner and then you can come to services with us. It's not a night to be alone in a hotel," Esther was insistent.

"I thank you," Anna said gently, softly, with a touch of French in her voice, "but I will be with my children."

"That is as it should be. My best wishes, then, for a happy year."

"The same to you," Anna said.

"And I must also tell you that I stopped at the Children's Home to leave a little something and heard that you've been continuing the good work of the Judge and I can only say God bless you."

"It's my pleasure," Anna said sweetly. "Goodbye."

Anna looked at her desk calendar. Her next visit to the Children's Home was two weeks away. She looked forward to the Thursday afternoons when she left her friends to their own meager resources and visited with the director of the orphanage and the other board members. They would discuss the numbers of pairs of new shoes, the painting of the bathroom, the cost of lettuce and vitamins. She often brought a treat with her; two hundred lollypops, two hundred Dixie cups or two hundred cupcakes. When she looked out at the children playing on the lawn, she liked to think that a little of each one belonged to her. She did not need to talk to them. She did not pat their heads or try to hold the little ones in her lap like Esther Schwartz. They were like her own children, distant, confusing, beyond her control.

"Open up for the police!" Hilda called from the hallway.

"Where do you think we've been? We bought a present for you," Elizabeth said.

"Why a present? What is the occasion?"

"The occasion is to cheer you up. We're too old to be so serious. Too many gloomy lectures. Too many long-hair concerts. We sat in my room and I mixed a little screwdriver the way my second husband taught me. Don't get scared, we didn't bring you any. But Annie, the world looks rosier this way. You're missing something." Elizabeth giggled and handed her the present wrapped in curled ribbons and gold paper. Anna was afraid. She didn't trust them.

"Open it! It won't bite you," Hilda urged.

They laughed hysterically while Anna opened the ribbons and slid the tissue paper out of the gold wrapper. Inside was a tiny ash tray in the shape of a toilet seat.

"It's charming," Anna said. "It will always remind me of you."

The afternoon slipped by. Anna lost twenty-six cents. She was annoyed by the Bassett hound that sat behind her chair, wheezing loudly.

"Tonight is a holiday," she said suddenly.

Her friends looked blank.

"It's Yom Kippur, the Jewish New Year."

"Get out the matzos," Hilda said gaily.

"Matzos are for Passover," Anna corrected. "Passover is in April."

"That shows you how much I know," Hilda said. "I never did take an interest. It's America for me and I say, let the dead bury the dead. I used to know a little something, I remember my first husband, Shapiro from the liquor chain, he once took me to some service and there were people crying over their sins. It was foolish. I said, honey, I haven't had the pleasure of a sin in a long time, and I'm not taking the blame for anything I didn't do. He was a character! Superstitious and dopey about food. The way I figured it, anything that was any good, he wouldn't eat. He drove me bananas."

"I wouldn't even care to hear about it," Elizabeth said. "After all, you have no idea of what it is to leave your house and your children. My husband left one of the best practices in Hamburg to come here like a beggar. Don't mention Jewishness to me!"

Anna was bewildered. It was during such discussions that she needed her man most of all. She did not have the words with which to demolish them, the vulgar ignoramuses with their ash trays. "I go to my daughter's tonight," she said. "We better put the cards away. I'm getting tired of gin."

"I was hearing the news just the other night," Elizabeth said. "The German war criminals and all that. And I ask, what about the American war criminals and the French and the British? I'm sick of all this hate for the German. Nobody knows what they would do if they were there. But I'll tell you they would do the same. Some day they'll have it all here and they'll see."

"Live and let live is my motto," Hilda said. "I don't care what a person is so long as he's decent."

Anna sighed with relief when they were on the other side of the door. She wrapped the ash tray in its tissue paper and put it in the drawer of the desk and prepared herself for the evening. They had not cheered her.

She muttered to herself while she dressed. It made her even more unhappy to think that she had forgotten the holiday. She took out her best black dress and chose a rhinestone pin and earrings to honor the occasion. She remembered to put some lollyppops into her purse for the children and went down to the waiting cab.

It was the rush hour out of Boston. People walked faster than the traffic moved. It took twenty minutes to get to Temple Israel, where crowds waited on the steps and women stood at their husbands' sides. She looked out enviously while the cab driver waited for the light to change. "My husband used to take me," she said to him. "Every year he would buy me an orchid and take me to hear the singing. He was very good to me."

"You don't say," the driver answered.

"Perhaps you know the name of Judge Samuel Cooperman? He passed away a year and two months ago."

"Here you are, lady," the driver said, "17 Emerson Avenue."

The children ran to the door when she rang the bell. She heard them fight for the privilege of opening it. Eight-year-old Larry opened it with such force that he tumbled backwards. His sister burst into tears. "It was my turn," she wailed. Martha came and kissed her cheek. "How fancy we are tonight, darling! How are you feeling?"

"It's the tone of her voice that I cannot bear," Anna said to herself. "It's not what she says, it's the way she speaks as if I were an idiot child."

"I am very well, thank you,' she said aloud. "I thought it would be nice to dress up in honor of the holiday. I have so little occasion."

"The holiday?" Martha asked.

"Tonight is Yom Kippur, it's the New Year. Esther Schwartz invited me to dinner and services."

"My God, is fat Schwartzie still around? Isn't it nice of her to think of you!"

"She's on the board of the Children's Home with me. I see her occasionally."

"Isn't that fine. Well, I'm changing into some clean dungarees. Would you like an apron, Mother? You're really too elegant for us. The children were painting today and I don't know how safe the chairs are."

"No, thank you. I'm very comfortable as I am," she said, but she took little Sara's hand off her lap. "Now be careful of Grandma's pretty dress, dear," she said coyly, "and do tell your mother to wipe your nose."

Anna looked around the disorderly living room for a place to sit. There were magazines and toys still on the couch. She moved them to one side and sat down gingerly. She looked around the room for some familiar things and found her silver tea set, tarnished from disuse, and a Queen Anne chair that sagged, and the reading lamp from her bedroom with the shade askew. It was all strange and unconnected like her daughters. Georgia and Martha were both built like their father. Georgia was five foot ten and Martha an inch shorter. Anna could not remember when they had not towered above her.

Georgia had her father's heavy nose and jaw and her mother's pale blue eyes. Martha had her mother's delicate features set on an oversized body. Both girls made her think of puzzles that had been jumbled, the features mixed up and the heads misplaced.

Martha came out of the bedroom in black gabardine slacks and a tight pink sweater. She had her hairbrush in her hand. "How are your lady friends, Mother? Do you still play cards every day?"

"We had a lovely game this afternoon."

"It certainly is lucky that you found each other. I was so worried that you would be lonely in the hotel."

"I'm not lonely," Anna said quickly. "We went to Symphony last night. Koussevitsky was marvelous."

"It was Charles Munch, Mother dear."

"I was there, Martha."

"I know, dear, but Koussevitzky died several years ago." Martha shoveled the crumbs off the kitchen chairs and wiped up the milk the children had spilled.

"It was lovely anyway. It was very lovely."

"Georgia will be here soon. She said she took you for a drive yesterday."

"Lovely colors," Anna said. "Your father loved such days. He would drive all the way to Vermont. Once we were all the way to Middlebury when I asked who he was going to see, and he said, the leaves."

"I was with you," Martha said. "Don't you remember?"

"Of course I remember," she said indignantly. "I see that the silver is neglected, dear. It's worth a great deal of money and you should polish it more often and my lovely old chair should have new springs. Mrs. Connelly was so devoted to all the things."

"I know," Martha said wryly. "I will never be able to compete with Mrs. Connelly."

"You should have some help then. I always said that a mother should take care of her children but there should be help."

"There absolutely should," Martha said, as she pulled her daughter's underpants down and carried her out of the room.

"Why don't you call Mrs. Connelly tomorrow and tell her Judge Cooperman's silver needs polishing. I'm sure she'll come."

"Mrs. Connelly is more than eighty years old, Mother, and if she were eighteen it would still be out of the question. I've explained so many times. The house gave us enough money so that you can live as you like, but that's all. I have to live on Sidney's salary."

"I don't see why he can't earn enough money to take care of his family properly. M.I.T. is such a big school and so elegant."

"Yes, my love, but our professor will be home in five minutes. Will you try not to speak of it? It hurts his feelings." She jabbed a potato baking on top of the stove. Sidney opened the door.

Sidney kissed them all. "And how is her Royal Highness?" he asked Anna. She begged him not call her grandma and it pleased her when he remembered.

"I don't like to look or feel like a grandma." She guarded her size fourteen and her high-heeled shoes. Her clothes were more youthful than her daughters'. Anna could remember when Larry was born and the Judge was asked a dozen times a day, "How does it feel to be a grandpa?"

"It's great," he liked to say, "it's just hard to imagine being married to a grandma." She never forgot his joke.

The children sprawled on the living room floor and watched television, while their parents ate. It was hard to talk under the noise of horses' hooves and gunfire. Anna's impatience grew. The noise, the table in the foyer, the tasteless meat loaf and canned peas all conspired against her. She was sorry that she had not gone to the Schwartzes'. At least they would have admired her clothes and talked of the past. She would have been introduced as the wife of Judge Cooperman.

"You're not eating, Mother," Martha said solicitously.

"It's not very good," she answered. "It's not nearly as tasty as we had at Howard Johnson's yesterday."

"That's too bad," Martha said, flushing.

"I'm sorry to hurt your feelings, but it really isn't any good. I've never cooked in my life but I know it shouldn't taste like this at all."

Sidney left the table to put the children to bed. Martha cleared the dishes. He brought the children in for their good-night kisses and she whispered, "If I get like that when I'm old, you can take me to the lab and use me for one of your experiments."

He kissed her quickly. "If I wanted a cook, I would have married one," he said.

Georgia and Ralph came in as they sipped their coffee. Ralph was a large handsome man with iron-gray hair and a pink girlish face. He began courting Georgia when she was twenty. She held him off until she was thirty-seven. "Because he's a perfect fool, Mother," she had said. But Anna preferred him to Sidney, who was short, pudgy, astigmatic, and half a head shorter than Martha. Anna swore they made a ridiculous pair.

"The most amazing thing just happened," Georgia Said. "Absolutely incredible! We were just finishing our dessert at Barbi's and I heard this familiar voice and turned to see who it was. I didn't recognize her at first, but it was Marian Carr and she knew me immediately. I haven't seen her for twenty-five years. She has three children. Two of them are married! She swore I looked the same as ever and was surprised to hear that I was actually practicing law. It's fantastic. I've been trying to remember what we did with twenty-five years. Four trips to Europe, three cross-country. But what did we really do? What did we accomplish?"

"Well, I always said you were working too hard. There's no point in a woman working so hard," Anna said.

"First it was Dad's office and then Steinberg's and then Ralph's."

"I couldn't have managed without you, honey," Ralph said.

"But twenty-five years! Do you realize I'll be fifty in July?"

Anna shook her head. "It's not true."

"I was born in 1907. I have a birth certificate to prove it," Georgia said bitterly.

"You don't look a day over thirty-five," her mother said. "I see no reason to harp on it."

"I'm not harping. I'm just asking myself, where did the time go. I never thought about it until I told Marian that I'm still living in the apartment I took when I left school."

"But it's a beautiful apartment and you've furnished it exquisitely. It's perfect," her mother assured her.

"But what about progress?" Georgia asked as if someone could answer her.

Martha collected the cups and saucers. "I can show you my rug. It's two feet larger than it was last week."

"What became of the loom?" her brother-in-law asked. "I knew something was missing."

"The children got into it," Martha said apologetically. "But more than that it began to be a terrible bore. You know, weaving is fascinating until you learn how. Once you have the pattern worked out, it's positively moronic."

"I thought you said it was relaxing?" her sister asked.

"Well, it is, but in a moronic way.'

"She's almost exhausted the arts and crafts field," Martha's husband said cheerfully. "In another six months she'll settle down and darn my socks and repair my torn pockets."

"Sometimes the lack of manual dexterity can be a blessing,"

Georgia said. "In the past year you've studied weaving and pottery. Before that it was tray painting and leathercraft."

"And the little blocks she stepped on in her bare feet," Anna added peevishly.

"And remember the year she rented a little piece of garden down near Fenway Park and grew the squash?" Ralph slapped his knee, threw back his head, and laughed.

"Nasty green things only an Italian could stomach,' Anna said with a shudder.

"Did she ever finish anything, Sidney?" Georgia asked. "I've never seen more than swatches of material or a single napkin."

Sidney shrugged his shoulders. "She has fun," he said. "I think you're jealous."

"Here's something that will be finished," Martha said. She pulled a rug, five feet in diameter, out of the closet. It was made of rags and old stockings that she braided. "I really need this rug. The one we have is falling to pieces. If someone will hold this end I can braid some more of these old stockings."

"Not tonight, dear," Anna said sharply.

They turned to look at her.

"Is it necessary to do that this night? It's a holy night. Do we have to sit here like rag pickers? I won't allow it. Your father would be humiliated."

"I don't remember that Father was so devout, Mother," Martha said gently.

"Not only was he not devout, but he laughed at the whole show," Georgia said.

"He took me to services every year. He never forgot the holiday."

"He was a politician, Mother. He couldn't afford to. He went to Irish wakes and Polish weddings and was a great pal of the Clan McNaughten. 'Stand on your own two feet,' is what he used to say, 'and don't get taken in by the hocus-pocus.'"

"You can say what you like, but I would rather be listening to the choir and Rabbi Liebman with people who know how to dress and behave, than working on your dirty rug that the children will surely tear to pieces in a few weeks. And I will ask to get me a cab, if you must continue."

"Senility," Georgia said between her teeth. "I told you. I knew it was coming. It won't be long before she'll be lighting candles for the dead."

"What are you mumbling?" her mother asked. "There's no respect any more. Is there?"

"It's late," Martha said, in the voice she used for balky children. "Georgia can give you a lift home. You've been out two nights in a row. It's no wonder you're tired. Let's see now, where did I put that glamorous hat?"

Ralph put his arm around her and led her to the door. "Why don't you wait here, Georgie? I'll take the Queen home and come back for you."

She liked the way he held her arm and helped her into the car. It was a big expensive Oldsmobile. She could not help but compare it to his brother-in-law's battered Ford, full of children's toys and cookie crumbs, that was parked behind it.

In a few minutes they were at the hotel. Ralph insisted on taking her up to her room. The desk clerk gave him the mail she had forgotten to take the day before. He was opening her door when Hilda came out of Elizabeth's room. Anna introduced her son-in-law and Hilda was obviously impressed. Ralph kissed Anna good night. "Take care of yourself," he said as he went into the elevator.

Hilda followed her into her room. "You had a good time?" she asked. "It must be nice to have your own children to visit."

Anna nodded as she took off her hat.

"Which one were you visiting, the artist one or the lawyer? Imagine a lady lawyer. She must be real smart."

"They were both at my younger daughter's house. She's the one that's good with her hands," Anna said.

"And those are her children?" Hilda asked as she pointed to a picture of Sara and Larry. The children sat on the couch, in party clothes she had never seen. "They're darlings! she said.

Anna remembered the lollypops that were still in her purse.

"My goodness," Hilda said, "is all that mail for you? Aren't you the popular one."

"I forgot to take it out all week," Anna said. "I'm ashamed. I forget so much."

Hilda counted the envelopes Ralph had left on the desk. "Twenty-six letters," she said incredulously. "It would take me ten years to get so much mail. You're lucky to have so many friends.

"My husband's friends," Anna said modestly.

"It's all the same," Hilda said. "Elizabeth and I were saying tonight that we envy you. That's why we like to make jokes. Sometimes we get scared that you're really sore. We know you're a lady and we're glad you hang out with us."

"I'm not really sore," Anna said.

"You see, I've knocked around so much, New York, Florida, California, always hotels and rushing around. No place is home. Nobody knows me anywhere. Family all gone. Elizabeth has had real hard times. Her children don't even bother to write her. All she has is her little bit of money and if she got sick and blew it, she'd be in a terrible fix. But see, now you've got friends and children and money to give away. It's the way to be."

Annie wrapped her velvet hat in tissue paper and put it away in its box. Hilda looked into her well-filled closet with envy.

"Well, listen," she said. "It's time for old girls like us to be in bed. So don't stay up all night reading those love letters. Good night, dearie."

"Good night," Anna said. "Thank you for coming in."

She sat at the desk and opened her mail. They were all New Year's cards from Kaufman, Clark, Klein, MacDonald, Fogarty. There were only three that she could identify, but she set them up on the mantel beneath her husband's picture and counted them again.

"Last year there were fifty-one and this year twenty-six and next year there will be twelve and some year there will be none."

Anna brushed her hair and put cream on her face and neck. She wore a blue satin nightgown that matched her eyes. She stretched out on her bed and said a prayer for the New Year. She prayed for health and better memory. She remembered her children and the children at the Home and even her neighbors. Her supplications, however, were not addressed to a distant, mysterious Almighty. It was easier to talk to her own Judge Samuel Cooperman, who had always been very good to her.

Thicker Than Water

Grandma Klein did not put her paper down until she was ready for supper. She had been reading all afternoon, her glasses low on her nose, the paper an arm's-length away. She didn't always understand what she read, but at least she read. It gave her a feeling of accomplishment and it didn't bother anyone else. To know what was read, one had to understand where everything was. She could not be sure. Was Paris in France or was it the other way around? Where exactly were Florida and California? Were they neighboring states? She had no way of knowing. But at least she felt she knew about Europe. After all, she had come from there. She knew how poor and broken it was; a place for war and devastation; a place where everyone grew old before his time from hunger and overwork.

At the supper table she listened while her daughter and son-in-law talked about a trip to Europe that her grandson wanted to take. At first she wasn't quite sure what they meant. There were so many things she did not seem to hear, or heard and misconstrued. When she had first come to stay with them they did not discuss things in her presence. Suddenly changes would take place that she was never prepared for. Of late, she found that though they did not include her in their conversations, they did not exclude her either. They did not hide things from her.

"What's this, Jackie's going to Europe?" she asked when she had had the last of her soup. She ate soup at the end of the meal, cold. She could never understand why the others insisted on having it first, hot.

Her daughter, at first, pretended not to hear. She carried the ice cream to the table for the rest of the family.

"About Jackie," Grandma Klein persisted, "why do you talk about him going to Europe? Are they catching him for the army? What are you keeping from me?"

Her daughter took the soup bowl away. "It's not the army, Mama. It's for a vacation next summer. His school is arranging a trip for the art students. Jackie wants to go and we think it would be nice for him. It's just for two months."

"You want him to go? Are you crazy? Don't you know what Europe is? What is the matter with you?"

"You don't understand, Mama. He's not going to fight. He's going to paint pictures with an art class."

"Don't tell me I don't understand. I have heard that already too many times these years. I read. I understand. I know what happens in the world."

Her son-in-law pushed his chair back. "Excuse me, please," he said politely. He threw his wife a look of understanding. With his eyes he said, "Good luck, darling! This is not for me."

Selma doggedly carried the dishes to the dishwasher. Her mother sat at the table and did not try to help. That much at least had been settled. Grandma Klein had not approved of the dishwasher. It had taken her job from her. At first she vowed that she would never use it, to prove that it was a waste of four hundred dollars. It took months before Selma had forced her mother to learn to use the machine. It was bought for a purpose, it was going to be used. Grandma Klein was never much of a dish-washer. They had become accustomed to eating out of egg-streaked platters, out of ringed glasses, and encrusted forks. At the beginning Selma had taken the dishes out of the cupboard every day and rewashed them. Her complaints were tallied with, "So it's a little dirty. What is it, poison? It won't kill you." Later on she rewashed them only for company. The dishwasher was her husband's idea. It made his wife a little lightheaded and he was happy to please her. He knew the value of a mature wife.

The first time Grandma Klein used the machine she dropped a small piece of raw carrot into it. It caught in the impeller and shattered it. The impeller was replaced but she refused to touch it again. She fingered some bread crumbs left on the table and wondered how to impress her daughter with the seriousness of the boy's trip. "What's the matter there's nothing to paint in America?" she asked. "What black year has to drag him to Europe?"

Selma did not answer her.

"I'm talking to you, Selma," she said angrily. "It's too good for you here? I'm thanking God he has a heart murmur and doesn't have to go away and you'll send him over the water yourself. You must be out of your head."

Selma carried the food to the refrigerator as if waiting for the subject to change without her help. "What's going to be with Jackie anyway?" the grandmother asked. "How is he ever going to make a living? The house is full of paintings. Can he sell them? What's the good of them? I told him already that he should stop and do something else. If you sell out what you have then you make more, but just to smear paint all day, what is the purpose? Wouldn't it be better if he went for a doctor or a lawyer?"

Selma rubbed the grease off the stove. "It's not even stylish to have so many pictures all over the house," her mother said. "I'm telling you, but you can ask anybody."

Selma went for the broom, wincing a little as she bent for the dust pan. Some nights she went to bed as early as eight-thirty because of her bad back. Lying down seemed to help it. "Don't bother Jackie, Mama," she said. "He has lots of talent. There are plenty of jobs for artists. Don't worry about him." Still she, herself, worried. She worried all the time.

The grandmother went into the living room to watch a television program. Louise, her fourteen-year-old granddaughter, did her homework at the desk opposite the set. Louise turned her chair so that they wouldn't look at each other. They weren't speaking to each other since Louise's birthday party the Sunday before. Selma, her husband and Jack had gone out for the evening so that Louise could have the house for herself. The grandmother had promised to visit with a friend of hers down the street until she was ready to go to sleep. The last minute, however, she had changed her mind and sat down in the foyer three feet behind the mistletoe to watch the party. When the boys came they sat slumped in their chairs with their feet over the arms. The girls danced together and put layer over layer of lipstick to pass the time. They played charades, but the party never acquired the right spirit. Grandma Klein enjoyed the sight of so many young fresh people. She was as pleased as any of them with the balloons and decorations. Her eyes caressed the platters of delicatessen, the chocolate layer cake, and the punch with pink ice cubes. She did not go to her room until her head began to slip forward on her chest. She kissed Louise and said, "It was a beautiful party. It would have been a shame for me to sit with old Mrs. Kauffman and miss it."

In the excitement over her departure one of the boys did a frog stand and backed into the table so that the bowl of punch toppled over on the floor.

When Selma came home the hallway was full of boys and girls. She reminded them that they were disturbing the other people in the house and they reluctantly went down the street, six abreast, so that no one could pass them.

Louise was crying while she cleaned the kitchen. "She stayed all night and spoiled my party," the girl said. "She sat right in the living room feeding herself peanuts like a monkey in the zoo." Selma clapped her hand over her daughter's mouth. "Hush," she said. "She's your grandmother."

In the morning Grandma Klein scolded her daughter. "How can you trust a bunch of young hooligans like that alone? They were quiet as long as I watched them, but as soon as I went out of the room they were standing on their heads and making a wreck of the house."

"They don't like to be watched," Selma said without force.

"So they don't like it. It would be a fine world if we did as they liked." When Louise came down to breakfast, however, her grandmother took a little ball of tissue paper from her pocket. She unrolled it and took out a pair of diamond earrings. "It's a present for you, Louise," she said. "I was saving it for you anyway, you may as well save it for yourself."

Louise didn't even look at them. "Thank you," she said. "I don't want them at all."

It had been a long hard winter for the family. Grandma Klein had nowhere to go and nothing to do. Some sunny afternoons she sat on the street corner with the young mothers. She carried her folding chair till she found a patch of sunlight between two store awnings. There she would stay until her hands and toes froze.

The intervening months, from February to April, were the worst. The gray bleak days put the grandmother in a terrible mood. She spent whole days in bed, weeping. The tears were a purge, as relieving as a funeral. She encouraged them with memories of all the hurts and disappointments in her life and she looked constantly for the small irritation that would give her a chance to indulge her feelings. At night before she went to bed she poured pots of water down at the cats that ran beneath her window. "Go! go!" she shouted. "Who needs you?" In the morning she vented her feelings on the pigeons. Selma heard the water splashing and the swish of their wings as they hurried out of the way. She heard her mother chase the children who lived upstairs till Selma begged her to let them be. "My head is broken," she complained. "How can I listen to the noise?" But whether she scolded them or not they drove around and around outside her windows with wagons tied to their tricycles and metal cans tied to the wagons.

Grandma Klein relinquished her winter habits one by one when the days became longer and warmer. It was easier to persuade her to change to fresh clothes; she wore the same crumpled cotton dress for weeks during the winter. "Who sees me? For who should I dress?" she would ask her daughter when Selma pressed her.

"We see you," her daughter said.

"You?" she would say in a way that was designed to hurt.

It was different when she sat on the bench in front of the house, greeting the people that passed on their way to the store. "Are you still sitting, Mrs. Klein?" one woman would call.

"Jealous, hah?" she answered. "I worked enough in my life already. I don't have to work any more."

As soon as the ground was workable, the landlord came to clean up the little garden in front of the house. He tried to keep the children out but they hung on the thin-trunked catalpa when he wasn't looking. They tore the first buds off the rosebush that climbed a broken trellis under Mrs. Klein's window and they cracked the stems of the purple iris with their balls and toys. Mr. Schwartz bent stiffly from the waist to twist a broken old kitchen knife in the dirt. Someone had once given him a hand rake and trowel to make his work easier, but he left them to rust on the basement window ledge. "This is also good," he had said.

Mrs. Klein sat with her hands in her lap and watched him work. "How's the farmer?" she called to him. "You're fixing it nice so the children can ruin it for you? Hah?"

He didn't answer her. He picked up the pieces of paper, glass, and ice cream sticks. He covered the garbage pails that were chained to the fence and he brought out bowls of milk for the alley cats, the ugly insolent street-walkers that preened themselves in the sun.

"I throw water on them to chase them and you feed them," she said. "What's the sense of it?"

He looked at her coldly and said, "They're living things too."

One spring afternoon Grandma Klein watched the neighbors' children playing outside her window. She was so amused by their conversations that she forgot for the moment that these were the same children she could not bear when they ran shrieking under her windows. They played house on the front steps. They made boundaries with egg boxes and paper cartons and moved in with their dolls and carriages, dishes and pieces of cloth. "My baby has the measles," the little girls upstairs said.

"And mine," her younger sister echoed.

"My baby died, but he'll be better soon. He's just a little bit died," the girl next door said.

A little boy called Peter was the father. He rode to work on a tricycle and ate the meals of stones and paper the girls prepared for him.

Grandma Klein smiled to herself as she watched them and finally took her folding chair and a bag of sticky old Christmas candy and went out to them. She carried her chair right into their house.

"We're playing here," one of the children protested.

"It's all right," she said. "I brought you some candy. It's better than stones to eat." She held the candy out to them. She had recovered it after Selma had thrown it away. "What are you throwing it away for? It's a waste," she had said. The littlest girl had moved to take some.

"Don't take candy from her," her older sister called. "How many times did Mama tell you?"

Mrs. Klein kept tempting the little one. "Take a small piece, darling. Your mother won't mind."

The little girl reached out again but her five-year-old sister hurried to stop her. "Look at it," she shouted in a voice like her mother's. "It's filthy. It'll make you sick as a dog." The little girl turned away reluctantly and Mrs. Klein nibbled the piece herself.

"Don't do me a favor," she said. "Don't take it."

The children meanwhile tired of their housekeeping. They hesitated for a minute while they decided what else to do.

"Play, children," Mrs. Klein begged. "Play a little. I like to watch you." But Peter took a handful of sand that they had used for cereal and threw it at one of the girls and then the oldest girl threw the egg boxes over.

"Let's jump! Come on, everybody," she called. She turned to go up the steps and the others followed her. First they jumped one step, then two, then three.

"Stop jumping, children," Mrs. Klein begged. "Stop jumping. You'll hurt yourself."

"Shut up, we know how to jump," Peter said and he led them higher and higher, four steps and five and six. The little girls leaped high in the air and slid on their bottoms. Mrs. Klein felt her heart pound in fear for them, but they jumped and wouldn't listen to her. She hurried up the steps into the house and went up to the second floor where two of the children lived. She knocked loudly on the first door she came to. She could hear the sound of footsteps, dishes rattling, and a baby's cry.

"Who is it?" someone asked.

Mrs. Klein didn't answer. She knocked again. Finally the mother came to the door with a baby in her arms. "What do you want?" she asked disagreeably.

"The children are jumping," Mrs. Klein said. "They're jumping on the steps."

"So?" the mother asked. "What do you want me to do?"

"Stop them," she begged. "They'll rupture themselves. They'll break their legs."

"Why don't you just let them alone?" the younger woman asked.

"It's for your good I'm telling you. They're your children."

"Please, Mrs. Klein, go sit someplace else. Don't look at them if they make you nervous. Just leave them alone and don't bother me. I have enough to do without you bothering me."

Then she shut the door. She shut it gently but firmly and there was nothing for Mrs. Klein to do but come down again.

"Did you hear her upstairs?" she asked her daughter when she came in. "What did I do so wrong? I wanted to save her children from harm."

"She has her hands full with three children, Mama. Don't pay any attention to her. She doesn't realize."

"I had children too. I know. It's no excuse to shut a door in a person's face if they want to help you. But take her part, Selma. Take her part. Take everyone's part but mine. I know what you say. I know what you think."

"What did I say, Mama?" Selma said in exasperation. "What are you making a fuss over nothing for?"

"What fuss? When fuss? Selma, I know all about it. I know how much you need me. I still remember the greeting you gave me when I came. You looked me over just as the women outside look everyone over. You're no different than they are."

"What are you talking about, Mama? Don't you remember we weren't even home when you came? We didn't even know you were coming till we found you waiting in the hall for us with all your bundles."

"I remember. Till I dragged those things in the house—it wasn't a job for my strength. I kicked them with my feet because I couldn't lift them. I remember."

"What are you bringing those things up for? That was six years ago, Mama."

"I bring it up because I haven't forgotten it. What were in my bundles? An old coffee pot, a few dish towels, some old silverware, and a few little things I saved over the years. 'Junk' you said. 'Throw it out, it's junk.' It was mine. Everything I ever owned I had to sell when Papa died. I saved a few little things to remind me I once had a home and you had to throw them out. What if it was junk even? It was still mine. When I sold everything away it was like chopping off my head. When the truck drove away with the things I saw my whole life driving away. And the little I kept you had to throw away."

"Do we have to talk about it again, Mama? Can't you remember that we didn't have any room? There wasn't an empty dresser drawer or a closet with two inches in it. Why are you so foolish? You came from Florence, angry. You said you couldn't stay with her any more. Did we turn you away? Did we argue with you? We gave you Louise's room. What more could we have done?"

"I should give you a medal. Louise still hates me for it. It would have been better if I slept in the hall or the living room like I wanted and she should like me a little better."

"You couldn't sleep in the hall. O Mama, let's not start in again."

"I only know I take up too much room here. That's what I know."

"What's the use," Selma said, "if we have to go over the same old thing a thousand times." Her mother went to her room and shut the door.

Selma dressed. She left lunch on the table for her mother and went out.

Mrs. Klein kicked off her shoes and lay down on her bed. Soon the tears began to flow. At first she wept without reason but then she wept because she thought of death. People her age were dying everywhere. Only a week before a friend of hers down the street had gone to the hospital and not returned. Fear and dread were with her always. It had been so since the morning she had awakened to find her husband cold at her side. She still woke up trembling almost as badly as the first years when she could not sleep at all. She used to sit in the living room with her newspapers and health magazines until she fell asleep on the couch. She would wake up at dawn in her clothes with the light on and the papers all over the floor. Her children had forced her to sleep in a room of her own, but she still lay awake for hours at night hearing the trains and the footsteps, watching the shadows the passing cars threw on the walls and the ceiling.

Lying there she heard footsteps in the outer hall. She hurried out of bed to lock the door. Her daughter always forgot. Selma seemed to be fearless in a city of thieves and murderers. The steps ended at her door and she heard a knock. She looked down at her crumpled soiled clothes and her bunioned toes poking out of worn old scuffs and she knew she could not ask who it was. The knocking persisted and then she heard a strange but familiar voice asking for her, not for her daughter or one of the children. It was a visitor come to see her. "Wait," she shouted through the closed door. "Wait a minute, I'm coming."

She tore off her clothes and stuffed them into the hamper. She pulled on her corset and a black crepe dress. She brushed the tangles out of her hair and rushed back and opened the door for an old friend.

The two women embraced and almost wept to see each other. "Come in. Sit down," said Mrs. Klein. "How wonderful to see you!"

Her friend at one glance took in the living room. She did not miss the china figurine lamps, the Persian rug, the brocaded draperies, or the knickknacks on the coffee table and the shadow boxes. "Beautiful," she said. "How lucky you are to have a place like this for your home." But soon they talked of trouble and misfortune only as childhood friends could. Even though almost ten years had passed since they had seen each other they could take up all the old intimacies. There was no shame between them. In the pleasure of real conversation they exaggerated everything. Both the trouble and the joy were enlarged and dramatized.

"When I go to see my daughter," the friend said, "it's always 'shur, bur'—I'm scarcely in the door and I'm out. I envy you."

"You don't have to envy me," Mrs. Klein said. "I don't spend my days licking honey either. After all, Selma is an American girl with an American education. What does she need me for? I haven't done anything here that's right. One would think I never had a home or I never brought up children. Not that we fight about it, God forbid. I'm just telling you you shouldn't envy. If I was in perfect health, I can tell you I would live by myself and be free as a bird."

"Count your blessings," her friend cautioned. "If I could tell you how I've felt these years wandering around, welcome nowhere, at home nowhere. For this I struggled with them. For this I wiped their noses and their bottoms. Ai, there's a great deal to tell and nothing to hear. But when you raise children for nothing, you know what bitterness is. You give them your strength and all they want is to do bad and outsmart you. Every step of the way. They're smart when they're little and smarter when they're big. They know they have you and right to the end they eat you alive."

"I hoped to hear better things from you," Mrs. Klein said.

"Sometimes I think I'm being punished," her friend said. "Do you remember my mother? She had asthma and a weak heart. She must have been over seventy when we took her to a home and they wouldn't take her. If I live to a hundred I won't forget the director screaming at us. He was a very nervous man, wild as a tiger. After all we didn't come for charity, we expected to pay, but he made fools out of us. 'Ten children,' he hollered. 'Eat straw,' he screamed. He told us to take turns. He said, 'You'll live through it. She may not.' I never took my turn. I put it off and put it off until she went. Maybe that's why I don't have a place to put myself."

"What are you talking? So what if I took care of my mother? How many years did I suffer with her, old and blind and useless? And what is my golden portion today? Listen, it's all a lottery. Everyone lives according to their circumstances and nobody can judge anyone else."

"It's not well to speak ill of the dead. May she rest in greater peace than I am living, but you remember the kind of woman my mother was. It was me, me, me, all her life. It was hard to take care of her."

"Of course I remember," said Mrs. Klein. "Who could forget her?"

Selma spent the afternoon in the stores. Sometimes she caught her reflection in a mirror and wondered for a moment, why am I here pushing and shoving; do I really need these things? It was almost a compulsion of the season. It was as if spring could only be assured by purchases. Country folk could measure the height of the shoots in their gardens. City people had to change their clothes and cut their hair to feel the season. For a few moments she would be distracted, but then she resumed the conversation with her mother. She could not buy her way out of it. Still, her arms were filled with bargains and she told herself that her mother was like all other older people, that the problems could not be resolved. They would be settled only by death, so she could not even wish it to be better.

When she came into the hallway she heard her mother's voice and the friend's. They were laughing shrilly and she stopped to listen. She could not remember when she had heard her mother laugh with such abandon. The other woman said, "What am I laughing? I'm laughing at myself. The nights I went to sleep and wished not to get up in the morning, you wouldn't believe."

Selma opened the mailbox. She took out the Edison bill, the soap coupons, and a request for funds for the blind. She put her bundles down again to open her door, and then put them all on the kitchen table.

"Selma darling, look who's here," her mother called. "It's a friend I grew up with, a friend of fifty years, or is it more?"

"Don't count, don't count," the friend said coyly.

"Imagine, I almost didn't let her in. I heard the door after you went out and I said it's probably a peddler or something. If I didn't hear her asking for me I wouldn't have even let her in. Imagine!"

"How nice," said Selma. "How nice for you to have some company. Can I fix you some tea?"

"Don't bother yourself," the woman said.

"If you don't mind, I appreciate it," Mrs. Klein said.

Selma busied herself in the kitchen. The two women talked in the living room, as if she weren't there at all. She poured the tea into glasses and put the bowl of lump sugar on the table. She took out a bag of special cookies that she bought for her mother. The children called them dog biscuits. "The tea is ready," she called.

The women came into the kitchen smiling. "You'll never guess what we're talking about, Selma," her mother said. "I'm surprised myself."

"Here is Mrs. Schwartz all alone looking for someone to live with her. She wants I should take a room with her. What do you think, Selma?"

"There's no hurry," Mrs. Schwartz said. "You don't have to make up your mind this minute."

Mrs. Klein shook her head. She fingered the familiar ridges in her glass and shifted on the old pillow she kept on her chair. The kitchen clock ticked noisily during the silence. Selma waited at the stove for the kettle to come to a boil again.

"It's hard to move," Mrs. Klein said. "I wouldn't know anybody in a different section. Besides I don't have any furniture any more."

"What are you talking about, Mama?" said Selma as she turned with the kettle. "Where would you find a place to live now?"

"You get so used to everything," said her mother, "the children, the house, even the neighbors. A few years go by, you know, it's hard to pick yourself up and change."

Mrs. Schwartz sipped her tea. "It's only natural," she said. "But think it over. I know myself, family comes first. There's nothing like having your own. What do they say?" she said turning to Selma. "Blood is thicker that water. If they say, it must be so."

Grandma Klein broke her cookie in bite-sized pieces and her friend lifted her glass so that Selma could refill it. Then they heard the doorknob turn and Louise with arms full of school books pushed the door open with her knee.

Celia in the Garden of Eden

Celia Abrams stood in the middle of the room with her hand over her mouth. "God in heaven," she said to herself, "what is a person? What is it that he is?"

She shut her eyes against the disorder and pulled at her hair. There was no place to sit down. Dishes were on every chair. Bedding and curtains were heaped on the kitchen table. The closets were emptied onto the beds and there were boxes still to take out of the corners, from behind the piano, from under the beds. Fifty years of living were strewn around her feet.

The buyers came in a steady dribble all day. They offered fifty cents for her ironing board and dollar for her bed. They did not care for her dishes or her piano or her leather-covered rocker. Some looked for a television set. Others wanted picture frames. A woman came hunting for Wedgwood china.

"How should I know what china I have? Three sets dishes from my wedding and from the movies my girls collected and a few pieces from my brother. Look over and see." The woman wouldn't even look. She walked out without a word.

"Go and let me think," Celia said as the door shut. She felt as if she were on the verge of understanding. One more thought and she would know. What? She wasn't sure. Six weeks had gone by like a ride on the steeplechase tornado. She had not yet recovered her balance.

Celia opened the last box in the closet and found gowns from all the weddings she had attended. Her own wedding dress was at the bottom, wrapped in yellowed tissue paper that was falling to pieces. The embroidery was stiff and the beads were crumbling, but she didn't cry. She had cried out all her tears, even the ones she didn't know were in her.

The first two weeks after Morris had gone she lived in a stony silence. Friends and family came to console her but she accepted no condolences. Everyone knew that she had had forty years of poverty and quarreling. There was nothing to say. Yet she found it hard to believe that there would be no more anger between them. It was as if they had argued and he had gone out for a walk. When they quarreled, he would not eat and she would not talk. He would taunt her while she ate his supper as well as her own. "Eat," he would say, "eat yourself into an early grave."

Celia waited until her children went back to their work and the relatives stopped coming. It was on a Friday that she looked at the clock and it was the exact time it had been the night she found him bent over the sewing machine in the store downstairs. Anguish came in like a tide. It was as if she were drowning.

The children and the relatives came back and a doctor brought sedatives. During that week when she scarcely knew whether she was alive or dead, everything was settled. The store was sold. The apartment was put up for rent and the furniture for sale. Her youngest daughter would take her. She would live in the country in a white-shingled house, surrounded by trees and flowers. She had never been there, but a relative had brought a report.

"I sat there on the porch," she said, "and listened to the birds twittering. And I said to myself, I must be dead. Otherwise how would I come to the Garden of Eden?"

"Twittering birds I can live without," Celia said. "It's my daughter Marilyn I have to live with. I'm afraid of her. I don't know what's in her mind. I don't know what to say to her. It's God's truth. I'm her mother, but I don't know her."

After the commotion at the cemetery, Celia was even more frightened than before. No one had known what to do or say. Morris

Abrams had been a belligerent atheist. Marilyn, however, stopped the pallbearers with a shriek. "Say something! Say something for my father," she screamed. She ran wildly through the cemetery till she found an old gray-beard at the gates. Everyone had to wait while she gave him her father's name and the name of his father and the names of his children so that the Hebrew words could be said. Morris' sister was furious. "It's just what he hated, just what he didn't want. What are they but actors and thieves full of blessings and hocus-pocus."

All their words rang in Celia's head as she unearthed a box of old bathing suits, her son's tennis racquet and ice skates, and her youngest daughter's baby clothes. Her memories were as unrelated as the things in her hands.

"I wanted to help him," Celia told herself. "That was all I wanted." As she said it something became clear. She had tried to save him from poverty and loneliness, but poverty didn't bother him and he liked to be alone. He had tried to save her too. He was always reading to her. "Look what goes on in the world," he used to say. "Don't be like the other beasts who sleep and eat and eat and sleep. See what goes on before your eyes!"

"Do me a favor and don't make me over," she would say. "I'm satisfied to be a beast. It costs you dear?"

Yet when his sister argued with her, he always took his wife's side. Celia tried to remember when it was that her sister-in-law had shouted, "Why do I waste my time talking to an illiterate fool?"

He told her to go and laughed at Celia. "An illiterate, my dear wife, is a person who cannot read. Since you can't read you can't keep it a secret forever. But if you aren't a fool then you will shut your ears when my sister talks. She hasn't said two sensible words in ten years."

In retrospect, his words seemed gentle, but at the moment she had turned on him. "Shut my ears," she said, "and sew up my mouth and close my eyes. Then your educated sister with her three diplomas and her Bolshevik papers can talk all she wants."

Celia wondered whether he knew that she would have given an eye for one of those diplomas. Could his sister have known how many times she tried to go to school? In each school it was the same. All day she worked like two horses. When she sat down in a class at night her eyes began to close and her head grew heavy. She told her friend, the Tante, all about it many times and the Tante sympathized. She had known the same feelings.

"All day I have the strength of iron," Celia said. "But God forbid I should sit down. Sitting down I'm not worth two cents."

It was not as if she had given up. Only a year ago she had bribed a little girl with cookies and candy, hoping that she could teach her. Susie was in the first grade. She came into the shop to show Celia her first book.

"See," she said arrogantly, "I can read."

After she read all the words she knew, Celia said playfully, "Teach me the words. Teach me the words and I'll give you an ice cream."

For a week the little girl came to "play school" with her. Celia knitted her brows and mimicked Susie. "Alice and Jerry. Alice and Jerry have a pet pony. Alice lives in a house. Jerry lives in a house. . . ." Susie covered the pictures with her hand and Celia guessed the words. But on Friday, when they came to page nine, Celia found she could not remember page one. On Monday Celia said sharply, "Go home to your mother, I have no time."

"What hurts me," Celia told the Tante while they sipped tea together, "is that Morris has anything you would want in his head. You need figuring? He can figure. You want to know what goes on in the world? He knows. You want languages or philosophy? He's there waiting. When Marilyn was home, the two of them could sit and talk two hours and I couldn't understand one word. What is there to talk that I shouldn't know what it is?"

"It's the same with my boys," the Tante said comfortingly. "Do you think I understand when they talk to each other. Sometimes it's hard for me to believe they're talking English."

"With the same brains, couldn't he figure the rent or the grocery? I hear he tells a friend they should change the laws the world should get better. But he never looks in my face to see if I'm laughing or crying. And he couldn't change himself from here to there. You know him! If somebody sits down in his chair, there could be ten empty chairs in the house and he has no place to sit. What can I do with him? They leave a hem for him to make. He asks a dollar. They leave fifty cents. He takes it! Doesn't say a word. Is this a man?"

The Tante, a true friend and comforter, shook her head agreeably. "He's been this way sixty-four years. You can't do anything now."

"Oh, if I only had the head for it and the education, I would know what to do," Celia assured her. "I wouldn't bury my head in a book or a newspaper. I would open a little business for myself. I would fill my pockets and I wouldn't be ashamed. With money you can live. Without it you drag yourself along. You look like nothing. You are nothing."

A Puerto Rican couple felt her bed and opened the dresser drawers and shook their heads as they turned to go.

"It's not even good enough for them," Celia said bitterly. She put her coat over her shoulders and went down to the drug store to call her eldest daughter.

"Sarah darling, please take some things," she begged. "I can't stand it any more. They'll never buy it all and I can't stay here and sell my life away. Take something!"

"I have everything I need, Mama," Sarah said. "I have no room for old things."

"Then take a little thing for a remembrance."

"Mama, I don't want a remembrance. I have my own life. I don't need remembrances."

"I'm sorry," Celia apologized. "I only mean the best for you."

Sarah called the dealer for her. The truck came on Friday morning with two strong red-faced men whose indifference terrified her. She watched them lift the sagging couch on experienced shoulders. The lamps were carried off casually as if they were umbrellas. The rocker in which she had nursed her children was upside down on the sidewalk. Celia walked nervously from window to window, cracking her knuckles while they took the pictures and mirrors off the walls. The rug that she has washed in ammonia twice a year and wrapped in camphor for thirty summers was dragged down the steps like a rag.

"Look what you're doing!" she shouted. "Are you crazy?" But they didn't hear.

She was panic-stricken. She was sure they wouldn't pay. They would fill the truck and drive off. She didn't know who they were. How could she chase them? But she would stand in front of the truck, they would have to run her over before they could leave. She began pulling old shopping bags from the cupboard next to the sink where she kept her store of bottles, jars, and pieces of string. She ran from room to room picking up a chipped ash tray, a picture, a battered frying pan. When three bags were filled, she hid them in an empty closet. Then she went down and waited beside the truck.

"That's it, grandma," the driver said. He counted the money and put it into her hand. "Sign here, please."

She stuffed the bills into her apron pocket and signed her name, slowly, carefully, in the German script her father had taught her when she was a child. Her eyes filled as the truck disappeared down the street, but she knew that the women were all at their windows, watching. She wouldn't give them the satisfaction. How they would like to tell their husbands, "Abrams is gone and did she cry." Instead Celia turned to a toothless, deaf old crone who sat on a box in front of the house all day. "I feel," she said, "like I was coming to America. I came with a pillow and two shopping bags and that's all I have left today."

The old one grinned and shook her head, delighted that some-one spoke to her.

"I tell you," Celia said bitterly, "a man of straw is better than no man at all."

The Tante came out of her fruit market, next door, in time to overhear. She wiped her hands on her apron and said "You're cor-rect, my dear friend, absolutely, a hundred per cent correct. When your partner's gone, you know what I've struggled for twenty years. It's a terrible thing to run a business alone. You did right. You'll never be sorry."

"Sorry? I'm sorry already. You know where I'm going? That's how much I know."

"Don't be foolish," her friend chided. "May my best friends have no worse. A son-in-law a doctor with a beautiful big house, and children good as gold. You'll live like a queen. Listen, any time you want to come and live in a hole, come here to me. I'll rent you my daughter's room. Go in good health and don't worry."

Celia looked sadly at the little shop, hidden behind the sign "Will Open Under New Management, May 20." She knew where every variety of button, snap, and lining was stored. She knew the prices that were never marked, the sizes of thimbles, shields, and welting. The young man who bought it would not believe that she had never taken inventory.

"Someone asks me for something and I don't have it, I buy a few," she said. "We made a living from this store for thirty years. We sent a girl to college. We didn't have big eyes, but we always had enough to eat."

His smart young wife turned up her nose. "I never in my life saw such a pile of junk." She spoke of fluorescent lights and new counters. She would not consider it without new flooring and venetian blinds.

The thought of it made Celia burn. "Money poured down the drain," she told the old crone when her friend went to take care of her customers. "I gave everything away to those young smart-alecks. I gave it away for nothing like a crazy woman. Abrams was my eyes. Without him, every piece of paper is the same. It's worse than blindness. It's better to be an eight-year-old child who can read a street sign and know what subway he's crawled on to. That's why I sold the stores. That's my only reason. I need to be a queen in my daughter's house? I should better be a scrubwoman in my own house. Suddenly you don't wake up a queen. You have to be born to it. Alone, your soul's your own. That's what I believe!"

The old one looked ahead vacantly. Celia shook her head. "I'm blind and you're deaf. We're a pair."

Celia's eldest daughter and son both begged her to spend the night with them until Marilyn came for her in the morning. She was stubborn. She borrowed a chair and an old army cot and spent her last night in the apartment. She woke with a start at half-past five. She had been dreaming that she was waiting at Castle Garden, resting her head on a burlap sack. She was twelve years old and alone. While she waited Morris ran past her. A mob of people were chasing him. She found a stick and beat them off.

Celia was trembling when she sat up, clutching the wooden support she had pulled out of the army cot. Her cheek was sore from the rough cotton. She could not remember where she was. The apartment was unrecognizable without furniture.

At seven-thirty, however, Celia sat at the window in her slip and sipped a glass of hot water, in which she dropped a quarter of a lemon. People were hurrying to the subway. Cars were going by. It gave her a feeling of accomplishment to see them go by. She noticed the clothes the people wore; the new hair colors and styles. The contents of the refrigerator were on the window sills. She carefully finished the left-over cottage cheese, a cucumber, and a hard-boiled egg.

At nine, she was ready in her winter hat and leather gloves. She wore her best dress and carried a pocketbook new and unused for six years. She carried her bags and boxes down, one by one. The suitcase was tied with twine. Most of her clothes and the family album were in a heavy corrugated carton that took an hour to tie. She stood in the doorway and waited.

Marilyn double-parked the car and ran out to her. They embraced quickly.

"Thank God, you're here," Celia said. "If I had a penny for every foolish thought that comes in my head, I'd be a millionaire."

"I thought Phil or Sarah would come to help you," Marilyn said.

"Who needs them? I can't help myself?" Celia said peevishly. Marilyn opened the trunk and together they struggled with the boxes.

"Just one favor," Celia begged. "I promised I would leave an address in the fruit store. She's my best friend in the whole neighborhood."

Marilyn left her address at the store. The Tante embraced her and wished her well. "Your mother is a wonderful woman. May she have what I wish her! Let me give you a few grapes for the way. She loves the purple grapes. Crazy for them!"

Marilyn worried about the car while the Tante carefully pulled off the bruised grapes. "I was here first," a customer grumbled. "How long do I have to wait?"

"I'm sorry," Marilyn apologized. "I'm not a customer."

"Business first and pleasure later! Give me some apples they would have a taste. I pay fifteen cents a pound for apples and they taste like potatoes, like raw potatoes. What's the matter with everything?"

The Tante pretended not to listen, but finally she turned and said, "Nothing's the matter. May I drop dead this minute if you can get better apples. When is the season for apples? Ask this lady here, a doctor's wife lives in the country. Ask her when apples come."

Marilyn looked out impatiently. "Tell her, darling," the Tante begged.

"In September," Marilyn said wearily.

"So what did I say? September, October, November, December, January, February, March, April, and May. What taste can they have nine months later? You're lucky they kept the worms away so long."

"I have to go," Marilyn said as she reached for the bag.

"Go in good health and come in good health and write me a postcard. Tell me how she is. I love her. I love that woman."

Marilyn ran to the car while the arguing continued. "I'm not a farmer and I'm not interested in the seasons. I only know if I pay a price, I want something for my money."

Marilyn shuddered as she opened the car door. She had been away for fifteen years but the neighborhood and the people in it still upset her. It was as if she were still in danger of being sucked back into the ugly rooms and the subways. She recoiled from the nagging voices and was depressed by all the people waiting at windows and stores for time to go by. When she was eighteen she imagined it all to be monstrous and subhuman. Fifteen years later it was only sad and poor, utterly depressing.

"Is the door locked, Ma?" she asked with studied gentleness. "I don't want to lose you."

They drove across Brooklyn to the highway that would take them to Connecticut. "It's another world," Celia said. She enjoyed the traffic, the houses, the bright-colored cars. "Palaces," she said. "Little palaces, each with a garden and a porch. If your father hadn't been so stubborn, we could have come a long time ago." After an hour had passed, the towns looked alike and the forests and fields ran into each other. Marilyn turned on the radio to fill the silence.

"It's only six weeks since Papa went away," Celia said. "We can live without music a little longer."

"The children are fine," Marilyn said for the third time. "And Sidney is busy at the hospital."

Celia looked for something to say. "Your aunt came last week to say goodbye," she said cautiously. "She found me in the fruit store and blabbled for two hours. She's angry with you for the prayer at the cemetery. She's angry with me for my whole life, for everything I did and everything I didn't do. My intelligent, educated sister-in-law. Her learning fits her like a hat fits a horse. Do you know what she said to the Tante? She says, 'I'm living with a man for fifty years. I have children and grandchildren. In a few months I'll have a great-grandchild. But if I had married him, I couldn't have stayed two weeks with him.' And she laughs at me," Celia said.

Celia dozed fitfully during the last few miles and awoke with a start when the car stopped.

"We're home, Mama," Marilyn said.

Celia took her daughter's hand so that she could pull herself out of the car. She looked up at the large white house, screened from all the neighbors. "It's big," she said, "bigger than I thought." She put her hands to her ears. "How still it is!"

Then the children came running. She devoured them with her eyes. "Country children with apple cheeks and brown legs. From whom did they get so beautiful?" The older ones ran away, but the youngest let her press her nose against the nape of his neck.

Marilyn took care of the packages while the girls pulled Celia through the house.

"And this," Joan said, is the living room. ... and this is Daddy's office. ... and the dining room. ... and upstairs. ..."

"Take me back to your mother," Celia begged. "I'm lost. I could never find my way back."

"Do you like it?" Marilyn asked proudly.

"It's like a magazine picture," Celia said. "It's so perfect, I'm afraid even to sit down."

"You'll get used to it," Marilyn assured her.

"It's too nice," she said. "It's too nice for me."

Celia examined the bright yellow kitchen and admired the gleaming stove that had no flame and was governed by little buttons. Marilyn showed her all the clever gadgets, while Celia smiled and didn't listen. "It's not for me," she said. "It's altogether not for me. I'd be afraid to touch anything."

Marilyn opened the last bag and found the soap dish with a sliver of soap, a battered frying pan, a coat hanger, a fly swatter, and a kitchen clock that had not worked for fifteen years.

Celia watched her with embarrassment. "It's nothing with nothing," she said. "I was frightened. I thought maybe I would need some things."

Marilyn pulled out the remnants of an old kitchen curtain. "What would you need this for?"

Celia opened her mouth and closed it without saying anything. It was too much to explain. "It caught me here," she said and thumped her chest. "Look it over. If you could use something, keep it. If not, throw it all away."

Marilyn looked worried. "Why don't you lie down and rest while I get supper?" she asked.

"I couldn't help you?" her mother begged.

"You can unpack your things, if you're not too tired?"

"Who's tired?" Celia said. "What hard work did I do today?"

She had trouble catching her breath when she climbed up the steps to her room. "You would think I never climbed steps before," she said jokingly as Marilyn put her boxes on a chair. She insisted on opening everything herself and told her daughter to go.

First she draped an old housedress over the pink chair so that she could sit down on it. She pulled off her shoes and rubbed her toes against the soft blue carpet, while she examined her room. The wallpaper was pink with red roses. The chintz curtains matched the pattern of the paper. She shook her head at her reflection in the mirror over the dresser. Her face looked green against the pink. Her wispy gray hair was as brittle as straw. She hung up one dress and put some underwear in a drawer. She stopped to finger the smooth edge of the bed. The walnut was polished as smooth as glass. She had always insisted on metal beds to discourage the bedbugs and roaches. She tested the mattress and found it smooth and resilient. The children played beneath her window and the baby cried. An insect hummed on the sill and leaves blew against the roof. She tried to think of the empty apartment she had left that morning, but it was in another world. Though she fought to keep them open, her eyes closed.

Something in the breeze that shook the curtains made her dream of a house she hadn't seen in fifty years. It brought back the feel of the dirt floor and the brook that trickled beside it and the mildew that covered her clothes in the morning.

"We're here to help you, Grandma," a shrill young voice squealed into her ear, suddenly. The little boy jumped up on her bed and sat on her as if she were a horse. Two icy little hands covered her eyes.

"Guess who?" the voice said.

Celia hugged them with one hand and pushed them off with the other.

"You didn't unpack," the older girl scolded.

Celia struggled to her feet. "First let me wash," she said. The three children followed her as she opened the closet door and the door to the attic.

"Where could the bathroom have gone?" Joanie giggled.

"Where could it be?" her sister echoed.

"Laugh, little ones," Celia said. "Laugh at an old grandma. She can't even find the bathroom or turn on the faucet. She doesn't know how to work the stove and won't even be able to boil herself a pot of water."

"I can turn on the stove for you," the older girl offered. "I'll turn it on any time you want."

Celia bent down and kissed her head. "That's a good girl. Now take everybody downstairs and I'll come soon."

When they were gone she pushed the valises and boxes into the empty closet. She brushed her hair and spoke to her reflection in the mirror. "The Garden of Eden is no place for you, Celia." She knew that in a few days, a week at the most, she would return to her friend the fruit lady and live in a familiar hole. "Oh, dear husband," she said, "when it comes to changing myself, I'm no better than you. May you sleep well, you in your Garden of Eden and I in mine."

The Salesmen

In March, the forsythia buds swell and the ice in our unpaved driveway turns to mud that tugs at the soles of our shoes. Swarms of tiny black bugs appear whenever the sun comes out, and the salesmen arrive. They bring paint and vacuum cleaners, insurance for this world and the next; samples of cosmetics and kitchen utensils; and bushels of last year's apples, rotten on bottom, firm and polished on top.

The first to come after the winter hibernation was a blond young man, bent under the weight of a vacuum cleaner. He stood in my doorway with the rain dripping from his hair and the heavy box of attachments dragging him down on one side. I didn't have the heart to send him away. The living-room rug was sprinkled with cracker crumbs. I thought I had nothing to lose but a few minutes of a gray day.

I gasped when he turned a bag of cork shavings on to the floor. He cleaned it up efficiently, however, and left a light colored square to show what might be done.

"You have a bad sand dust condition here," he said, like a doctor urging an operation. "This is what you permit your children to breathe," and he showed me the contents of his dust bag.

Originally published as "A Suburban Note." Reprinted from *Commentary*, March 1957, by permission; all rights reserved.

He made it plain that only a calloused mother and inept house-keeper would live with an outmoded cleaner. I found myself admitting that my cleaner was ten years old and even agreed to discuss the matter with my husband.

"I'm sure he wants the best for you and the children," he said. "The offer is just for today. Why discuss it? Why put it off?"

The company was offering a new suit of clothes and a trip to Miami to the young man who sold the most the fastest. "This sale means an awful lot to me," he said.

I had to tell him the truth. I did not plan to buy a vacuum cleaner. I did not care whether or not he went to Miami. Did he care whether I went to Miami?

He swore softly as he gathered his hoses and brushes. He had no use for people who weren't serious. I had wasted his time and lessened his chances to win the contest.

The rain turned to sleet that day and icy roads protected me from the outside world. But several days later, as soon as the sun came out, two women came to my door. One was middle-aged and stout; the other a young girl with a pony tail tied in a pink ribbon. She smiled as she spoke. "We come to bring you word of the true religion."

The older woman shook her head in agreement. "People have fallen into bad ways. We live in a corrupt world," she said, and I could not disagree.

"It's like in Noah's time," the young girl said. "God saw the earth and it was ruined. All flesh ruined its way on the earth."

My daughter hugged my knees and shared my uneasiness. "What does she say?" Nancy asked.

"It's in the Bible, deary," the older woman assured her. "God's word is all in the Bible."

"I'm sorry," I said. The baby rattled his crib impatiently.

"For your good and the good of your little children," the girl begged. "The time is at hand for Jehovah to bring his punishment upon us all. Terrible destruction awaits us." Her voice trembled. I thought I saw tears in her eyes. "True religion brings great blessings and love," she said desperately, pressing some pamphlets into my hand. "A little gift," she said. "Only ten cents for this little gift."

I took a dime from the change the milkman had left and gave it to her.

"God bless you and teach you repentance," the older woman said as they turned to go.

"Tell me," Nancy pleaded, "tell me what they were selling you?"

On Friday, the paint salesman came. The children were playing in the sand box. I was typing at my desk near the window while I watched them. It was the first quiet moment of the day and I was not happy to see a car in the driveway. A heavy young man in a leather jacket pulled a briefcase out of the back seat. He came up to the front door with a confident smile and waved when he saw me at the window.

"I would like just ten minutes of your time," he said cheerfully.

"I'm sorry," I said, "I'm busy now."

"Come on," he urged. "I'm here to do you a favor. What can you lose?"

"My place," I said angrily.

"What are you doing, writing a book?"

"Yes," I said sharply.

"You're kidding," he laughed. "Look, when I decide to do someone a favor, I do it. So relax. I'm not selling anything. I just want to offer you a once-in-a-lifetime opportunity. I don't have to tell you that your house needs paint." He scraped his fingernail along a shingle and the blistered paint flaked off. "Your friends and neighbors must have told you already. It's just your luck that we have a special this month. We just finished the Cory house down the road and they gave us your name. Now if you take advantage of our offer Cory gets twenty-five dollars off his bill. Now I'll be happy to give you the same amount for every person you recommend. You recommend fifteen people, you get your job done for free."

"We're not painting the outside this year," I said firmly.

"Why not? Give me a good reason why not?"

"I don't have to give you any reason," I said angrily. "We'll paint when we're good and ready and we'll do it ourselves. You're just wasting your time."

"It won't cost you a cent," he said. "I put it on your mortgage and you don't lay out a penny. Let me show you a sample of the work we do. You could never do it! You'll paint this house yourself? What are you talking? It's impossible!"

He did not look at me, but stared rudely at the dining room behind me. The table was set for a Friday night supper. There were candles and a braided *challeh* on the white tablecloth.

"Isn't this nice. I haven't seen this since my old grandmother died. How nice you keep it up! I really like this kind of thing, I really do. I'll tell you something. I'll take off fifty dollars for being you're in the family. What do you say? Do yourself a favor!"

I couldn't get rid of him until the baby fell and cut his lip on his pail. "Where's your doctor?" he asked solicitously. "I'll give you a lift."

"Will you please go?" I found myself screeching. "Just go!"

In the course of two weeks I resisted a photographer, a tree nurseryman, and people wanting me to subscribe to magazines I had no time to read. But all my experience could not prepare me for Mr. Stern.

He came out on a Sunday morning when I was trying to turn a day that was neither Sabbath nor Monday to some account. I imagined that I could hurry spring by painting kitchen cabinets. The children squatted at my heels. My husband helped without enthusiasm.

"Not company," I groaned when I heard the doorbell. Dishes and cans were piled on the living-room couch. The children had turned the kitchen furniture into a train.

I knew in a moment that the visitor was a stranger. Our friends did not wear gray felt hats.

He asked for me and I assured him that I was myself.

"I pictured you older," he said thoughtfully. "My wife and I love your stories. They have a mature point of view, an understanding of life. I've wished a long time for the opportunity to tell you."

A flush of embarrassment and pleasure went from my cheeks to the back of my neck. I found myself staring down at my green-speckled dungarees, one leg rolled to my knee, the other slipped to my ankle.

"We're painting now, but won't you come in?" I said as I turned to take a pile of dishes off a chair.

"There aren't many people I can drop in on like this," he said. "You can only do this with a mature person, who takes life seriously. ... Is your husband in. I would like to meet him too."

It was then that I first noticed the leather briefcase. Nancy ran to get her father.

Mr. Stern stood up to shake hands, but withdrew from the green fingers. "I'm sorry to interrupt your work, but I was passing by and I had to speak to you and your wife. We're expanding every day and prices are going up. It would not be wise to delay."

"I don't understand," I said. "I don't know what you're talking about."

"I'm sorry," he said. "I thought I mentioned that I am on the staff of the Hillside Memorial Park."

I still looked blank until my husband said, "You mean the cemetery?"

"You mean you're trying to sell us a plot in the cemetery?" I said.

"I'd like you to think of it as insurance, as an investment in the future. It's protection for you and your children and a chance to get the most for your money. That's exactly the proposition I want to offer you."

I took a deep breath. "We're painting this morning," I said tightly. "Why don't you come back in about twenty years?"

"I'm glad that your wife has a sense of humor," he said. "But in all seriousness, if you wait for an emergency, a plot can set you back as much as five hundred dollars. If you buy now you can get two for the money."

He was ready, pencil in hand. "How many children do you have?"

I shook my head mutely.

"I have a site on the hill," he said. "The view is breathtaking. It's right beside the chapel where memorial services are held, which is a real convenience. I can show you on this diagram that it's a perfect location, right on the path. The inside plots are not as desirable because you can't go right up to them."

The baby crept in quietly and knocked his leather case over. "No!" he shouted, so sharply that we all jumped.

"I'm not interested," I said.

"You can't ignore it, my dear," he said. "The five hundred dollars you save by purchasing now can go toward a child's college education."

Stevie sat under the dining-room table sucking his thumb, looking with yearning at the hat on the mantel.

"It's not only the money, it's the aggravation. Why not protect yourself from a difficult decision at a time when it's hard to make decisions? I offer you here the most beautiful, the most dignified cemetery in New England. You'll never be ashamed of it. It's the best, the very best that money can buy."

He spread his glossy photographs out on the floor. Some looked like a well-tended golf course; others like a botanical garden. There were fish ponds and weeping willows, formal flower borders. Outside my window was a bumpy lawn, bounded by a tangle of blackberry brambles, goldenrod, and sumac.

The only cemetery I had ever seen was the one in which my grandparents were buried. It was a poor man's place, stone against stone, treeless, as crowded and ugly as the tenement in which they had lived. The ivy we brought each year grew reluctantly, looking like the sweet-potato vines that once trailed around my grandmother's kitchen.

"It's too fancy and too expensive," I said, while my husband studied the photographs. "We bought two acres of land for five hundred dollars. Why should a tiny little plot cost that much?"

"You would look for a bargain?" he asked, as if I had hurt him deeply. "You are thinking of the place where your great-grandchildren will come to pay their respects. You *owe* them a spot that is dignified, convenient, and refined. This is a memorial garden, insured perpetual care by a trust fund. It's a democratic cemetery, no difference between rich and poor. What more could you want? You pay it out in monthly installments and you won't miss the money."

He gathered his pictures and papers together. "I'll give you a week to consider the special offer. Five hundred dollars for two, twelve-fifty for six, which not only saves you money but is the only way to keep a family united in a fine type of family estate. Think about it. I'll be back."

There was something ridiculous about this lugubrious little

man in a dark suit and hat and carrying a briefcase full of contracts for final resting places. We laughed hysterically as he maneuvered his car in our narrow driveway.

I returned to the kitchen cabinets and the drying paint, determined to forget Mr. Stern, but my husband, whose vanity had not been wounded, could think of practical considerations.

"What if something happened to me at work? What if we were both in a car accident? Explosions, plane crashes, fires—anything can happen!"

"I'm responsible for so many things," I argued. "I don't want to worry for my great-grandchildren and I'm not so serious and mature that it's time to bury me. We could buy a rug for the money, or a new vacuum cleaner. We could have the house painted instead of doing it inch by inch ourselves."

The vacuum cleaner and paint salesmen did not come back, but Mr. Stern appeared week after week, a mortal angel of death in a dark gray hat. First he came to see if we had made up our minds. Then he came to tell us the prices were *really* going up. The third time he came to announce that two of our best friends had bought their plots from him and we could arrange to have congenial neighbors in the house of eternity.

I refused to speak with him. My husband hurried out to the steps to assure him that we had not been waiting anxiously for his arrival. The fourth time, however, I was not at home and Mr. Stern followed my husband around as he raked the debris of winter out of the gardens. He insisted that it was protection for me, an impractical and unstable woman; it was a favor to the baby playing in the sandbox; it was a man's duty to look out for his family.

My war with Mr. Stern was lost that morning. A letter of congratulations was in our mail on Monday. We were prepared for anything the future could bring. I was too angry to read the details.

A subdued Mr. Stern paid a final visit two weeks later. "I want you to see it with your own eyes. I don't feel it's right to take your money without you seeing what you get for it. All I want is you should be satisfied."

He drove us to the cemetery, past the gates, through the lavish gardens, the rolling lawn, past the fish pond and the formal arrangements of cedar, cyprus, and arbor vitae. When the road ended, Mr. Stern led the way on foot.

"You can't expect much for such a small investment," he said. "It may take five or ten years before the landscapers get to this section. It was your idea, sir, and if it's what you want, you're welcome to it."

Our "estate" for two was in uncleared woodland, a tangle of thorns and young trees sprung up since last year's fire and hurricane.

"It looks like our back yard," Nancy said.

Mr. Stern pulled burrs off his coat. "Are you really sure that this is what you want? I can still change it."

I picked the baby up out of the path of the poison ivy. "It's fine," I assured him. "It's just as ready as we are."

A few minutes later we were home again. Mr. Stern shook hands with us.

"The service and the contract are the same whether you pay a hundred or a thousand. Once they clear the area it will be as beautiful as the rest of the park. It's just a question of time. I wish you a good life, free from sorrow, and I want you to know that I am your personal memorial counselor, ready to serve you in any way, at any time."

He gave my hand an extra squeeze. "I hope we'll be reading something of yours soon. My wife is a very literary person and has so many ideas. It's a pity that she doesn't have the time to write them down, but she was just saying this morning that if you ever need some ideas, she would be happy to talk with you and share some of her experiences."

Home for Pesach
...And Back Again

Home for Pesach! It has a good sound, like home for Christmas, or for Thanksgiving, or the Fourth of July. Where is home? Home is where grandparents live. The children's books still say that Gramp lives on the farm and the city children come to visit to see the chickens and the cows. In our family, it's the other way round. The children live in the country and come to visit Grandma in her city apartment.

"My grandma's house is bigger than the Town Hall, the Library, and the Post Office put together," boasts my daughter.

"It's like a castle," says her sister. "It's a red brick castle with a drug store downstairs for emergencies, a candy store around the corner, and a bakery that you can smell all day."

We pack for a three-day visit as if we were bound for a trip around the world. Who knows what the weather will be in April? We're prepared with snow suits and straw bonnets, boots and pink sandals.

I make a list. I must tell the cat-sitter where the food is. The water and electricity must be shut off. A capricious dishwasher once turned itself on while we were gone. Like an idiot sorcerer's apprentice, it nearly washed the house away before the pump gave out.

The phone rings as I shut the last door. It's a Mrs. Johnson to ask a favor. She has been invited to play the violin at a Women's Club tea. She would like me to accompany her on the piano. I agree, and explain that I cannot stop to talk. "I'm going home for ... Easter," I say.

"Of course," she says. "I forgot, you lucky girl. I love New York. I adore the lights, the shopping, and the shows. Have a marvelous time and be sure to come see me as soon as you come back."

Finally I join the family in the car. We take leave of the half-opened narcissus nodding into the swollen brook and the crocuses strewn like orange peels across the lawn. Goodbye to our own little piece of exurbia!

The drive is supposed to decompress me and offer a transition from my hurried, disciplined life to the one I will lead in Brooklyn. At home, every morning, I count out the hours of the day like money in the bank; so much for the children; so much for the typewriter; so much for the garden and so much for the stove; so much for the piano and for friends and so little for miscellaneous interruptions. Two friendly telephone calls or a bloody little nose can wreck the accounting system.

Ahead of me yawn three days of visiting with relatives, hours in the kitchen, gossiping, while I sit with empty hands. I might enjoy it if I were more adjustable. But I grow tense at the thought that I will have to stop running. Once I visited a friend in her trailer and moved so fast I cracked my head in a low doorway and knocked myself out. I tell myself to remember it. Running in my mother's house will have the same effect.

Ready or not! Five hours and two hundred and fifty miles later I pull the lollypops out of the children's hair and wipe the graham cracker crumbs off their cheeks. We're home.

My father has been sitting at the window waiting for us. My daughter jumps into his lap before he can get up. She strokes his last white hairs, kisses his ears, and takes the pennies out of his pockets. My mother wipes her hands on her apron, and stares at us hungrily and smiling, as if we might disappear if she blinked.

While we carry in our valises, I notice that the couch sags a little deeper than last year. The linoleum is worn a darker brown and the cracks in the ceiling have not been repaired. But everything is in order and very clean. The furniture gleams and the cotton doilies and net curtains are stiff with starch. Every corner has been scrubbed in honor of the holiday and even scrubbing isn't enough to make the surfaces suitable for Passover.

The kitchen table is covered with three sheets of heavy cardboard. The cupboards where everyday dishes are kept are locked. The stove has a sheet of tin over it to hide the porcelain that been touched by leaven and the sink has a Passover drain board. If anything falls into the sink, it will be thrown away.

Grandma explains what can be touched and what must be left alone. The children listen eagerly, entranced to discover that there's a taboo in every corner. They obey without questioning. In an enchanted castle, spoons, dishes, and cloths may have a life of their own that must be respected. Kitchen closets containing cereal, beans, and cans of salmon may be locked as if demons would escape if they were opened.

When the car is emptied and parked, my husband stretches out on the couch and goes to sleep. There's little else for him to do. Two children find tricycles and ride them up and down the long hallway. The television blares though no one looks at it. My son beats a drum, abandoned by his cousins, with his fists, while I try to hush him.

"Please," begs my mother. "It was quiet last week and it will be quiet next week. I hear them only once a year. Let them!"

I stand in the kitchen, looking for work to do. The beet soup bubbles in the pot. Three potato pies are in the oven and my mother pulls pinfeathers out of the fourth chicken. She refuses to tell me how I can help her but I know enough to find the chopper and the chopping bowl. I pound away at the onions, the chicken livers and hard boiled eggs, and glue them together with globs of golden chicken fat. The chopper thumps rhythmically while I watch my fingers. One year I left a piece of my thumb in the bowl. I remember how surprised I was to find it didn't hurt. I wondered whether all losses could be borne if they were not premeditated. Thinking brings the pain, the guilt, and the understanding.

My mother and I work in silence for a little while. We both

fear that words will obscure the waves of affection that flow between us. She does not scold me for being too thin and I watch her devotion to super-abundance and do not say, "What do you need it for?" The children take turns bolting into the kitchen. Each time they get cookies and kisses. The look at me with questioning eyes, asking for permission.

"I've had five already," admits the eldest.

"Don't ask," says my mother. "If Grandma gives, take."

I'm proud of my self-control. I don't warn her that she will make them sick or remind her that she tried to fatten us all to obesity. I refused to eat, but my sister knew years of struggle and discipline before she came back to normal size. My brother is still huge.

It pleases me to be indulgent and passive, a grown woman, no longer impatient with my mother and angry at my father. My brother and sister have ceased to be inadequate extensions of myself and have miraculously turned into real human beings with dreams and sorrows of their own. It seems a pity that it has taken me thirty-five years to come to these discoveries. No harm would have come out of learning sooner.

When silence palls, we look for safe subjects to discuss. I ask about aunts and cousins and hear that they are all, "Thank God, the same." The familiar phrase reminds me that in our family change has a connotation of trouble if not outright disaster.

"The old lady with the fiddle," Mamma says, "how is she? She has still trouble with her children?"

Mrs. Johnson, who wants me to call her Mary, is the old lady Mamma means. I sent home clippings from the local newspapers when we last played together. The last time I was home, Mamma stared at the pictures while I told her of Mary Johnson's accomplishments, noting again and again that she was almost as old as Mamma.

"What could be missing to such a woman," said my mother with such unabashed envy that I stopped telling her about the rose garden and the beautiful white house, about the trips to Florida in the winter and the Cape in the summer. Instead I shared Mrs. Johnson's troubles with her. Her thirty-year-old son had no interest in work of any kind. Her daughter had just divorced her second husband.

Mamma dispensed with all comfort and luxury with a wave of her hand. "I won't trade with her then," she said. "I wouldn't want to live if I didn't have pleasure from my children."

That night is the first Passover Seder. My younger sister and older brother come with their children. The dining table is opened as far as it can go and two bridge tables are added for the children. The white tablecloth is covered with a sheet of plastic so that the wine can be mopped up as fast as it's spilled.

My father makes the blessing over the wine. My youngest nephew begins to ask the four questions that begin the ceremony. He stumbles. His father glares at him and the boy bursts into tears. He runs away from the table with his mother after him.

Papa asks himself the questions and gives himself the answers. He tells the story of the Exodus in Hebrew which only he can understand. He chants in a monotone, stopping only to point to the chicken bone that is supposed to be the paschal lamb, to the celery that symbolizes bitter herbs, to the chopped apples and nuts that remind no one of mortar or clay. The younger children do not even look. Two older ones beg to sing the portions they have learned at Hebrew school, but my father doesn't know the tune they know and he can't stop to wait for them. They get even by giving each other sly pushes and kicks and wiggling the rickety table. A little one chokes on a crumb of matzah. Another throws up his taste of horseradish that he thought was cherry jam.

Papa doesn't look up from the Haggadah. He reads doggedly without changing a word or skipping a sentence. When he is done my mother brings the food she has been preparing all day, according to her own unchangeable ritual.

I help carry in the soup, made exactly as it has been made the twenty-five years I've been carrying it. The smell of it reminds me of all the battles and quarrels against the rigidity and stubbornness in my father's house—all lost battles. But they look so different now that I've established a secure beachhead for my own rigidity. I imagine that whatever dignity my parents have comes from their refusal to accommodate themselves to me.

The second day is the same as the first. Cousins and aunts

come to visit in the afternoon. I hide in the kitchen with my mother. Each guest is offered a dish of pancakes and a glass of wine. I beat the eggs in batches of four and pour the fat into the frying pan. Nieces and nephews roll nuts in the hallway. My children are delighted with the timelessness, the freedom. They can run around the block whenever they feel like. They can play hide-and-seek under the high, old-fashioned beds and they can eat all day long. They wallow in the noise and confusion.

My mother is in her element. Her face is flushed at the stove. Her hair is disordered and her apron is streaked with food. We're together, doing women's work, gossiping about relatives, and discussing the prices of apples and potatoes.

The second Seder is the same as the first. The chanting, the squirming, and the soup are unchanged. But this time my nephew doesn't stumble. The food, the wine, the Haggadah, and the children make conversation impossible. My brother, who sells fabrics to dress manufacturers, says that business is good. My brother-in-law complains that television sets are not moving. A sleepy child cries and gets everyone's attention. Boredom settles on us all, like a frost.

We ask the family to excuse us the last night before going home.

"Where are you going?" they ask.

We don't know. We're going out to find Mrs. Johnson's New York. We'll look for lights, for shows, for something to take home. First we call our old friends. They've all moved to Larchmont, Bellaire, or Darien. We take the subway uptown, alone.

We think that we might eat a huge lobster as an antidote to all the potato pancakes we've eaten. Perhaps, we'll see a show. It doesn't matter what it costs. We'll find a Modigliani print in a bookstore. We can even go to a night club.

Instead we wander around Times Square, like lost teen-agers. There are no tickets for anything we would care about. We're too full to eat, and are really not interested in a night club. We want desperately to be frivolous but have no idea of how to begin. We don't speak of it, but feel that there is something improper about spending as much money for an evening's entertainment as the family could use for a week's food. No matter where we go, we will come back to sleep on the broken sofa and wake up to see the cracked ceiling above our heads.

When we're tired of walking, we permit ourselves an Italian movie, and a pastrami sandwich and a glass of beer. The best part of Italian movies is that when you come out of the theater to American reality, you feel so lucky.

In the morning I call my sister and sister-in-law to say goodbye. I know that we've said very little to each other, not only because children didn't let us, but because we don't know how to talk to each other. I ask, "What are you doing?" They answer, "Nothing much," and the fence is up. I imagine that they think I'm boasting or complaining when I volunteer information.

"May we be together again next year," says my mother.

'If God wills," says my father. "May next year find us alive and in good health!"

The children cry because they want to stay longer. But our visit is over.

All the way home I make lists of what I shall do. The children sing nursery school songs. I feel as if I were coming out of a tunnel. The way home to the country always seems shorter.

The next morning I find that the rain has washed the crocuses away, but the narcissus has opened and the violets are showing their heads. I have a light-headed feeling when I take the children off to school.

Mrs. Johnson is at her mailbox when I drive past. I have to stop. She insists that I have some coffee with her. I can tell that she is troubled and needs someone to talk to. It doesn't seem right to have troubles in her beautiful white house. She grew up in it. But its paint is always fresh. There are no cracks in the ceiling. It's in perfect order and repair.

"There ought to be a way to protect parents from the greediness of their children," she says bitterly.

I'm embarrassed to listen. Sometimes she complains of problems, years old. I never know whether she is remembering her daughter's adolescent rebellion or her adult dependence; her son's indolence or stupidity. She speaks of the younger generation with anger, forgetting that I am of the younger generation.

The dogs, three boxers, jump around us, and I pretend I don't mind. I really dislike their firm, warm bodies against my legs and wish they would go away. Mary Johnson pats them affectionately and talks baby talk to them. "My best children, my best sweet children! No problems with these babies!"

Mr. Johnson has coffee with us. He looks on patiently while his wife shows me a new black and gold tray that she has painted and reminds her of some plants she said she would give me for my garden.

I don't say much at first. I always feel something strange about my friendship with my neighbors. Perhaps it's because they assume that we understand each other and they know nothing about me. All I know of them is that Mr. Johnson is a retired businessman. He fishes and plays golf in the summer and goes to Florida or Arizona for the worst of the winter. I see his name in pieces about the local Rotary. Mrs. Johnson is still a pretty woman, well cared for. She's the secretary of the County Historical Society, a vice-president of the Women's Cub, and she paints trays and plays the violin very nicely.

Some rainy days we play sonatas together. She brings me the perennials that she thins out of her garden and samples of her jelly when the strawberries are ripe. Though she's not known to be a warm person and prefers dogs to children, she's always very friendly and warm with me. We have a kind of symbiotic relationship. I need someone older to look after. She needs a daughter who can play the piano and be independent of her parents.

I'm embarrassed when her children are at home. She scolds them as if they were infants or pokes fun at them as if they were her enemies. Conscious of her voice, I hear my own, and I find I have three separate sets of vocabulary and inflection.

I have an everyday voice for children, husband, and old friends. I have my Brooklyn voice, half dead-end, half Yiddish, that I affect as soon as I see my family, and then I have a special voice that I hear in Mrs. Johnson's living room. I hear myself as if in a record at the speech clinic. My—brown—cow. . . . What am I doing? I'm imitating Mrs. Johnson. I do so well I could pass for a Wellesley girl.

Mrs. Johnson wants to hear all about New York. . . . What can I tell her? For the first time, she asks about my family.

"What does your father do?" she asks.

I redden slightly, angry at myself that I do, and tell her that he's a presser.

At first she doesn't seem to understand, but finally she says, "Like that nice little tailor in the square."

I get a feeling that she's pleased to be a liberal person who can be friends with a tailor's daughter who plays the piano. But it may be all in my imagination.

"How old is he?" she asks.

"Over seventy," I say.

"He must be terribly strong," she says enviously. I cannot help but look at Mr. Johnson, well-tailored even in the morning, and smelling of shaving lotion. His cheeks are pink from the winter and summer sun. I think of my hollow-chested, bent father, with dry, trembling hands and sunken face. His whole body screams exhaustion, but he refuses to rest, afraid that a day's uselessness will condemn him to death.

I think I have to explain it to Mrs. Johnson. I tell her that he's an Orthodox Jew, an immigrant from Poland, whose English after forty years in America is still unsure. She knows, of course, that we're Jewish, but she is so pleased that we look just like anybody.

I find myself describing a Seder. I tell no lies, but neither do I tell the truth. I let her get a vision of a genial patriarch and his respectful family acting out an ancient play. She thinks of a great feast, not hard-boiled eggs and boiled chicken. She enjoys the sound of the words and repeats them after me so that she will remember the paschal lamb, matzah, bitter herbs with ginger and apples and nuts.

"I love old customs," she says, "especially when they're happy." She thinks I should write down what I have told her for the Historical Society newspaper. "It's absolutely charming," she says and remembers that someone had once explained the Jewish New Year to her, but she had not liked it at all. "It was morbid," she said with revulsion, "but the Seder is delightful. Thank you for telling me about it."

When I get up to go she gives me some music, a Victor Herbert medley that we will play at the Women's Club tea. We both prefer Beethoven but the ladies begged for something lighter when we played the "Spring Sonata" last time and we promised to find something familiar.

I'm ready to go, when her daughter comes down. I smile. She nods.

"Don't you dare go downtown in those vulgar red pants," says her mother. She turns to me and in another voice, "It was lovely, dear. Come again soon!"

I have the door open when she adds, "That girl of mine has always been demanding. When she was little she wanted me to be in the house waiting for her whenever she came home. She still does."

I look back at the house and see her at the window, surrounded by the dogs. One is up at her shoulder snuggling his nose against her cheek. The other two have their paws on the window sill. Something about the composition reminds me of my mother with my children clinging to her, the purest devotion in their faces.

I race the motor. I don't know the time. I'm terrified that the littlest one may have come home before me to be frightened by an empty house.

I rush for nothing. When I get to the driveway, I see the nursery school station wagon, a little bit down the road behind me.

Cats and Christmas Trees
The Old Struggle in New Suburbia

Selma Applebaum and I are neighbors but not friends. We're not a pair. When my father saw her he said, "A pretty little woman! She makes me think of a new-born calf." I've been likened to many things, but never to a calf.

Selma and I grew up in the same apartment house in Brooklyn, under a cloud of depression that was not an era but a world. We played in a sour-smelling hallway in winter and on our adjoining fire escapes in summer. It didn't trouble us, however, because we knew no other world and had no one to whom we could compare ourselves.

We clung to each other because we were the only two girls, the same age, in the house. We tapped signals on the radiator pipes to wake each other in the morning and tied vital messages to a string that we lowered from her window to mine directly below.

Though we had been inseparable until we were ten, we said goodbye when our parents moved us to more prosperous neighborhoods and never saw each other again until we accidentally bought identical houses right next door to each other. Not in our wildest dreams had we seen ourselves in split-level houses, carpeted, draped, furnished with the latest Paul McCobb. But two years ago I painted my house brown, because hers was pink, and we shared the cost of the cedars that we planted on the line between our properties. Only friendship and understanding elude us. We have but to meet each other outdoors to clash, like a scythe against a stone.

Take the question of the kitten, for instance. Selma called my children to her door one day and gave them a present of a six-weeks-old kitten, a beautiful ball of gray fluff with surprised blue eyes and trembling legs.

The children, overcome with their good fortune, came running to tell me the news.

"I'm sorry," I said sadly. "Take it back!" It was as if I had opened a faucet. They all began to cry. It was not a time for me to get weak. I led the parade back to Selma's followed by three crying children and one small cat.

"Why didn't you ask me before you gave it to them?"

"You won't let them keep it?" she asked in amazement.

"I don't like cats," I said firmly.

"But the children adore them. You should see them playing on my porch with the kittens. It's selfish to deprive them of such a little pleasure."

"It's not a question of depriving," I said. "I had a cat once and it didn't work out. The cat was miserable and so was I."

"What do you mean, miserable," she said with a laugh, and the children listened hopefully.

"I mean that I can't stand a cat walking between my feet. I can't bear it on the kitchen table, the couch, or my bed. I won't let it tear holes in the rug. All day long, I'm throwing the cat. . . . And it's hard to throw a cat when you can't bear to touch it. I have to find my gloves every time I want to pick it up. It's no life for a cat. Your kitten will be better off at your house where you'll love it."

"If you feel so sorry for it, then love it," she said.

"You can't make up your mind to love something," I tried to explain. "For me, a cat is a scapegoat. When the children drive me crazy, I throw the cat out in the cold. If I get angry with my husband, I don't feed the cat. My mother hated cats, my grandmother hated cats, and I hate cats. What do you want from me?"

"I want to know why," she said stubbornly. "My mother hated cats too. I used to plead with her for a kitten and she would holler, 'Dope, in your own house you can have fifteen cats and twenty-two dogs with my blessing, but not in my house.' As soon as I was married I bought two collie pups and three cats. Sidney nearly went crazy, but I had to get it out of my system. I can't understand you. Cats are clean. You can train them to stay off the table and they keep the field mice away. They're so nice and fluffy to touch. What are you so excited about?"

"I would only enjoy a cat if it would behave like a human being. I don't like animals, even trained animals."

"How unreasonable can you be?" she said sarcastically. "It's hard enough to get people to act human, let alone cats."

"Why do I have to be reasonable?" I asked. "Maybe I don't like cats because they're beautiful, self-centered, and lazy; all the things I would like to be. Maybe it makes me too envious to have a cat in the house, sleeping and stretching itself while I work."

"Now I've heard everything," she said. "You have a phobia. It's too much for me." She bent down to the children's height and said, "Now don't be like your mother. Any time you want to play with kittens, you come right over here and don't pay any attention to her. OK?"

I went back to the house alone. She had already alienated my children.

It was practically a campaign. The day before Christmas Selma came to the kitchen door at three-thirty. The children were eating cookies and milk. They had just come in from school and their boots and coats were still on the floor where they had dropped them.

She had a package behind her back. "I have something for you," she said. "Promise you won't get angry!"

"Why should I get angry?"

"I bought a little Christmas tree at the A & P this morning and Sidney just came home with another one his boss gave him. Take one! The children will have a good time with it. I have plenty of tinsel and decorations."

The children stopped chewing and listened. The eldest, full

of eight-year-old piety and conviction, shook her head. "We can't have a tree," she said. "We're Jewish."

Six-year-old Judy was not so burdened by conviction. She jumped out of her chair and began to hug my knees. "Please, please," she begged, "let us have it." Four-year-old Joe took life in his own hands. He pulled the tree out of Selma's hand and said, "Thanks, we'll keep it for you."

I felt my face grow hot and red.

"Well, that's settled," said Selma. "Alice can come back with me and I'll give her the decorations."

I shook my head. "We can't keep it."

"Your father won't come till Sunday. You can throw it away by then."

"My father has nothing to do with it," I said angrily.

"Of course he has," she said. "I'll never forget our first tree. It was only about ten inches high. Marla was only a baby. Pa walked in unexpectedly and I thought I'd die. He took it off the table and threw it in the wastebasket. . . . But even he's learning. A few years ago he began bringing presents for the children. He's almost a changed man and so comical. Last year he stared and stared at the tree as if it would explode in his face and finally he said, 'At least you can't say it's ugly.'"

"My father isn't your father and I'm not you," I said stiffly. "Take it back."

"What are you fighting?" she asked. "A little tree with a few strings of tinsel? What would happen if you bought the children a few presents and made them happy? How foolish you are."

Judy loosened her hold on my legs and Joe put the tree down.

"Christmas doesn't belong to me," I said. "Please, just take it back."

"The trouble with you," said Selma, "is that you think too much. You're always looking for trouble and you don't know how to enjoy yourself." She waved the tree at me and said, "It's for fun. You're an artistic person. You could make it pretty."

"I've decorated a Christmas tree," I said. "Once is enough."

"What happened?" she asked. "Did it fall on you?"

I suppose I would have tried to tell her then, but she didn't give me a chance.

"You're the one who goes to the Andersons on Christmas Eve," she said. "If that's not against your principles, why such a fuss about a tree?"

Words couldn't help us. We were not talking about the same thing. I wished that the Andersons would invite the Applebaums instead of the Schwartzes one year; or perhaps both of us at the same time so that the other neighbors could learn to tell us apart. But the invitations were not mine to give and Selma might sit at her window for a lifetime of Christmases, looking at the cars parked on the other side of the street, feeling like an eight-year-old left out of a birthday party. I knew, though we never spoke of it, that she wanted me to stay at home because she wasn't asked.

One year I made the mistake of telling her that it was not as gay as she thought. There were only about a dozen couples. The men talked about their businesses and the women about children. A few people danced to old records in the den. When Jack Anderson reached the proper state of relaxation, he played the piano and everyone sang the great old songs, "Clementine," "I've Been Working on the Railroad," and "Old Black Joe." It was as cheerful as a PTA supper.

But Selma wanted to know what we ate and what clothes everyone wore. She wanted a recipe for the eggnog and the ham spread. She was annoyed when I evaded her questions and asked me point blank, "If it's so uninteresting, why is it that you go every year?"

I went—because they asked me. A few days before Christmas Betty Anderson would bring the children a dish of Christmas cookies and ask me to stop and have a drink with her and her husband on Christmas Eve. It was the extent of our relations. The rest of the year we waved or smiled when we passed each other. Though there was only a narrow road between our houses, weeks went by in winter without our greeting each other.

She invited the same people year after year. They all lived in our development and knew each other from church meetings and

the school PTA. My husband and I were not members of the crowd
and were treated with the respect reserved for outsiders. Someone
always came to tell us of a lovely Greenberg family they knew in
Brooklyn, or a clever boy by the name of Shapiro their son had
met in college. We were asked if we knew Goldsteins in Los Angeles
of Kleins in Richmond. Last Christmas, a neighbor by the name of
Hill—or maybe it was Hull, or Hall, even—came up to me, took my
elbow, and led me carefully to a chair opposite his.

"Let me tell you something, Mrs. Applebaum," he said, with a
smile.

"I'm Martha Schwartz," I reminded him, but he only waved his
hand to show that it made no difference so late in the evening. The
punch bowl was nearly empty.

"The most important thing to remember, Mrs. Applebaum, is
that we must not judge each other. Do you agree with me there?"

"I agree," I said, without knowing whether or not I really did.

"Good," he said. "Then we needn't forgive each other. You
can't forgive, without judging. Do you agree?"

Before I could make up my mind, his wife came to save him
from himself.

"You're a nice girl," he said in parting. "I hope Santa Claus is
real nice to you!"

Selma called the next morning to ask if we had fun at the
party.

"It was interesting," I said.

"What do you mean, interesting? Either you had a good time
or you didn't. Listen, you don't have to tell me about it if you don't
want to."

Two years had passed, but she hadn't forgiven me for keeping
secrets from her. "Well, I guess you're going to the Andersons tonight,"
she said as she opened the door to leave. "Have fun!"

The children whispered at the table, but they didn't wheedle.
They were used to me. They hung up their coats and went down
to the basement to play.

I was left alone to think—too much, or too little. It didn't
matter. What *was* the matter with me? Another phobia? Why does

Selma need her little tree so badly? Why should she make me so angry?

In the house where Selma and I grew up, Christmas was a wreath on the hallway door and a dollar bill for the superintendent. It was carols at school and little baskets of candy the teachers gave us in exchange for the scarves, brooches, and boxes of chocolates we brought to them. The only one who had a Christmas tree was Mrs. Gerrity, the corsetière. Mrs. Gerrity and the Negro superintendent, who slept in the basement, were the only outsiders and the only representatives of the majority which we pretended didn't exist.

I remember enjoying Mrs. Gerrity's Christmas lights against the dirty brick walls. I was shocked once when I overheard a neighbor say, "Oh, how she flaunts that tree, flaunts it in our faces." I always felt sorry for Mrs. Gerrity. No one came in to share a cup of coffee with her. Voices changed when she came by with her valise of laces and stays. She had no children, only a fluffy, tan little Pomeranian that wore a blue bow around its neck in summer and a plaid wool coat in winter. On Purim I would bring her some *hamantashen,* and on Passover a small package of matzah that she liked. I would leave them at the door and run, frightened by the barking dog.

One night my father and I came out of the subway and found Mr. Gerrity walking in front of us, singing at the top of his voice. Not only was he singing, but he stopped at every fire hydrant, jumped over it gaily, calling out, "Johnny on a pony, in a one, two, three." I thought it was very funny until I saw my father's face in a grimace of pity and revulsion.

"Shiker iz er, trinken miz er," he said sadly, *"veil er iz a goy."* [Drunk he is and drink he must—because he is a goy.]

There were others watching Joe Gerrity on his way home. No one said, "There goes a happy man!"

How strange to think of the Gerritys whom I haven't seen in twenty-five years! I lose my car keys every day and have trouble remembering my own telephone number.

There was a knock at the door. Selma was back. "You wouldn't have an onion?" she asked. "I forgot to buy onions this morning."

"I can always find a spare onion," I said, as I reached into the vegetable bin. I took out the onions, closed the metal door, and suddenly remembered so clearly why I sent the tree back with such determination.

"Don't think I'm just stubborn, Selma," I said. "It reminds me of things I don't want to remember."

"I didn't say you were stubborn," Selma said.

I wanted her to understand me. I tried to explain a day, seventeen, eighteen years ago. It was just after the war began in Europe. I went up to an insurance office on Wall Street, looking for a job. I waited in line with the other girls, all of us holding the same advertisement from the *New York Times*. I was there at seven-thirty, was interviewed at nine, and was working at the filing cabinets at ten-thirty. The salary was eighteen dollars a week, twice as much as I had been earning as a doctor's assistant.

I felt so lucky that morning. I was only eighteen, but I imagined that I had waited on countless lines, only to be rejected at the end. I filed the cards and apportioned my money; so much for home, so much for clothes, for lunches, for entertainment. The girls around me were friendly and talkative. We ate lunch together and hurried back to decorate a Christmas tree that had been set up in the lobby. I helped unwrap the glass ornaments and tossed the tinsel. I passed the silver angels and cotton-bearded Santa Clauses. I felt myself expanding, opening up with joy and freedom and the smell of pine in the dusty city. It was the big world and I was in it!

At three o'clock the personnel manager sent for me. 'You were hired by mistake," she said. "We don't take Jews."

"Why?" I asked boldly.

"You take too many holidays," she said.

"I won't take any holidays," I promised.

She shook her head and handed me the pay envelope. A slip of paper counted out the hours and the social security. The two dollar bills were crisp and clean and the change rattled.

I stood there, stupidly, waiting. The woman turned her back to me and looked out the window to let me know it was time for me to go.

"It's no wonder there's a war," I said, as the tears started to fall. "No wonder people are always killing each other." She didn't turn around.

I was sobbing in the elevator, but the operator didn't ask me why. The tree was glistening and shimmering in the lobby. Wreaths hung from all the windows and the Salvation Army Santa Clauses were ringing their bells. I walked from Wall Street to the Eighth Avenue subway with tears streaming down my face.

Selma listened with her mouth open and her head cocked.

"That was years ago," she said. "There are laws now. It doesn't happen any more."

"A Christmas tree always reminds me of it."

"You're mean," she said. "Because you had a bad experience, you'll take three innocent children and mix them up with memories that would be better forgotten."

My jaw was set. I gave her the onions.

"Thanks," she said with a shrug. "I'll pay you back tomorrow."

It was almost dark when she left. Christmas lights were lit in all the houses across the street. Was it fair to look at their lights while they saw darkness in my window? The symbols were misleading, but was I the one to change them? How could I? Anxiety had a hold on me. I braked the floorboard of the car when my husband was driving. I watched the propellers in a plane, sure that they would stop turning if I stopped looking. I was afraid to forget the past for fear that it would come back to remind me . . . an ugly chain; small unkindness and huge atrocity, petty discourtesy and murder, all linked together.

The children were so quiet. I tried to open the door to their playroom but it was locked. "Don't come yet," someone shouted. "We're not ready!"

I waited for Judy to open the door with a flourish. "Come see what we made for you," she said proudly.

A branch of pine was pushed into a pot of begonias. Buttons, beads, and small toys hung from every twig. My best earrings formed a star at the top.

"It's all right for us to have it," Alice said with authority. "It's not real. It's only homemade."

"We'll put everything back," Judy promised.

"I won't break anything," her little brother added.

"Look who's watching," Judy said, pointing to the window.

Selma's two cats snuggled against the warm windowpane. Their eyes burned like coals in the dark.

"Can I let them in for a minute," Judy begged.

"They can't hurt anything down here," Alice said.

"Another time," I promised.

"When, when," they asked all at once.

"Someday," I said, hopefully.

What should I tell three innocent children?

Anything is possible. I may someday bring Christmas presents to their children and stare at their tree, comforting myself to see that it isn't ugly. Who knows what the world will be then?

A Feather and a Wooden Spoon

Holidays? What can I tell you about holidays? Passover has always come upon me like an attack of malaria. For the early symptoms, I clean cupboards, scrub floors and polish windows. Later developments respond only to a full-blown cooking orgy. I watch myself working like a madwoman but cannot stop. "Idiot! ... Fool! Why must you carry on like this year after year?" I ask myself while I hurry. But by the time I find the strength to answer, the seder is ready—the guests are invited, the fish is settled in the jellied broth, and the *taiglakh* heaped like marbles in the honeyed glue.

In the first years of our marriage my husband was astonished by my seasonal enthusiasm for tasks ignored the rest of the year. As years went by, however, he came to accept my holiday madness—and to expect it.

Our children, having no basis for comparison, were amenable when young. They learned early to ask the four questions, steal the *afikomen* and open the door for the prophet Elijah. I caught them up in my own fever, so they would know what I knew, feel what I felt. Later, they could accuse me of "indoctrinating" and "brainwashing"—and I would plead guilty. My defense was that I wanted them to be *my* children—my friends, not my enemies. Of course, I knew no more about what went on in their heads than my mother

Reprinted from *Hadassah,* March 1975, by permission.

knew about what went on in mine. I didn't even wonder what they made of me and my rational and irrational passions.

I saw Passover as a holiday of rapprochement between generations—not only the distant ones sojourning in Egypt, but the closer ones wandering in modern deserts. Making Passover is my message to *my* mother, who is no longer with us. "See Mama, what a good daughter I am," is behind those sudden attacks of domesticity. Polishing my father's silver wine cup—the one with his name and wedding date on it—kept his presence alive. Small gestures. Compensations. Tangles of guilt and affection.

There were other elements to contend with. When I was a little girl growing up in Williamsburg, the seasons didn't come and go as they pleased. My mother forced them to change. She turned off the summer by baking honey cakes for Rosh Hashana and warned the winter it was on its last legs by grinding poppy seeds for *hamantashen.* As soon as Purim was out of the way, she attacked the winter as if it was her worst enemy. She drove it off with brushes and brooms. Every piece of furniture was pulled from the wall to be sure that not a vestige of the dead season was trapped in the cobwebs. When there was no doubt that the winter was beaten, she made Pesah out of chicken fat, crates of eggs from a Lakewood farm, and matza from a special bakery where you could watch it slide out of the oven into your own box.

The frenzy of activity did not end until the evening before Passover. Then, my father went through the apartment with a feather, a candle, and a wooden spoon to exorcise the last invisible crumbs. I, myself, took the feather and spoon with me when I went off to school. Somewhere between home and P.S. 19 I would find an old crone warming her hands over a smoldering pile of broken apple boxes. From a safe distance, I would toss my sacrifice, an effigy of winter as well as *hometz,* into her flames.

I tell you this only to explain my restlessness when it is time for seasons to change and holidays are brewing. I need no calendar. I awaken one morning sure that there is something important I must do, remember, find. The tension builds until I get to work. Do you believe me? When I used to tell this to the thirteen-year-old girls I taught in Sunday School, they listened with bored, mocking faces, closed to mysteries.

"How can you prove it?" asked little Enid Grossman, skeptically. "Maybe someday you will be in another country without a calendar or any way of making a holiday, and you will see if what you say is true. Till then, I prefer not to believe you."

"I will let you know," I said to have the last word. Who would have believed that ten years later she would be a witness to such an unlikely experiment?

Let me explain how it came about. In February 1973, my husband and I stopped in Vienna on our way to Israel. His work as a consultant was expected to take a week or two at the most. But every time we prepared to leave, he was asked to stay just a little longer. After three weeks, we left the hotel to move into a furnished apartment where I could at least cook our own breakfast.

By then, I had visited all the museums and palaces and really didn't know what to do with myself. When the snow and ice melted I would walk for miles along the Danube Canal communing with the gulls, childishly collecting the feathers they dropped in my path.

I watched the haughty peacocks in the Stadtpark and sat in cafes for hours without hearing a word between the *"Gruss Gott"* when I came in and the *"Auf Wiedersehen"* when I left.

One day, I stood at a street corner, turning my map this way and that, trying to decide which direction to take, when an elderly woman touched my elbow and asked, "May I be of help to you?" Bright eyes glistened in a face like a withered peach. Wisps of white hair slipped from the shawl that covered her head. She might have been a peasant in the marketplace, but she spoke the first English I had heard since my arrival.

While she found our corner on the map, she explained that she had worked as a translator for the Americans at the end of the war. "If you like, I can show you places tourists miss," she said. "I can tell you some interesting history if you have time." I admitted that I had plenty of time on my hands and was weary of wandering by myself without a soul to talk to. She took my address and telephone number and promised to call soon.

The brief encounter with a woman whose name I didn't even know raised my spirits for a day or so, but she didn't call and the melancholy settled on my head like a mist. The days grew longer. The air was softer. The winter smog lifted and there were patches of blue sky, but a kind of panic was growing in my head.

"What day is it?" I asked my husband before he left for the Institute one morning. "What difference does it make?" he answered impatiently. "I promise that we will go on to Israel just as soon as I can get done here."

He wanted me to enjoy freedom and aimlessness, but it was too late. I had no talent for it. I went to the market and watched the carp swimming in the tanks. I admired the pyramids of eggs and the bushels of fresh chickens. A stall heaped high with wooden bowls and spoons grabbed my attention. Irresistible spoons! The peddler watched me run my fingers over the polished spoons, testing till I found one just right—long enough, round enough.

"What do you need it for?" I asked myself. But by then I had already paid fifty schillings for a spoon worth no more than five. It was sticking out of my pocketbook, ready to poke any stranger who came too close.

When I added the wooden spoon to my other paltry treasures, mostly gull and peacock feathers, museum tickets and concert programs, a light went on in my head. My trouble was clear as day. I had only to see the spoon and feather side by side to know it must be close to Passover. I was finally in another country without a calendar, without children to feed, closets to clean, friends to invite.

All of my unfocused holiday fever went into a search for a Jewish calendar. Hopeless! But in Steffle's Department Store, where they had no calendars, I saw a man coming up the escalator with a box of matza under his arm. It came from the Israeli section of the foreign foods at the back of the grocery department. I put a box in my own cart and stationed myself in an inconspicuous corner—a Passover spy in Vienna! It seemed reasonable that customers who bought matza might know when Passover would be. I was prepared to wait all afternoon for one to turn up. The first, unfortunately, was a Swedish lady who liked matza without knowing the significance of it. The second was a Viennese gentleman who didn't talk to strangers. The third scratched his head for a minute and decided that it was two days later.

Two days? Two weeks? What difference could it make? We didn't know a soul to share a hard-boiled egg with. The thought of the two of us alone with a box of matza, while our children were at colleges thousands of miles away, was too lugubrious to contemplate. My husband's practical suggestion that we forget Passover for one year and go out to dinner and the opera as usual was a reasonable solution for *him*. He had not grown up in Williamsburg with my father and mother.

What could I do but be as rational as possible while I hoped for some small miracle. "If we're supposed to have a seder in Vienna, we will," I told myself. "If anyone needs me, I'm here." The trouble was that no one knew where to find me. My sisters in New York were the only ones who had my phone number.

When the phone rang the next morning, I ran to the door in confusion. "Long distance from Zurich," said the operator when I finally pulled my wits together and lifted the receiver. My heart stopped pounding. We didn't know anyone in Zurich. But a second later I heard a young woman asking for me. "It's Enid, Enid Grossman, your Sunday School brat! Can I come to see you?" She spoke as if we were old friends instead of enemies. "My mother met your sister and got your number. Isn't that amazing?"

"Come for Passover, Enid," I shouted so I could be heard in Zurich.

"When is it?" she shouted back. "I thought it was over."

"Tomorrow night," I said, thinking it would be too soon.

"O.K. I'll be there," she said enthusiastically.

I began to give her directions, but the operator was asking for more money and all she had time to say before we were cut off, was, "Don't worry! I'm hitching. See you at noon!"

Of course, I worried. The inner city where we lived was like a rabbit warren. I often got lost two cobblestoned streets away from our apartment, and I never left the house without a map. Before I could give Enid my full attention, however, the telephone, as if pleased with its own sounds, rang again. This time I heard a quavering old voice. "Do you remember the old woman who showed you the way?" she asked.

"Of course," I said. "I've wondered what happened to you."

"I have been a little sick, but thanks to God I am now better," she said. "Can you come with me tomorrow night to a lecture at the university? Interesting things. I will translate for you."

I had to tell her I was sorry, that I was expecting a young guest from Zurich.

"Bring her along," she said quickly.

"I cannot," I said. "It is Passover. I need to celebrate the holiday at home."

"The Jewish Passover?" she said, as if there were other kinds. "All my life I wished to be in a Jewish house on Passover. My friends were all taken away before I had the chance."

"Then you must come here," I said as if I were back in Boston where a dozen strangers could come to our seder with hardly any inconvenience.

She worried about imposing on us, about not having the right clothes. "I am vegetarian," she said, explaining that she lived on herbs, grains and yogurt and feared she would be a bad guest at a feast. I assured her that our guest would be wearing dungarees, that she need not eat anything she didn't want to, and that our feasting would be modest since I had only a two-burner stove and refrigerator the size of a hatbox.

"Then I will come," she said. "It will be an honor."

My head was already spinning with the challenge of making Passover in a closet kitchen with three wobbly pots, four plates, and a set of tin spoons. The melancholy feelings that had been hanging over my head like a fog, however, disappeared. I ran off to the market to see what I could buy.

Why bother you with details? Two wooden boxes tied to the iron window railings tripled the size of the refrigerator. There was room for a jellied carp, a cold fried chicken, a box of hard-boiled eggs and a bouquet of parsley. I polished the tin silverware and filled a vase with flowers. By the time Enid arrived at noon, I felt I had created a new season, single-handed.

An older, wiser Enid than I remembered threw her arms around me even before disengaging from her backpack. "How good it is to see you," she said, taking deep breaths of the onions sizzling in chicken fat. "Fantastic," she said. "Smells like my grandmother's house."

Enid told me of how she had left home in search of her "self."

She had been looking for it in Amsterdam and Copenhagen, London, Paris and Zurich and was now on her way to Athens. She spoke of her "self" as if it was a small trinket mislaid somewhere, inside or outside, to be found only if she were far from home and parents. Why had she come to me, then? Didn't she know that I was the last person to sympathize with her search, that I believed in roots, connections, links in the chain of generations, everything she was against. "What luck," she said, "to get a lift right to your door." As if that were the place she needed to be.

My elderly friend was not so lucky. She lost our apartment number and went from door to door asking for us, a grandmotherly Elijah looking for a seder. We were just ready to give her up, when we heard a timid knock on the door. I assured her that she was in the right house and helped her take off her shawl. She tucked her feet under the chair to hide her torn shoes and we began to improvise our Viennese seder.

Of course, we had no Haggada. Enid asked what she could remember of the four questions. The parsley, matza, egg, horseradish, chicken bone and salt water served as notes. When my husband lifted the dish of chopped apples, ginger and nuts, asking. "What is the meaning of this?" there was a kind of sincerity in his voice that had been missing all the years he had asked the question.

When he had finished telling the story of the holiday, our elderly guest asked if she could tell of her "exodus from Egypt." Her voice deepened. Her breathing changed. It was as if she were an actress declaiming from a stage, rather than an impoverished old woman talking to an audience of three at a small dining table. She told about her role as a resister against the Nazis in a city where anti-Nazis were few and far between. She slipped out of English into German as she described hiding and fleeing, imprisonment and escape, the loss of identification papers. Her son, she said, was shot for helping Jews. Her husband disappeared. When she saw the bewilderment on Enid's face, she remembered to speak English again. Enid listened with moist eyes to terrible tales from a time before she was born. "Unreal," she whispered to herself, shaking her head. "Absolutely unreal."

"Only one thing more," said the old woman. She reached into

her bag and took out two small, bent silver goblets. "For making Passover blessings," she said. "Not for guzzlers and drunkards! . . . Sacred things left with me by a neighbor who did not return. . . ."

We stared at the goblets as if they were ghosts. "Please to take them," she said, "to use at right times in memory of people who were slaves with me in Egypt."

My husband, a rational, secular man, blew his nose for a long time before asking Enid to open the door for Elijah. He filled both goblets. One for the Passover of 1973, the other for all the years before. Our guest closed her eyes when he made the blessing and then she tasted her first matza, which she called, "holy bread."

Troubled that I didn't know her name, I asked our guest. "What may we call you?"

"You may call me Mutter," she said.

"Only Mutter?" my husband asked curiously.

"Mutter Anna, if you will," she said, as if divulging a great secret. To Enid, she added, "Anna is a holy name, the same forwards and backwards."

She left as soon as we finished eating, without telling us where she lived. She would not let us take her home. With the shawl back on her head, pressing my hands in hers, she kept thanking us for taking the goblets, for letting her come into a Jewish house on Passover before her life was over, for welcoming a Catholic woman as if she were a member of our family.

Enid, exhausted from a long day, fell asleep on the narrow couch. I covered her with her sleeping bag and put one of the goblets in her pack for her to find after she left us. If this night had seemed unreal while it was unfolding, it would be even harder to believe now that it was over.

The other goblet I set beside the feather and the wooden spoon, the beginnings of a seder that was evidently destined to take place that year in Vienna. It was done at the next to the last minute . . . just in time.

The Christmas Tree

I do not like to lose people. Isabelle, however, slipped out of my life as if she had never been an important part of it. We came to the first parting of ways when I was married and left New York to settle in Boston. A few years later, she and a new husband I had not met moved to Ohio or Pennsylvania. I was never sure which it was.

The letters I sent to Isabelle's parents at the old Park Avenue address were never answered. There was just a formal thank-you for the wedding present we sent. I wondered about them for a while but then decided that they had lost interest in me. I gradually gave up the fantasy of welcoming Isabelle and her parents to our proper house. It would have pleased me to show them what had become of the poor girl from Brooklyn they had once helped and patronized.

More than twenty years had passed since we had seen each other when the phone rang and Isabelle was back in my life. She was calling from Massachusetts General Hospital, where her husband had come for some tests. They were to stay in Boston until a decision could be made about a heart operation.

"You must stay with us," I said even before she finished

Originally published as "The Christmas Tree on the Lawn." Reprinted from *Hadassah*, December 1976, by permission.

explaining the situation. "Tell me where I can pick you up. I'll be right over."

"Bless you Ellie," she said emotionally. "Bless you! Bless you! You're saving my life."

Just hearing her voice, as breathy and girlish as ever, made me feel twenty years younger. She still had the accent she had acquired in private school. She sounded as if nothing had changed between us, as if we could easily pick up the threads of affection and friendship we dropped so long ago. We met in the forties. She turned up on the assembly line of a defense plant. I was only two years older than she but I was her supervisor.

It was so strange to find her among the Irish and Italian working-class girls. Her inflection, her clothes and conversation were from a world totally unfamiliar to all of us. The others responded with hostility. I was just curious about who she was, where she came from and why she was there. It never for a moment occurred to me that she was Jewish. Her nose turned up. Her honey-colored hair was straight and long.

I was pleased when she asked if I could leave my family on Christmas Eve to come to a party at her house. I didn't know her well enough to try to explain that Christmas had no place on our family calendar. I worried a lot about what to wear. Even without any clues about where she lived or how, I knew it would be very different from anything I was used to—that I wouldn't look right or feel comfortable.

She made it easier by insisting that I come with her from work. I was grateful. There was something intimidating about that house on Park Avenue. The canopy, the doorman, the paneled elevator— each in its way seemed to be asking what I was doing there.

The apartment itself was the most elegant I'd ever seen out of the movies. A glittering Christmas tree was almost as high as the ceiling. Some of the guests wore evening clothes. A long table in the dining room was covered with beautiful and forbidden things to eat. It was the first time I was so close to ham, lobster and shrimp; to mysterious shells with slimy little animals still inside. Absolutely another world!

Isabelle's parents, however, were not at all forbidding. They greeted me as if I were her counselor at summer camp, her elementary school teacher, some older supervisory person I was not prepared to be. Before the evening was half over, the mother beckoned me into the library and quickly answered all the questions about Isabelle I had not dared to ask. Isabelle had been expelled from Radcliffe College a few months before she came to work in my department. She had been involved with some radicals and had spent more time on picket lines than in classes. The school psychiatrist had recommended that she take a job and learn something about the world.

Isabelle's mother was convinced that she was responsible for her daughter's happiness. She assured me that she had done everything in her power to make Isabelle feel good about herself. Her nose had been fixed by the finest plastic surgeon. Her hair was colored by an artist among hairdressers. A teacher of models had taught her to walk. A drama coach had trained her to talk. Her clothes were made to order to bring out the best in her. There was no excuse for her low opinion of herself. She seemed to have no idea of who she was, and her parents decided that I might be a good influence. At any rate, they said Isabelle admired my strength and wanted me to be her friend.

A bizarre Christmas! Isabelle's parents and all their friends were Jewish, my first uptown Jews! No one I had known in Brownsville had prepared me for such people. Their willingness to adopt me and include me in their celebrations astonished me.

After Christmas I became a frequent guest. They took me along when they vacationed in the Berkshires. I learned gradually to eat their strange food and to stop gawking at the antique furniture, the crystal chandeliers, and the oriental rugs. I learned to take the view of Park Avenue from the twentieth floor for granted.

It was not easy, however, to go back and forth between my parents' humble apartment and Isabelle's city palace. In each place I pretended the other didn't exist. It was the only way I could handle the quick swings from our long hallway lined with boxes and seltzer bottles, the linoleum-covered floors and shabby furniture to the silk-covered walls and chairs, the Chinese porcelain and gold-plated faucets at Isabelle's. It was not envy, but a kind of esthetic confusion that unraveled me. The most valued possessions at Isabelle's were not considered important in my parents' house. The qualities my parents treasured were not visible in her family.

My father was sure, for example, that there was some heavenly scale weighing out *nahes*. The rich, he believed, were doomed to have trouble with their children. The poor, on the other hand, were more likely to be rich in *nahes fun kinder*. He wasn't at all surprised to hear that Isabelle's family were plagued with troubles. She had an older brother in a mental hospital. A young uncle who lived with them was rarely seen sober. It was not a peaceful house. I heard quarrels that embarrassed me. When I stayed overnight there was often the sound of weeping, shouting and a harsh slamming of doors that the thick carpets didn't cushion.

When we knew each other better, I brought Isabelle home with me on Friday nights to share our supper of soup and boiled chicken. When the days were long enough, I tried to come in time to hear my father make *kiddush*. My mother was sometimes uneasy about my rich friend slumming in her Brownsville kitchen, but there were times when Isabelle seemed more relaxed with us than she was in her own home. She made herself at home in our kitchen, even though I agonized about the differences in our worlds.

All of this was going through my head as I drove to the hospital to pick her up. The city was glittering with Christmas lights that encouraged memories of that Christmas when I first met Isabelle's family. I wondered if they knew how much they had helped me define my life and my plans for my children.

If I had not followed in the tradition of my parents, I had learned to avoid the excesses of Isabelle's as well. My parents had left me with a deep concern for the separations and disciplines that were so important to them. Their appreciation of kosher and *treif* began in the kitchen but branched out into all areas of life. Isabelle's family, by having everything that money could buy, had made me very conscious of the value of things that money could not buy.

I pulled up as close to the hospital as possible but saw no sign of Isabelle. There was only a drab middle-aged woman in the doorway who attracted my attention because her coat was unfashionably long in a year when everyone's knees were showing. I waited a few minutes and then double-parked and ran up the ramp to see if she was waiting in the lobby. I was about half-way to the door when the middle-aged woman opened her arms and began running toward me. The kerchief on her head slipped. She couldn't run very fast because she was wearing heavy shoes, the kind worn by old ladies with fallen arches. "Ellie," she called, "how wonderful to see you!"

It was Isabelle, all right. I tried to hide my consternation. Her face and her bearing were unrecognizable. Only the voice had remained the same. I helped her with her valise and hurried her into the car. I thought it might be easier to talk if I was driving and not looking at her directly.

She had a long, sad story to tell me, but I will just give you the basic, unvarnished facts. She married a Hungarian refugee. Soon after their marriage eighteen years ago, they became Orthodox. Their three sons were in a yeshiva in Montreal.

Her parents had never reconciled themselves to her choice of husband and life. Whether they had disowned her or she had refused their help was not clear, but she was living a poor, hard life. Her husband had a small appliance repair shop close to downtown Cleveland. They lived in a rented house near their favorite rabbi. My offer of hospitality was welcome because she had little money.

Imagine my feelings! After all the years in which I wished I could show her that I had come closer to her standard of living, we were no closer to being peers than before. I quickly rattled off the details of twenty years of family life, making as little of them as possible. My husband was a successful engineer with his own company, just as her father had been. We had two daughters away in college, a son in high school and a foreign student from Sweden living with us. I was a columnist for a local newspaper. Nothing earth-shattering! A typical suburban Jewish family!

Isabelle went from room to room, admiring possessions as I had once admired hers. Her enthusiasm embarrassed me. The last thing I wanted was to be envied. But then we came to the kitchen and the full impact of our reversal of roles shattered us both. I was serving coffee and Isabelle asked where the milk spoons were kept. "Take any one," I said easily, unprepared for the wall that sprang up instantly between us.

"You're not kosher?" she said. "Why didn't you tell me? I would never have come if I'd known."

I didn't know what to say. I was determined not to hurt her feelings. She was very worried about her husband, whose life was in danger. She needed a place to stay, and it was not likely she could find a hotel room the day before Christmas. I begged her to stay and assured her we could work things out. I had a box of glass dishes, paper plates and plastic spoons. I offered her anything we had that would make her and her husband comfortable.

I had the feeling that she wasn't listening. She was sitting at the edge of the chair waiting for the phone to ring. She kept calling the doctor and reaching only an answering service. Finally, she called a cab and went back to the hospital. Our son and the Swedish student were coming in as she was going out. There was time only for an exchange of greetings.

When the cab pulled out of the driveway, I found an old photo album and showed the boys what my friend looked like twenty years before. There was Isabelle in a picture hat at the entrance to the Park Avenue apartment, Isabelle on the veranda of the pink villa in the Berkshires, Isabelle and I sprawled on the grass in Tanglewood. They hardly looked. A mother and an old friend were of no interest. It was the day before the vacation began. They were planning a Christmas party for the International Club at their school.

I tried to create some buffers, some protection against the confusion that I knew was in store. I called my husband to warn him about unexpected house guests. The list of necessities for a kosher kitchen grew longer and longer. I went out for a supply of cottage cheese, cans with a U label, kosher soap and baked goods. I cleared a shelf in the refrigerator and lined it with tin foil and set apart a burner on the stove.

Isabelle did not return till after ten that night. She was exhausted and had missed supper. She appreciated my shopping expedition. My husband tried to engage her in conversation, but she made it difficult. She sensed his disappointment and disapproval. The silences filled the room.

It was agreed, however, that she would stay and that her husband, Yitzhak, would join her the next day. He was able to leave the hospital for two days and then had to return for further testing. Isabelle hung a few things in the guest room closet, but I could see she was having difficulty settling in. The more I kept assuring her that things would work out for us in the same house, the more uncertain she seemed to become.

Insuperable problems! She said they would not eat with us and did not want us to be offended. Her husband would get up early to pray. I assured her that I had awakened every morning in my father's house to the sound of *davening*. There was still another problem. She needed a *mikve*. I had no idea of where it would be, but Isabelle looked it up in the telephone book and found it listed between Mikulshik and Mil-Maw Home Products. She went off early the next morning to find it and came back in a couple of hours to report that it was well-cared-for and clean and the hair-dryers worked.

The longer I waited for the arrival of Yitzhak, the more anxious I became. It was a relief finally to see him come out of the cab— heavy-set, bearded, not healthy looking but not decrepit either. His English had only a small trace of an accent. Something strident and provocative in his way of speaking, however, suggested that he was a difficult man, quick to judge, slow to accept explanations, not at ease with himself or others.

He spent most of that first afternoon in bed. When he got up I was in my study typing away to meet my weekly deadline. He opened the door without knocking and, without any apology for disturbing me, asked: "What polemic are you writing there? Show me what you're doing!"

I shook my head emphatically. Nobody saw my unfinished work. Even my husband saw the articles only after they were published. "I'll send you a copy when it comes out," I said, trying to finish a paragraph as I spoke.

"I wanted to see what could be so important it takes your time from koshering meat and making a Jewish house."

I didn't answer, but that didn't deter him: "Isabelle is so disappointed in you. She told me so much about your saintly parents. She went through such a struggle to bring *Yiddishkeit* into her life she can't understand how you could throw it away. You had it for a gift. How could you do such a thing? It must have broken your parents' hearts. Is that piece of pig so important to you?"

"Pig?" I said without turning around. "We do not eat pig."

"Ah," he said, "that is very nice. You do not eat pig. Christmas, however, you must celebrate."

"We don't celebrate Christmas either. Please," I pleaded, "excuse me for just a few more minutes. I must finish what I'm doing."

"I saw all the presents wrapped on the table downstairs. Cards are set up on every window sill. What do you call that? Isn't that celebrating?"

Isabelle's husband had a talent for infuriating me. In a few minutes he turned me into a rebellious adolescent. "You have chosen your life," I said curtly. "We have chosen ours. It's a free country."

"Freedom for a Jew comes from following the Law. Without the Law, freedom means nothing."

"Let's talk a little later please. I just need a few minutes to finish the paragraph."

"So you're giving me the brush-off?" he said. "I can take a hint." He went back to his bed but left the door to my study open. I closed it. The thread was lost. I couldn't concentrate.

I found myself thinking of my gentle Orthodox father, who never would taunt anyone this way. He was always so worried about hurting anyone's feelings. "The biggest sin," he liked to say, "is to humiliate another person." I once tried to apologize to him for breaking his laws and his answer was quick: "It was my responsibility to teach you the right way. What you do with your life is your responsibility. There is only one judge." He pointed his finger toward heaven to let me know where judgments came from.

I would have liked to explain this to Yitzhak, but he was not interested in explanations. He didn't listen when I told him that the Christmas packages in the hall were given to my husband at work and had nothing to do with our commitments. The cards came from people all around the world who wrote me only once a year. They were other friends from the past, like Isabelle, that I didn't want to lose.

He would come into my room with a direct attack. "What harm did keeping the Laws do you? Didn't it make you a better person? Tell me the truth! Do you regret your upbringing?"

"I do not regret it," I almost shouted, as I gave the typewriter carriage a shove.

"But you think you are wiser than the Sages. You know better than they do."

"I didn't say I was wise," I answered quickly.

"But you make the decision to deprive your children of *mitzvos*. You bring them up as *goyim*. You admit you're not so wise, but you dare to make such a crucial decision."

I couldn't answer every taunt. But I couldn't ignore him either. Speaking to him gave me as much satisfaction as banging my head against the wall. Isabelle stood quietly behind him and listened. That aggravated the pain. She knew I loved and respected my parents and that I was not ambivalent about my Jewishness. If I didn't raise my children in the Orthodox tradition, it was because I wanted to save them from the rebellion that tormented me as an adolescent. I was looking for another way than the one I knew as a child, and I didn't want to apologize for my search to a stranger whom I welcomed into my house and wished no harm.

A memorable Christmas Eve! Our son and our Swedish student were away at the school party. My husband was so offended by our guest's behavior that he hid himself behind a magazine and didn't show his face till bedtime. Isabelle and Yitzhak waited until we had finished dinner before eating their cottage cheese and cucumbers out of the paper carton with plastic spoons. They turned each bite into a reproach and made me feel like a stranger in my own house.

Tension grew, hour by hour, to climax on Christmas morning. I woke early, as usual, still worried about the last two paragraphs of the piece that had to be in the mail the next day. I put a robe over my nightgown and slipped quietly into my study. It was always easier to collect my thoughts when everyone was asleep.

In a few minutes, I was down to the last few sentences. I was so absorbed I didn't hear the first knock. The door opened at the second knock. "Good morning, early bird," said Yitzhak. "One thing only I want to ask. I see a Christmas tree on your lawn. If this is not a Christian house, why is there a tree outside?"

"There's no tree outside," I said.

"I am not a well man, but my eyes are still working," said Yitzhak. "I tell you there is a Christmas tree outside your door."

I thought he was out of his head but still left my desk to see what it was he imagined. There, however, in the middle of the lawn, was a tree about six feet tall, festooned with cranberries, popcorn and cookies. It was a little crooked in the wooden bucket, but there was no denying that it was there.

"So what do you say?" asked Yitzhak. "What is the significance?"

"I have no idea," I said. "I didn't put it there."

"Take it away, then, before the neighbors see it. They'll think you converted."

I was in no mood to go out in my nightgown to carry away a tree in ten-degree weather.

"If you don't take it away, I will assume you like it there," said my guest.

"Later," I said, going back to the typewriter. "I will finish these last few words." I no longer cared what he believed. All I wanted was a little peace.

"There must be an explanation," he said, to be sure the last word was his.

Of course there was an explanation. When the boys came down for breakfast a little after noon, they said they had left it on the lawn for the birds. "Someone had to take it," said Oleg. "The Christian kids had trees and the Jewish kids didn't want one. I thought it would be nice for the birds. A pity to throw it away. Also— I'm a little homesick. This is the first Christmas I'm away from my family. I hope you don't mind it for a while."

It was the first and last Christmas there was a tree on our lawn, even for the birds. Yitzhak muttered about it until he and Isabelle returned to Cleveland. They didn't stay as long as they had expected. The operation was indefinitely postponed. There was rejoicing in the congregation in Cleveland. Their friends had been saying *teh-illim* since he left for Boston.

I took them to the airport three days after Christmas. Not till the last minute did I ask Isabelle how she could live with such a provocative man. "How can you stand it?" I asked after he had barked at her for some small error. "Why is he so hard to reason with? How can someone religious be so insensitive?"

She looked at me with brimming eyes. "Ellie, he's so much better. He's come a long way since the Rebbe took him under his wing. The *halakha* is just beginning to have an effect on him. . . . He came from a family even worse than mine. Rich and coarse and without any discipline! He bummed around a lot before he became a *baal teshuva*. My parents could never understand, but you should be able to—you, of all the people I ever knew."

Yitzhak was checking their baggage. Isabelle talked as fast as she could before he returned. "Do you think it's easy for us to live as we do? We have to think of every little thing we do. There are so many temptations to guard against. You cannot imagine how we struggle to remember the right way. We didn't have it all given to us. We were cheated out of our inheritance. That's why it hurts us to see how you've thrown yours away. I guess you had it too easy. It's not good for things to come so easy."

Easy? Easy? "Nothing is easy Isabelle. Nothing in this life . . ." was all I could say as her husband approached.

"Enough gossiping. Time to go. I will not thank you for your hospitality. It was your obligation to open your door to us," said Yitzhak graciously. "Perhaps it would be right for you to thank us for giving you the opportunity to have a *mitzva.*"

Isabelle and I were both in tears when we kissed each other goodbye. We knew we would not try to see each other again. The Christmas season, however, brings thoughts of her back every year. Though some years have gone by since her stay with us, I admit I still have not gotten over my dislike of cottage cheese.

After the Revolution
An American Passover Story

It would begin when the days grew short, this uneasiness my mother called "the heaviness on the heart." First twinges came in December, growing stronger in January; and in February I needed only a glimpse of the premature stacks of matza in the supermarket to feel previews of the misery to come. March was imminent, and then there would be Passover to live through.

The holiday we had once loved the most was an ordeal. In the season for family rejoicing we were alone, a childless old couple — except that we were not so old, not childless and too sensible to risk spending a holiday all by ourselves. We collected Russian immigrants, lonely Israelis, widows, orphans, hungry students and curious non-Jews to simulate a family. On Passover our children were not *our* children. They had flown to the four winds, and whom they belonged to, God alone knew. In their absence, a haze of melancholy had settled on the house. Sadness seemed to drip from the crystal chandelier. It flaked off the ceiling like poisonous lead paint.

I tried to escape the gloom one year by accepting an invitation to a friend's house in another city, but I missed the therapy of the preparations. I needed the bustle and rush of making a holiday, the

Reprinted from *Hadassah,* April 1981, by permission.

aggressive chopping and peeling that worked off some anxiety and depression. I missed the fantasy that the phone would ring and one or two of our straying lambs would turn up.

They gave me no reason to expect them, but each year I hoped for a change, for some miracle that would turn them around. Our old rabbi, who remembered our rebels when they were his good, bright children in Hebrew school, called every now and then to see how they were doing. "They'll be back," he promised as if he knew them better than I. "For my funeral," I once said angrily, "when I won't care a fig."

He remained rabbinical to the core. "God is good," he said. "You have nothing to worry about. I know how much love and care you poured into them, and they had Sabbaths and holidays and a good Jewish education." He was very impressed with Susie who had just published her first book on anthropology. He always asked for Barry who was making a name for himself as an economist in Washington. Ellen, however, was his favorite, the best Hebrew student he ever had. She was a linguist, had mastered Sanskrit and was perfecting her Japanese in Tokyo. He urged me to *shep nakhes* from their accomplishments.

I did. I did. But I didn't have the heart to spoil his memories of a loving, caring family with soft-voiced, respectful children. He was not there when, one by one, they exploded into adolescence, going off like time bombs. I had trouble convincing him that his "darling children" one day turned on us like enemies, dripping hostility, watching to catch us at some misdemeanor, some failure of style or sensibility for which there was no defense. We were pronounced guilty—without a trial. The endearments of childhood disappeared like last year's snow, and suddenly words were flying like darts, stones, whole quivers of poisoned arrows.

"I owe you nothing," said my daughter, light of my life, for whom I would have once cut off my right hand if she needed it. "I didn't ask to be born," said her sister. "You are not my friend. I can't confide in you." But hardest of all to hear was, "Jewish? What do you mean Jewish? I'm a citizen of the world. I don't want to be Jewish."

My husband, gentle professor, was outraged by the behavior

of *my* children. I was equally put off by the heartlessness of *his* children. We blamed each other for being too good, too generous, too permissive, but then clung to each other, partners in crime and affection, while we waited for the future to unfold.

A friendly psychologist assured us that there was nothing abnormal going on. "Your children are asserting their individuality," he said, as if we couldn't figure that out for ourselves. "Separation from family is very important for self-development," he explained. "You're just suffering from the empty nest syndrome," he added, as if the name for our trouble was also a cure. He recommended that we go off an a cruise and have a good time in some unfamiliar place.

My husband was loath to leave his laboratory. I found other excuses. The children remained distant strangers. We saw them once or twice a year at times and places of their choosing. Afraid of saying the wrong thing, I said nothing. Their father heard his questions hang unanswered. They were individuals with private lives of their own which they were not ready to share with us.

When holiday seasons came around, however, a long-distance call could still make my foolish heart leap and then fall if it was not Ellen or Susie or Barry. When our old neighbor Zelda called from California, I had trouble concealing my disappointment. "Zelda?" I said, as if I'd forgotten about her altogether.

"Are you all right?" she asked all the way from Berkeley. "And how is Lou—and all those marvelous children?" She didn't wait for an answer, but just bubbled on. "I swear, I think of you every Passover. I've never forgotten that last night in Boston at your seder. I'm telling you the truth—I've just had this fantasy that I'd get back some day, and you'd open the door for Elijah and find me there. So what I'm calling about is to say I may actually make it this year. I'm alone, I'm sorry to say. Dave and I were divorced a few years ago. Please forgive my silence, but I'll explain when I see you. Is it O.K.?"

"Sure," I said.

"Then it's settled. Save me a place and a few of your feathery *knaidlakh*. I love you all. Say hello to the kids. I'm sure they've turned into fantastic people."

The phone clicked before I could ask about her children, or

where she planned to stay and how long. It was really a jolt to hear from her after so many years. She had been my neighbor, and our husbands both taught in the same university. She taught elementary school and I then worked in the school library. Our girls were old enough to be her babysitters. It was long, long ago in the days of innocence, when we thought marriages were for a lifetime and the family was a permanent sanctuary. It astonished me to think that she expected to find us just as she had left us when her husband got an appointment at Berkeley.

Even more astonishing was the way she remembered her last night with us at what I thought of as the mad seder of 1971, the year I felt that some crucial thread was pulled that left our family coming apart at the seams. Suddenly, my head was as full of flashbacks as a Woody Allen movie. All the repressed details of our last family seder were as clear as if they had happened the day before.

The seder night that Zelda remembered with such affection was a disaster from beginning to end. I invited her and her children because, for the first time since they were born, we weren't expecting our own. Barry had called from Yale to say that he had no time for a seder and in any event it was hypocritical to take part in something he didn't believe in.

Susie was at Radcliffe, which was only ten minutes away but somehow was as distant as if she were camping out on the far side of the moon. She tried to explain to her father that she couldn't possibly be a member of the Chosen People and a citizen of the world at the same time. It ended badly, with her shouting, "You don't listen. You don't understand me. I don't want to live your kind of life!"

He went around for days asking himself what was wrong with his kind of life but found no satisfactory answers. Ellen at least said she would really like to come home for Pesah but it would not be comfortable if the others were not there. So for purely selfish reasons I asked Zelda to join us with her two children. Her husband had already gone off to Berkeley. She stayed on to sell the house. We needed someone who would be pleased to be with us to salve our wounded egos.

The night before the holiday, Ellen called to say that she would come if she could bring some friends. Barry sent us a message that

Ellen would be picking him up on her way from Columbia; and Susie, feeling better now that she made us feel worse, deigned to join us after all. She, too, would bring some friends. The exact number was in doubt.

My husband was amused by the contretemps. He thought this early skirmish was the end rather than the beginning of the battle. His confidence in his role of father was restored, and he was quite glib about the need for faith in our children. He swore that he knew all the time that they were just testing us. What for, however, I couldn't figure out. My problems were practical, not philosophical. The seder I planned for three adults and two children had to expand to feed fifteen or sixteen.

Rushing madly the morning of the seder, I realized that the dining room table was too small. In that manic mood, the solution came in the form of a Ping-Pong table in the basement. Full of adrenalin, laced with anger, I tried single-handed to fold it and drag it upstairs. I prefer not to remember how this beast of a table sprung open half-way up, wedging itself between the steps and the ceiling, trapping me between it and the wall for what seemed like an eternity, while the hard-boiled eggs burned to the pan. If Zelda had not stopped to see if she could be of help, our motley collection of guests might have found me there, the prisoner of a Ping-Pong table and with nothing to eat but burnt eggs.

I guess she forgot about that rescue. I remembered how I rushed, checking things off my long list of duties, proud of my strength and angry that they had made it so unnecessarily hard, knowing I wouldn't be able to say, "Never mind. Don't come. I don't want to meet your friends." It would have been unthinkable, which is why it never occurred to me.

When the children and their friends began arriving, the Ping-Pong table was covered with three tablecloths. There were flowers, candles and wine glasses. My father's *kiddush* cup was polished for Elijah. It would not have looked much different if I had had two weeks to prepare, and I was quite pleased with myself, this self-created self I had organized in opposition to the person I imagined my mother to be. I wanted to be an open-minded, flexible woman with one foot in the tradition and another in the modern world. I thought I was succeeding—until the young people came piling in the door.

Suddenly, I felt myself stiffening, aging. Our children and their friends seemed in disguise as if it were Halloween or Purim rather than Pesah. It was not the beards. My grandfathers had thicker, longer beards. It was not the jeans and the programed scruffiness or the boots marking my polished floor. The headbands on two of the young men made me nervous, however.

It bothered me that they all seemed to look alike and they had no second names. The Black girl was welcome and the Harvard undergraduate from Egypt as well. But something made me feel not at home in my own house that Passover night. My children avoided my eyes. I felt a fence of brambles sprouting between us and didn't know how to stop it. It made me feel foolish and inadequate in spite of the excellence of the *knaidlakh,* the tasty *haroset,* the nicely browned turkey.

We began the seder as we did every other year with the same Haggadot, the same questions, the same songs. My husband took on his new congregation in his best pedagogical style. One of the guests brought Arthur Waskow's *Freedom Seder* and we encouraged him to read from it. Zelda's children read the questions, one in English and one in Hebrew. The Black girl lifted her eyes when we sang of slavery. And the Egyptian undergraduate seemed to be hearing about the plagues for the first time. My husband was too busy with the Haggada to notice the looks exchanged. He paid no attention when our young guests left the table briefly. He might have thought they were helping me in the kitchen.

There was no one helping me in the kitchen that night, but a mysterious whirring sound from my sewing room in the attic led me upstairs to check what it was. I was more than a little astonished to find a young woman I'd never seen before sitting at my old sewing machine surrounded by yards of red material. "I'm making the banners for the demonstration tomorrow," she said. wiping the matza crumbs from her lips with the back of her hand. "You daughter said it would be all right."

Susie had brought her samples of the dinner we were eating downstairs, and she was nibbling and sewing, paying no attention to me at all. Not knowing what to do, I returned to the kitchen in time to see a headband emerge from the basement. An unfamiliar, pungent odor floating up from below sent me down to investigate.

Somewhere between the kitchen and the basement I became more like my mother, may she rest in peace, than the flexible modern parent—neither assimilated nor fanatical—that I imagined I was. My nameless young guests were surprised by my fury. "You will not smoke pot here," I said, grabbing the elbow that held the waterpipe. "Do you understand? We are separated enough as it is!"

My son came to rescue his friend, sensing the violence in my voice. "I told him it was a celebration," said Barry. "It's just his way of celebrating. Don't get hysterical, Ma. It's O.K."

I was not hysterical, but it was not O.K. My husband, oblivious to what was going on above and below him, was singing his way through the Haggada. Zelda's kids had bargained for the return of the *afikomen* and were having a wonderful time, but I could see that our other guests were bored and looking at their watches. With nervous giggles, Ellen admitted that they had to leave before ten. There was a bus to Washington they were going to catch in Harvard Square. They were marching on the Pentagon the next day.

The young people bolted at ten, leaving Lou and me with a mountain of dishes and that alien smell of grass trapped in the air vents. Zelda offered to help, but her children collapsed and she had to take them home.

Lou was sure the evening was worth the trouble. I felt used and abused. If there had been other seders after it, the mad seder of '71 would have taken its place in the family chronicle as a hilarious comedy of errors; but it was the last. To think of it brought back the queerness of the time, so much of which was still with us. I thought of it as if I had tried to get out of bed in the morning and found the floor missing. For ten years we had been living as if it were back, but I still missed a secure foothold.

I thought of all that while waiting for Zelda. For a while I thought of collecting some lonely friends with empty nests and simulating a seder for Zelda's sake. But I couldn't summon the strength. I decided that there would be just the three of us, catching up on the years we had not shared.

When the phone rang, it was Zelda I was expecting, not Susie just back from Guatemala. Susie, in the formal voice she gave lectures in, asked for my health and then said she was calling to ask a favor. A professor she was working with had asked her, the only Jew in her group, to organize a traditional Jewish seder. She was calling for recipes. She had forgotten what I put in the *haroset,* how I made those feathery *knaidlakh.* She wanted to know which of the brands of gefilte fish was best, since she didn't think she could make it from scratch. She wondered where she could buy some Haggadot. I told her I had thirty copies neatly packed away if she wanted them.

Susie called more times that week than in the year that had passed. The last call was the one I found hardest to believe. "Ma," she said in a voice I had not heard for a long time, "I really can't do this seder thing all by myself. There's only five of us, but I'm supposed to know everything. I just don't feel comfortable. I was wondering whether I could bring Professor Johnson's group to your seder. You probably have a lot of people, but if there's room for five more I'd come and help. Is it possible?"

"Is is possible?" she asks.

The seder night had a dreamlike quality. Zelda came late. We embraced tearfully. She had gotten leaner. I was fatter. She was delighted to see Susie, her old babysitter, just turned thirty, a success in her profession. We introduced Professor Johnson and his assistants. Barry, eager to see his sister, surprised us by flying up from Washington. Zelda, bemused and emotional, said it was just like she remembered. "What was so wonderful about this house," she said, "was that the door was always open, and there was always a welcome for strangers." Professor Johnson was reminded of Abraham's tent, the flaps open on all sides.

Lou and I exchanged looks. Bewilderment? Surprise? He came to the kitchen to ask if I was happy, but I didn't trust my feelings. I was still a bit numb from the long wait, but defrosting fast. Two of our children had come home for Pesah bringing flowers, Barton's chocolates and kosher wine. Barry wore a jacket and tie. His beard was neatly trimmed. Susie was singing *Dayenu,* swaying as if she were "really into it."

Professor Johnson looked a bit moist around the eyes. He found our "service" very moving, an important experience. The *knaidlakh* were a great success as usual, and one of Susie's colleagues had a passion for horseradish, which she had never tasted before. She took one spoonful after another without blinking.

There was polite conversation before we parted, as if it was the most natural thing for us to be together. In this new era, everybody helped with the dishes at the end, including Professor Johnson. We kissed Susie and Barry goodbye, aware that they had not told us very much about themselves, but we picked up our ears when everyone said they looked forward to coming back the next year. The extraordinary seder of 1980 would have seemed ordinary to anyone but us.

Zelda stayed on. There was so much to explain. There were sad stories to tell. Her husband left her for one of his students. Her children were overwhelmed by the divorce. She spoke about them in a flat, frozen voice. Her son, for a while had joined some cult. She had not heard from her daughter.

"I couldn't create a home that was a sanctuary for them," she said. "They can't forgive me. If only I could have given them traditions, the stability you had. . . . I always envied you because you knew what to do and how to do it. You had roots, and I was like a leaf blowing in the wind."

I hated to spoil her fantasies, but I to tell her that the revolution blew through our house as it did through everyone else's. She sat there staring in a funny way. "I was sure your sanctuary would hold," she said, but then admitted that it made her feel less a failure to hear our story. When I told her my version of the mad seder of '71, I found myself clowning, softening the pain of the night with the hilarity of it. It was, after all, not the night we lost control; it was the night we lost our illusion that we once had it.

The day before Zelda left, our old rabbi turned up to see how we were doing. "So what did I tell you?" he said. "And next year Ellen will be back as well." I had a sudden shiver of uncertainty: "And we can do the seder in Japanese?" But I was grateful for the change. I didn't know what the future would bring, but there was no sadness flaking from the ceiling. The floor was not as solid as I'd like it be, but this year I will dare to put my foot down.

Like Father...

The glass, half full of wax, stands on the shelf for weeks, hidden behind the boxes of cereal and tuna fish cans. The fear of forgetting begins early, so I remember to remember. On the appointed day, I pull up the buried wick and put a match to it. The small flickering light sets shadows dancing on the smooth surfaces of the stove and refrigerator and my head fills with memories. Old events and half-forgotten conversations come back with jolting clarity. It is my father's *yortzeit*. The anniversary of his death brings back all the unfinished business between us.

I do not, of course, need a *yortzeit* candle to remember my father. I see him in the set of my son's mouth and in the line of my daughter's cheek. I find him in my own quirks and prejudices; in what I do and say and don't do and don't say. Though once positive that my life was a rebellion against his and certain that I was another kind of person, his very opposite, I'm no longer so sure.

One evening at the end of a lecture I was giving, a stranger in the audience asked, "Why do you write? Do you get paid well for your work?" When I recovered from the impertinence of the question, I astonished myself by answering, "My father got up every morning, put on his prayer shawl and phylacteries and *davenned*. I get up and go to the typewriter and write something."

Reprinted from *Hadassah*, January 1982, by permission.

The more I thought about it, the more I was sure I told the truth. How else could I account for my behavior? My life differed from my father's in many superficial ways, but we were both powered by energy we couldn't control. We were bound by the same fences and values. He had taught me what was *kosher* and *treif.* Though I was free to do what I pleased, the labels could not be changed. *Kosher* remained *kosher* and *treif* was *treif* in all aspects of my life. The Jewish calendar that dominated his life is my memory bank as well.

The first dates I mark are the *yortzeits.* Holidays and Sabbaths are already there. The birthdays and anniversaries are added last. Work assignments and lectures are noted on my English Gregorian calendar. My Jewish calendar follows the phases of the moon, which cannot be changed. The other, like my life in America, seems more negotiable. The two hang side by side in my kitchen. It pleases me to see the year structured right from the beginning. Obligations and pleasures neatly choreographed; seasons under control. Time is holy stuff, not to be wasted, squandered, or, God forbid, killed.

A neighbor looked at my two calendars and said: "You must *need* a structured life. I couldn't stand having so little free time to do as I pleased."

Her words rang in my ears for a while. It had not occurred to me that I was not doing what I pleased. I had somehow lost the concept of "free time" without missing it. My neighbor was fascinated by the differences between us. "How disciplined you are! How organized!" she said, with a shake of her head that made me wonder whether I was envied or pitied.

In the early years of our acquaintance, we had talked a lot about choices. She worried about my habit of looking back for models. "You have to change with the times," she said, as if everything new was automatically better.

I tried to explain that we were shaped in different molds. Watching us, someone with a discerning eye could probably imagine the forms in which we were set. Meanwhile, we lived in identical houses. our children shared a sandbox and wading pool. We were both transplanted city Jews living in a development where farmers used to plant corn and tomatoes. We harvested babies instead of vegetables, and the little ones created a sense of urgency, pressure to figure out our objectives and plans for the future.

We would stay up till the small hours talking about who we were and what kind of people our children would be and whether we were Americans who were Jewish or Jews who lived in America. We agonized about the traumas of Jewish history and our concern for Israel.

It began with the two of us but developed into a little circle of worriers as the development grew. I found one night that I was the only one who would not have preferred to have been born a white, Anglo-Saxon Protestant. A minority of one, I found it hard to get my neighbors to believe I was sincere. "You've got to be kidding," one of them said, speaking for the others who could not imagine why anyone would choose to be Jewish.

The arguments would climax with some variation of the "three choices." It would be put as a riddle: If your daughter had three offers of marriage—one from an Israeli Army captain, one from a plumber who was an Orthodox refugee and one from a wealthy and well-born graduate of Harvard Medical School, not of the Jewish persuasion—which would you want her to choose. Since our daughters were all in diapers, it was a thrilling academic debate. But I was always out of step, hearing everything twice, first with my own ears and then with my father's, never able to join the majority.

The worst of those evenings was surely the one when my mother-in-law was visiting and joined the fray. She was an immigrant with a Yiddish accent, like my own mother's; but she sided with my young neighbors against me. She was proud of having emancipated herself from old-fashioned "superstitions" and obligations and she thought it inappropriate for a "smart, college-educated American girl" to be so backward. *"Vos zikhst du dem nekhtigen tug?"* she demanded. "Why look for bygone days? In America, you do what Americans do." She lit no candles and made no blessings. Nor would she set foot in our new, little synagogue.

My father's *yortzeit* brings her to mind. She was always embarrassed by my lighting of Sabbath and holiday candles. *Yortzeit* memorials were out of the question. "What are you doing? Are you trying to burn the house down? Candles make me nervous. What do you need it for?" If I talked of the "wisdom of the past," she reminded me that I wasn't there. As far as she was concerned it was foolishness to be jettisoned.

On the day of my father's *yortzeit,* I went about my daily chores, but the acrid smell of tallow and wick, the shadows on the ceiling and splashes of light in unexpected places pulled me back to other times and places. Suddenly, I remembered the race to the hospital, my heart pounding as if I'd run, not flown, from Boston to New York. My father was waiting for me, stripped to the bone, looking just as my mother warned he would if she were not around to tease a few morsels of nourishment into him.

Master of the art of not eating, he had resisted her culinary coquetry for forty-five years, keeping his fasts in a house that smelled of warm yeast and carmelized sugar, of rendering chicken fat and frying onions. Alone the last few years of his life, he lived on raw onions, farmer cheese and *mamelige,* the corn meal mush of his Bukovina childhood. On Friday, he would permit my sister to bring him a chicken in honor of the Sabbath; but most of it was left with the house superintendent, who had a better appetite.

He greeted me with, "Right you should come, Jennie," in the same breath apologizing for taking me from my husband and children. "This is how He wants it," he said. "If it was up to me, I'd be home taking care of myself."

He was so worried about troubling me. Only six weeks had passed since my last visit, but he was no longer his stubborn self. He had insisted on staying on in a neighborhood smashed beyond recognition and had turned down all our offers of help—even after young thugs had thrown him to the ground, smashed his glasses and ripped his coat. They didn't believe he had no money to give them; but it was the Sabbath, and he was on his way to the synagogue without a penny in his pocket.

I had come then to persuade him to move; but he stayed on, a prisoner in his apartment, connected to the world only by the telephone, an instrument he hated to use. I cried all the way home after that visit—for the pleasures he denied himself, for the way he let himself be beaten, cornered into a narrow, rigid life as if the slightest change would destroy his fragile equilibrium. And then, suddenly, I understood that he felt himself hanging by a hair. He had placed himself in God's hands and did not complain about his lack of options. It was not my responsibility to change him, as it had not been his responsibility to force me to follow his ways.

One visit, when the atmosphere was full of affection but conversation lagged, I tried to liven things up by apologizing for having been a difficult daughter when I was young; but he shrugged it off. "You were not a rotten kid," he said. "It was my duty to teach you the way to go, but the rest was up to you." He swore he could not remember any time when he was displeased with me or my sister. He was the father of "good" children.

I sat at his bedside and watched the hospital nourishment come into his veins from the jar above his head. His skullcap was pinned to his hair with two bobby pins. Prayers slipped from his lips like bubbles from a spring. His inner clock told him when it was time for *Shahris, Minha* and *Maariv.*

"Blessing us out," said the Irishman in the next bed. "Night and day."

The Puerto Rican on the other side hoped the Hebrew magic would bring him luck. The nurse who came to take his pulse smiled as she waited. "How's our rabbi doing?" she asked, not expecting so much praying from an ordinary Jew.

I told the nurse he was not a rabbi and turned away before she questioned me further. I wouldn't have known what to say any more than I did years ago in elementary school when the teacher went up and down the aisle asking about fathers.

One by one, we were expected to stand up and say, "My father is ..." a grocer, a shoemaker, a laundryman. Fathers were the subjects of sentences. Their occupations were put on the spelling lists on the blackboard. But I didn't stand up when it was my turn.

The teacher urged and scolded and pulled me to my feet while the giggles of my classmates fell like hail. Someone suggested that I might have no father, forcing me to whisper, "My father is religious." I had wanted to say *davens* but didn't know the English word.

"Religious?" said the teacher. "Is that an answer? We are talking about occupations, Jennie. Where have you been?" She gave me no peace until I said, "My father presses."

"Then you must say, 'My father is a presser.'"

But I looked into her angry Irish eyes and said: "He's not a presser. He just presses."

"I had to write, "My father is a presser and I am an insolent girl" five hundred times for punishment, but that didn't change my mind. I knew that pressers were a rough and ignorant bunch and that my father was a gentle, religious man held captive in a shop where he didn't belong. I listened when adults were talking and knew for a fact that he worked with pressers but was not one of them.

I used to wonder what he did during the long day he spent in the shop. My mother let me know it was a place where men and women worked beyond their strength and where there was a boss who squeezed the marrow from their bones. My curiosity grew until I persuaded an older friend to show me the way to the Broadway address on the little envelopes in which my father brought his piecework tickets home to count.

We left the playground near the Williamsburg Bridge and went all the way downtown.

My friend waited for me in the lobby, while I took the rickety elevator up to the ninth floor. The roar of the sewing machines was louder than the trains coming into the subway station. I felt the floor and walls tremble from the vibrations and just across from the elevator door I saw the boss sitting in his office. He was not the huge monster I imagined, not fanged or clawed, just an ordinary nervous little man with a bald head and metal glasses.

I watched the boss from behind a rack of dresses until I caught sight of my father in a corner of the loft. His back was turned to me, but I recognized his skullcap. He was hidden behind a cloud of steam at first, but when it lifted I saw him stripped to the waist, dripping with sweat.

My fantasy of surprising him, as I used to by meeting him in front of the synagogue, ended in the terror of being discovered where I didn't belong. I bolted through the door just beyond the elevator and down the steps at a dizzying pace, my palms scraping on the rough banister and my stiff oxfords thumping on the corrugated metal steps.

I never asked about the shop again. Some mornings, I opened my eyes and saw him in the kitchen, wrapped in his prayer shawl with the little black box on his forehead and the leather thongs twisted around his arm and I knew that when he was finished he would go off to the steam iron and the roar of the machines. I was only nine but already torn with some inexpressible sorrow for him and anger with a world I couldn't understand.

I had learned very early that there were two worlds to negotiate. The one at home was *eidel*—soft-spoken. Cursing, shouting, even a raised voice, were frowned upon. Slaps and punches, even playful wrestling, would be unthinkable.

Then there was the other world that began just outside the door—where the dangers lay. Listening to my father and mother, I sensed that life was something "to go through" with fear and trepidation. I pictured it as a thorny, unpaved road with wild beasts and murderous lunatics hiding in the underbrush. "If you don't go, you won't be sorry," was the message. "Look behind you, not ahead, and you will be content."

There were other messages in the air. I would hear my parents haranguing the Almighty as if He were a negligent landlord mismanaging his property. *"Riboino shel oilom*—Lord of the Universe— is this just? Is this right?" my mother would complain, letting me know that she was angry with the way things were, even though she showed the world a gentle exterior. My father lived against the grain of society, convinced that what went on around him was uncouth, barbaric, certainly disgusting. He would not "go native" in America. He would not become *Americanish*. In a country where everyone kept up with the Joneses and the Goldbergs, he urged us: "Look what people do. See how they behave—and don't learn from them."

I had been a good little girl for a long time when to be good meant to be able to sit quietly without jumping, to show respect to elders, to "act like a *mentsh,* not a wild animal." I remember that time of life as an endless summer Sabbath: The piano was locked and the radio silent. Work and play were equally forbidden. No pencil or scissor could be touched, let alone used. Toilet tissue was torn and stacked in neat little heaps in the bathroom, and covered pots simmered on the tiny flame that would flicker until sundown. The clocks ticked louder on the Sabbath than the rest of the week, as if amplified by the polished furniture and the freshly cleaned floor.

In that mythical time, I would stand against the hot brick of the Pearl Building in Williamsburg, wearing a starched organdy dress and shiny patent leather shoes, while my street friends wore bathing suits and jumped and splashed under the firemen's hose that sprayed cool water on our steaming street. In the afternoon they went off to the movies, while I sat on the stoop with my library book, waiting for the first liberating star to free me from the Sabbath limbo. The day that was supposed to be a taste of the peace of the world-to-come seemed to me only a preview of the grave.

I was good, good, good—and then suddenly I couldn't be good another minute. *A balduver iz in ir arine*—an evil spirit has got into her," my mother said, and I felt as if I were really possessed by some demon. Spasms of rage passed through me like lightning. I could feel myself spinning like a Catherine wheel. The Sabbath peace my parents savored felt like quicksand pulling me under, and I began to resist with all of my 12-year strength and *hutzpa*. The week's seething boiled over at the Sabbath meal before the table was cleared, before the *birkas hamazon*. My mother would give me the center of the stage by saying, "Please don't start in, Jennie," and I would start.

I announced that I was old enough to form my own opinions and that what was good enough for my parents was not good enough for me. I would make another kind of life for myself. I would become *Americanish* and enjoy myself without their fear and worry. I would play ball in the middle of the street like the other children. I would roller skate, ride a bicycle, take art and music lessons. I would journey alone on buses and trains to places they never even heard of. How could I look behind me and be content? I was desperate to move into a larger world than the family offered, with no idea of how to leave or where to go.

My sister would leave the table in tears, unable to witness my bad behavior. Carried away, I would even, may God forgive me, tell my father that he was ignorant and superstitious, that I would no longer say the prayers he taught me because I didn't think God was listening, if He was there at all.

"What do you want from him?" my mother would mutter angrily. "He slaves all week for us. Doesn't he deserve a little peace on Shabbes?" My father's cheeks would flush, and his eyes would sparkle. He never attacked me or told me to be still. Mostly he shrugged and said: "Where did she learn such things? Where did she get such a head?" He answered my cruel taunts seriously.

Could he have been flattered by my nerve? Everyone else treated him as if he were made of glass and easily shattered. I behaved as if he were forged of steel and as if I could bang my head against him as much as I wanted without making a dent.

What I wanted was not clear to me. I needed to challenge him for my self-respect, but I wanted him to resist me for his. I would have been devastated if he had given in and changed into an ordinary American father, a dad who played golf or tennis, who smoked a pipe and went fishing like the pictured fathers on Father's Day cards. I knew, even as a little girl, that Orthodox Judaism came naturally to him. It was not a yoke for him to carry, but the structure of his life and the source of his dignity. The Law was on his side; the Lord of the Universe, his friend and confidant.

I guess I needed everything to change for me, while he kept his world intact. I needed to be asked, "Will you become a Christian, Jennie, if you don't believe in God?" so I could jump out of my chair shouting, "No, no." And from there to, "Will you then join up with the *communistlakh* and sell their papers in the streets?" There, too, I assured him, I couldn't and wouldn't. I was too rebellious and independent and would not turn my life over to anyone. Obedience went against my nature. "A *davkenik*—a just-for-spitenik," said my father. "That's what she will be."

He was right. In the throes of adolescent atheism, I would lie awake half the night, because I couldn't fall asleep without saying the *shema* and wanted to break myself of the habit. Blessings on bread and fruit slipped out before I could stop them. Nothing could make me hungry on Yom Kippur. I tried to taste forbidden foods, but they did not look edible to me and it was hard to swallow something not meant to be eaten. I was at war with myself. My father was more witness than adversary. It was beneath his dignity to struggle with me. He kept his place and let me have mine, to the end.

That last day in the hospital, I watched him pray himself out of the world like an actor bowing himself off a stage. I held his hand, but he didn't hold mine. The last thing he said to me was, *"Gei gezinterheit un kim gezinterheit."* Go in good health and come in good health.

There was a package he had brought with him to the hospital. When they gave it to me I found his prayer shawl, an unfamiliar length of cloth that was a shroud, and a paid bill for plain pine box without nails. Independent to the end, he left us no decisions and no opportunities for errors. He was *der tatte*—the *paterfamilias*—and we were good, but not perfectly reliable, children.

So much to think about in a single day to the light of one flickering candle. My neighbor drops in just before dinner time to borrow a cup of sugar. The candle is still casting shadows. She acknowledges it with a nod, so that I will know she understands. She no longer challenges my need for a structured life. We accept each other as old neighbors of different Jewish persuasions. She will think what she thinks without any judgments from me, and I will do what I do without criticism from her.

I pour the sugar into her cup. She can't resist asking a question: "Do you think there's a chance *your* children will remember *you* with memorial candles?" Her eyes twinkle wickedly, as if she has made a point for her side.

"It's not likely," I answer.

She catches my look and regrets her question. "It won't matter for you. You've written lots of stories. Maybe they'll read them."

I give her the sugar without a word. She stops at the door, hesitates, and says: "Think of me. I haven't even written any stories."

The wick sizzles as it reaches the metal. I think of my father raising his eyebrows, shrugging his shoulders, saying, *Der mentsh trakht un Got lakht."* Man thinks and God laughs.

A Thousand Kisses

Russian voices echoed through the hallway. Russian noises trickled through the vents and the cracks in the walls. I heard shouts and whispers, commands and denials right under my window. Without understanding a word, I found myself straining to catch every syllable as I used to when I was little and Yiddish secrets were passed back and forth over my head. I had listened then until I magically broke the code and intercepted the messages. I kept hoping the magic would work again and organize the jumble in my ears.

The confusion, however, remained. I could catch feelings of joy and fear, affection and anger; but the actual words were beyond my grasp. The day that a Russian family moved into the apartment next door I baked a lemon bread to welcome them. I knocked and knocked, heard voices, but no one came to let me in. Just as I turned to leave, the door opened a crack. A woman peeked out anxiously. The man behind her grinned and I could swear he said: "See, it is not the KGB. What are you afraid of? We're in Boston." She laughed nervously when I said, "Welcome!" and handed her the warm bread. She responded with all the English she knew. "A thousand kisses to you," she said.

I promised we would be good neighbors when they learned English, but at that time we did not even exchange names. She

Reprinted from *Hadassah,* December 1982, by permission.

became the "thousand kisses lady," and he was her husband.

A few months later I heard a commotion in the hallway and opened the door in time to see the welcome for the grandmother just arrived from Moscow. I'd never seen such hugging, kissing and weeping. "My mother is here. My mother is here with us," said the lady of a thousand kisses. She took me by the elbow and pulled me into the bare apartment for a glass of wine in honor of her mother's safe arrival. Other Russians came piling in and the Russian swirled over my head for a few minutes before I excused myself. All that emotion overwhelmed me. I was afraid I might burst into tears if I stayed another minute.

At that time I had not admitted, even to myself, how much I was aware of the Russian voices on the other side of the wall. They invaded my privacy in a way the students who were the previous tenants had never been able to. They disturbed the boundaries I had set for myself and breached my defenses against family feelings and responsibilities. Long-buried feelings were creeping up like green shoots in an April garden. I was not prepared for unexpected yearnings for family connections. The independence and distance I had prized so highly suddenly seemed flat and stale compared to the intense feelings openly displayed next door.

On impulse I picked up the phone and called my mother in New York. "What happened?" she said. "What's wrong?" I blushed to think that a call to say hello was such a novelty. "I got lonesome for you," I said. "Come visit me in Boston."

"And what will I do in Boston?" said my mother.

I urged her to come to relax a little, even though I knew she was more relaxed bent over her sewing machine with her tape measure wrapped around her neck and her mouth full of pins than she'd be pacing back and forth, empty-handed in my apartment. She insisted that she was too busy and didn't want to get in my way, but I knew she would come eventually, if for no other reason than to make sure that nothing was wrong. I'd been trying for years to persuade her that no news from me was good news, that not hearing from me meant I was busy and having a good time. When I was a student she would call me in a voice breathless with terror to say, "Susie, how are you?" I spent a lot of time in the library when I was writing my dissertation, and she'd be overcome with angst when she couldn't reach me. She almost always picked up the phone after reading about a rape or a murder. She'd hear about a fire, a flood or a snowstorm anywhere in New England and call to make sure her Susie was all right. The sound of my voice was all she needed to allay her panic.

After my father died I began calling more often to spare her those feelings. If something weird was going on in Boston I'd call to assure her I was all right even before she heard about it. My telephone bills tripled, but I was no longer a student and could afford it.

It's true that my calls were dutiful and not emotional or affectionate. We had affected a cool style. Except for the occasional fits of panic, we did not show our feelings. In spite of that, calling my mother was an exhausting experience. We exchanged feelings. It was a regular Yankee trade. When we hung up she inevitably felt happier and stronger and I felt sadder and weaker. It happened every time. If I invited her to visit, I was not heartbroken if she said she was too busy. I thought it fortunate for both of us that she was so independent and successful in her work.

My mother is a fine designer and dressmaker with a rich, stylish clientele willing to pay well for her hand-finished pockets and buttonholes, for her beautiful linings and perfect darts. Everything she touches becomes a work of art. Her clothes are made so well you could wear them inside out and no one would notice.

My father had also been a perfectionist with high standards. I once heard someone ask him if he didn't get bored looking into open mouths all day. He assured his questioner that he found dentistry fascinating. "I see very mouth as a little world in need of delicate repair," he said. "Every tooth wants to be saved and live forever. It gives me satisfaction." My grandmother, however, worried that her son worked too hard. She was upset because he ignored Sabbaths and holidays and took no vacations. She was even more perturbed by my mother's work. *"Der man makht a leben,"* she would say. *"Far vus arbet zei azoi shver?"* [The man earns a living. Why does she work so hard?] I spent a lot of time with her when I was young, and she gossiped with me as if I was a grownup. She thought my parents were trying to earn more money than they needed. I knew, even as a little girl, that they were afraid of free time. They were both incapable of sitting around with empty hands.

By the time I was an adolescent I knew that they worked less for the money they earned than to keep their feelings of anxiety under control. Worry, more than heartbeat, pulse or breath, was a sign of life for both of them. Watching them, I decided that I would not fall into the habit of thinking of the worst that could happen, then imagine it had happened already. I was against unnecessary suffering over imagined catastrophes. I was on guard against moments of panic. I was not immune. I hid behind my books and papers as my mother hid behind her sewing machine and my father behind his drills.

When the anxious feelings passed, I felt foolish. That's how it was when I went to pick my mother up at the bus station. Many months had gone by since my impulsive call. The weather had been too warm and then too cold. My mother had too many orders to fill and I had too many papers to grade and an article to finish writing. Finally, we both ran out of excuses and there she was, getting off the bus, the best dressed woman in the terminal. She was wearing a dove-colored suit with flecks of teal and purple and a beige silk blouse. I had been cleaning house in her honor till the last minute and had rushed out in my dusty jeans and a loose flannel shirt, in heavy boots that looked monstrous next to her neat calf pumps.

Driving back to my apartment, I pointed out changes in the city since her last visit. From the critical way she looked at me I knew that she was waiting for the chance to ask why everything changed while I stayed the same. She waited until we were home and I had put her valise down in the foyer. We could both see ourselves in the hall mirror, and she said: "Look at yourself. Just look at yourself!"

There we were, the two of us. I am four inches taller and more than twenty pounds heavier. I have my father to thank for my bone structure and my mother to thank for my face. We have the same noses and chins, the same brown eyes and high cheekbones. Her mouth is set like her opinions. Mine wavers, not sure what expression to take. Her hair is short and curly and she has been dyeing it a honey color so long I don't remember when it became gray. Mine is long and unruly. I find a gray hair on my comb every now and then. "You could be a beauty," said my mother, "if you took care of yourself." She made her annual offer of a visit to the most expensive hairdresser in the city. I told her that she didn't acknowledge her age by dyeing her hair and keeping it curly and I didn't acknowledge mine by leaving it long and straight. "You never let me have the last word," she complained. "That's what I get for having a professor for a daughter."

The way mother says "professor" exposes her tangle of pride and worry. I know she boasts about me when I'm not around and fears for me when I'm there. She sure is that "Mr. Right" would beat a quick path to my door if I lost twenty pounds, put red on my lips and green on my eyelids and wore the beautiful clothes she keeps sending me. I cannot explain that the clothes are too beautiful and expensive, that I have no occasions to wear them and that they would separate me from my impecunious friends. She thinks I should find more affluent and fashionable friends. Coming from her world of clothes-conscious people it is hard to imagine why anyone who could afford beautiful and fashionable clothes would choose to go around in frayed jeans and torn sneakers.

When my mother says, "I cannot understand," she really means it. When my neighborhood was full of students I had a hard time convincing her that there were future doctors, lawyers and teachers hiding behind the fierce beards and wild hair. She could understanding "fixing" oneself *up*, but not the disguises of downward mobility. "Why look like a bum if you're not one? Why look like a lunatic if you're not crazy?"

I was finally old enough to know that some things would remain inexplicable. Our discussions were so predictable they seemed choreographed. We went through our familiar little steps and patterns, dancing our mother daughter parts with a limited number of variations. So I do not argue with her any more. I tell myself she has her reasons for her feelings and I have mine. Instead,

I try to protect myself from her open disappointment in the way I look and live. I try to see what she sees and understand our differences.

My apartment makes her uneasy because it reminds her of her childhood. The crooked old walls and uneven floors bother her. She isn't amused by my ancient bathtub on claws and doesn't appreciate the quaintness of my oak-paneled kitchen with open shelves for my unmatched dishes and battered pots. The wooden floor, untouched by linoleum, offends her idea of progress. She accuses me of going backwards, of aping my grandmother. She blames herself for letting me spend so much time with "the old woman." She too is looking for reasons and explanations. When I tell her I enjoyed my grandmother and was glad she taught me Yiddish, my mother makes a face that tells me what she thinks of my nostalgia.

My mother thinks that my singleness in an old-fashioned Boston apartment reflects upon her, a modern woman who believes in progress. She thinks life should be planned, mapped out, followed as she follows her patterns. She hopes to live to see me married to a good man, living in suburbia with a formica kitchen and tiled floors, with a microwave oven, a patio, a swimming pool and a baby in the nursery.

I began to tell her about my Russian neighbors to change the subject and force her to think of something besides my precarious future as an unmarried professor of English literature.

"Russians?" said my mother. "I wouldn't get involved with them. They don't belong here. They should be in Israel where they're needed."

I was sorry she said that. Just that morning I had met the lady of a thousand kisses and looking for something simple to say I had told her that my mother was coming to visit me from New York. "I am so happy for you," she said and it seemed natural to ask her to come in and visit us, to meet *my* mother. She placed her hand on her chest as if her heart was full of words she would soon arrange in English sentences. For the moment we settled on eight o'clock, that very evening.

Promptly at eight there was a knock on the door and there

they were with a bouquet of carnations to welcome my mother. I finally found out that my lady of a thousand kisses was called Galina and her husband was Boris. They had been taking English lessons at Hebrew College and could risk small sentences. They had both learned to read English before they came and could understand much more than they could express.

It might have been good at this first encounter that we had to count our words and test each one for comprehension. Communication took place in fits and starts with many rests while Boris and Galina conferred with each other as they searched for the right word. He was a mathematician, studying computer science. She had been a doctor and was trying to learn enough English to be able to take her boards. She was working temporarily as a cosmetician in a company that hired newcomers.

They looked around them and praised everything in sight. "Beautiful, beautiful," said Galina. She touched my mother's skirt and said, "Elegant and soft, so soft."

At first it was all politeness and little charades, but then we began to risk serious questions. Boris asked whether we were American or Jewish. When I said that we were American *and* Jewish he understood that to mean that one of my parents was Jewish and the other American. My mother, who had been listening quietly asked why they had not gone to Israel.

The look that crossed Boris's face made me jump to his defense before he could find the words to answer her. "And why aren't we in Israel?" I asked.

"Maybe we should be," said my mother. For the first time I heard her tell about her wish to go with her friends when she was eighteen. "Before I met your father," she said. "My parents wouldn't let me. They sent me to dressmaking school instead."

Galina shook her head sympathetically. "My parents were the same. Ten years I wanted to leave, but my parents would not sign. They say Russia is my country. I must go to medical school. My father is doctor. My mother is dentist. They are good Communists and do not want their daughter to be traitor."

Galina took a breath. It was her longest speech so far.

"What made you want to leave?" I asked.

Boris was not sure of the difference between "what" and "why." I asked for reasons and he shrugged as he repeated, "Reasons?" He counted them off on his fingers. "Grandfather at Babi Yar, uncle murdered by Stalin, cousin in *gulag* for writing *samizdat.* Jewish feelings, especially after '67 War."

He sensed that he had not answered my question and tried again. "For myself it was pain in my heart at father's *yorzeit*. you know what is *yorzeit?*" We nodded to show that we knew. "My grandfather was rabbi. My father was head of Jewish school ... serious Jewish man ... very fine. When he died I wanted to say *kaddish* ... to remember him in traditional way. Impossible in Moscow to go to synagogue. University professor of mathematics ... does not go through synagogue door. Instead I go to cemetery to say my prayers to the stones. I know is not right way but better to talk to stones than KGB. One year I have conference in Riga at time of father's death anniversary. In Riga I am stranger, unknown. I can go in synagogue. Who cares? From that year I plan conferences for time of *yorzeit* in far places from Moscow. Years and years I am planning conferences and all the time thinking ... what I am doing. I, Boris, trying to be Jewish in country where it is crime."

"When we hear it is possible to go to Israel," said Galina, "we think to pack up and go. If parents were not so stubborn, we would have gone in '73. Our daughter would have grown up as Israeli."

"You would have liked that?" my mother asked.

"Like?" said Galina. "We would like a feeling of being normal people ... that we have not yet known ... anywhere. In Soviet Union we try to be ordinary citizens ... but we are Jews. We try to be Jews ... and we do crazy things. ..."

"What do you mean, crazy things?" my mother asked.

"Passover," said Galina, shaking her head. "Going out late with doctor bag to pick up cookies ... year after year."

"Cookies?" my mother repeated. "What cookies?"

"Excuse please," said Galina. "We would not speak of *matza.* We had friend who has friend ... who has friend. Call would come to pick up cookies and I would go ... like a smuggler ... like criminal person ... to pick up the package and hide so neighbor should not see. Small thing . . . but added to many, many difficulties to give me angry feelings."

I asked how she persuaded her mother to give permission.

"I did not succeed," said Galina. "But my daughter's tears they could not stand. Her young man . . . very nice smart Jewish boy was arrested for Zionist activity. She, herself, was . . . how you say . . . pushed out from school. She came crying to grandparents that they must leave. She was only nineteen. We would not let her go without us. It was only way . . . to go together."

"How does one get arrested for Zionist activities?" I asked.

"For singing," said Boris. "For singing in public place, naturally."

"What kind of singing?" I asked.

Boris hesitated for a moment and then a nice baritone began, "*David, Melekh Yisroel . . . Hai, hai vekayom . . .* Zionist song . . . for arresting young people. They say to him when he comes out of prison he can leave country or go to mental hospital. . . . You understand?"

Galina pressed her fingers to her lips. "How can anyone understand? I am trying whole life to understand and cannot succeed. Imagine. My daughter's young man has parents like my parents. They have no Jewish hearts, only identity card that says they are Jewish. The mother is only half Jewish. They do not want to go to Israel. It is strange place for them. They agree to come to America to save only son. We are wanting to go to Israel and must also come to America because our daughter is in love with nice boy."

Boris pulled his wallet out of his pocket and showed us pictures of the couple. Wedding pictures. My mother looked at them enviously.

"Unusual young man," said Galina. "At Brandeis University. Will go to medical school when he graduates. Parents do not understand him. Before he married our daughter . . . he went to Beth Israel for . . . circumcision . . . then to synagogue for bar mitzva. Fantastic. Wants his children to be real Jews. Had wedding under *huppa.* First time I saw such a thing."

Boris said: "Good it all took place before her mother came. It would have been too much . . . too much."

My mother had begun wiping her eyes when Boris began singing. She kept lifting her handkerchief to her eyes. He touched her arm. "A soft Jewish heart," he said. She was embarrassed and said nothing.

"Some day," he said, as if he were beginning a story, "some day we all go to Jerusalem . . . to stay. Who knows? This is wonderful country. But not mine."

My mother shook her head. "I am too old," she said. "And afraid of fighting. It is too late for me."

"You cannot tell," said Galina. "My mother is here. It is unbelievable to me. When my father died she wanted to be with us. And she came. Everything is possible."

"Who knows," my mother agreed. "My daughter might marry an Israeli."

"So many reasons," said Galina. "For every person . . . another reason."

Boris looked at his watch. Galina took my hand in hers. "A pleasure to meet you," she said to my mother. To me, she added, "So we are good neighbors. A thousand kisses to you!"

Envy
A Story of Best Friends

I last saw Schatz the day before my family moved away from Williamsburg. I was twelve and she fourteen. We had just graduated from the Talmud Torah. We parted with tearful promises of writing letters and visiting back and forth that we both knew we couldn't keep. Moving to another neighborhood meant moving to another world and we were already old enough to know how hard it is to live in more than one world at a time. We were moving too far away for a Shabbos walk together and the Talmud Torah classes and services could no longer keep us together.

We had been "best friends." We told each other secrets we shared with no one else and risked confessions that we might have kept to ourselves forever if we had not found each other. We told each other stories that revealed our own psyches and the details of other relationships and experiences as they unfolded before our critical adolescent eyes. We came from different worlds though we lived only twelve blocks apart. She never came to my house. I was at hers only once. We had space in which to exaggerate and diminish what we did and didn't understand, what we had actually seen and only heard about. We knew our parents were not likely to meet.

Schatz would remain fourteen forever in my imagination. I

Reprinted from *Hadassah*, November 1983, by permission.

could not picture her older than she was that last summer in Williamsburg. Over the years some young girl with a long braid hanging below her waist would remind me of Schatz's golden *tsepel* and certain kinds of pretty symmetrical faces set on small-boned bodies would make me think of her. When it was fashionable to speak of "good things in little packages," I would think of Schatz, the way she looked and the way adults looked at her as a kind of treasure to be enjoyed and protected.

I envied her long before we were friends. I'd watch the teachers put their arms around her, pat her hair and feared that I would have to work very hard for the gestures of affection and approval she received just for being herself and looking the way she did. I didn't know in the beginning that the teachers were all her uncles or her father's or grandfather's students who had known her since she was born. She was also the child of her parents' older years, with brothers almost old enough to be parents. Her father was the head of a yeshiva and her grandfather a respected rabbi and teacher.

The *yihus* Schatz was born into I could neither acquire nor simulate. My envy was blatant but ordinary. Her sinuous *tsepel* made me feel my short hair, shingled in the back, like a castration. More than a head taller, I wished for her smallness and for the blue handmade dress she wore on Shabbos. I was obsessed with longing for the kind of rimless glasses she wore, so different from the heavy dark tortoise-shell frames I was stuck with. Our nicknames were a measure of our differences. She was called Schatz though her name was Esther. The boys taunted me with "Foureyes." There was nothing I could do about it but make her my best friend.

Long before we had said a word to each other, I was in the habit of waiting for her after the storytelling time on Friday night. The program at the Talmud Torah included classes after school Monday to Thursday, Sunday morning, services early Friday evening and Saturday morning. My favorite time of the week was the storytelling after Friday night supper. The only trouble was that the streets were dark and scary going home. Schatz walked safely between two uncles. I followed a few steps behind them for protection until we came to the large intersection where they turned right and I turned left, to run all the rest of the way home. My six years at

Talmud Torah included some unexpected track training. I mostly came and went alone braving the packs of nasty boys, barking dogs, my fear of the little fires lit at the edge of the curb for purposes I could never fathom. There were also the occasional drunks who stumbled out of the tavern in my path. My most unreasonable phobia had to do with construction sites. I ran especially fast to avoid any derrick or crane that might run amuck, snatch me up by its iron claws and lift me higher than I dared to be. My parents, of course, had no idea of my terrors. I had no wish to add to their troubles. They sent me forth with assurances that God was with me and watching over me. I was not altogether confident that He knew what was going on in my neighborhood.

One Friday night Schatz came out just behind me after the storytelling session and started walking home without any uncles for protection. I no longer remember whether birth, death or sudden illness had kept them away, but she set forth and I trailed behind as usual. I heard the hiss of the boys' voices before I saw them and shouted, "Watch out" too late for it to do any good. They caught her first and then me as well, trapped us their circle, shouting, "Goosem, goosem," while I pulled and punched, bit and kicked with all my strength. Schatz's rimless glasses fell to the ground and were broken early in the fray. One of our assailants was bloodied by the broken glass. "Run," I shouted as he let go for a minute and Schatz ran, weeping, and I pulled myself free and ran after her. The street was empty. There were no witnesses.

At the Grand Extension where we usually separated, I decided to walk her home. She was still shaken and crying and not sure she could see without her glasses.

I wanted to leave her at the wrought iron gate of the brownstone house she shared with her grandfather and one of her uncles, but she begged me to come in with her. She had already decided what to say to her mother and needed me for support.

When her mother opened the door we were both grateful for the darkness. The Sabbath candles were not bright enough to show the buttons torn off my coat and my scraped knee. Schatz introduced me as a friend who was kind enough to come home with her after she broke her glasses. Her mother seemed more sad than angry when she asked how she broke them. "I fell," said Schatz, neither lying nor telling the truth. Her mother put her arm around her and told her she should have been more careful. "I was running. I couldn't see," said Schatz.

Schatz's mother was very different from mine, but Schatz seemed as careful to save her from worry as I was with my mother. When told that she shouldn't have been running, she told a garbled story about boys fighting, without implicating us in their brawl. Her grandfather, from the next room, said, "Schatz dearest, fighting is forbidden. *Me tur zikh nisht shlagen*" [One must not fight]. And Schatz dutifully answered, "Yes, Grandfather, I know."

I was torn between staying as long as possible to avoid the terrifying walk home alone and leaving as quickly as possible because my mother was surely worried about where I was. I stayed long enough to see that Schatz lived in an environment totally different from mine. The rooms were all lined with bookshelves from the floor to the ceiling, with more books than I had ever seen outside the public library. She had a room of her own with her own private bed and desk, her own chair and chest of drawers.

Long after I forgot the nasty boys who frightened and shamed us, I remembered Schatz's house in the dim light of flickering Sabbath candles as a sanctuary from the cramped life I was used to.

I saw my own family in a different light after that glimpse into her world. My father's library was a narrow shelf of prayer books and a battered Bible. He was a passionate reader of Yiddish newspapers and selected the most important items in *The Day* and the *Morning Journal* to read aloud to us after dinner at night. "Listen to this," he would say and we would stop what we were doing to listen.

Most of my friends and relatives lived as we did in three cramped rooms. Our dining room, which was my bedroom at night, was a gallery of photographs of bearded European grandfathers in high silk hats and coats with fur collars. They looked like men of substance and wisdom, more accomplished and better educated than their sons who fled to America to become tailors, furriers and house painters. Some nights, before falling asleep on the narrow cot I shared with my sister, I would think of these faces above my head and their unknown and unknowable lives in that distant place called Europe. I would imagine my father, his brothers and my uncles as princes in disguise. Their hands were the worn hands of working men. Their faces resembled the portraits if I could imagine them smooth-shaven. Their voices and manners were not coarse. They were gentle people, *eidele mentshen,* as it was said.

I remember, however, that my mother's welcome when I finally got home was too distraught for gentleness. I ran and skipped all the way, praying to be invisible to any boys hiding in doorways. When I reached my street, I could see my mother hanging out the window waiting for me. I had my excuses ready and fashioned into a compelling story of bravery and rescue. I too omitted the boys and told about the rabbi's granddaughter who fell and broke her glasses. I planned to describe the house and the welcome I received, but she was not impressed with me. "And where was everyone else?" she wanted to know. Why had I taken it upon myself to look out for the rabbi's granddaughter while she waited for me at the window?

I was, after all, no more than ten at the time. My mother knew and feared the dangers of the streets whether I kept secrets from her or not. If she could only have known how desperate I was for praise and approval, she would have spared me the scolding. I just added another difference to the list that separated my life from Schatz's.

I was too young to think of class separations and had been only in the homes of relatives or close neighbors. I was more aware of the way I differed from children from non-Orthodox homes, who were playing ball in the street while I marched off to Talmud Torah every day. I also knew what my parents thought of children left to their own devices. *"Kinder auf hefker"* [Neglected children], they called them, confident that they would come to a bad end. I sometimes wished for a taste of their freedom, but no more than a taste. My envy was turned in another direction. I was already fixed in my need for an orderly life, fenced in by the clock and the calendar, the *mitzvot* and *aveirot.*

Schatz and I talked about this a lot when we began meeting on Shabbos afternoons while our parents napped. Once we had established the differences in our backgrounds, we turned to the areas we shared. The overwhelming difference was in education. Her mother had gone to university in Switzerland. My mother, raised in a small village in the Carpathian mountains, had missed schooling altogether. Schatz's father, grandfather and uncles studied the Talmud and taught others to study. My father was too worn out by his working week for such a luxury. In spite of this, however, and the minor differences in decor such as real Persian rugs rather than linoleum stamped with the pattern of Persian rugs and private beds rather than shared folding cots, we were more like each other than anyone we were likely to find outside our Talmud Torah.

We were both raised in households straining to be ready for Shabbos in time. The food we ate was kosher and fasts were kept. Lights and fires were not lit when it was forbidden and we waited for the same three stars to appear before declaring the Sabbath over. There were, however, sharp differences in the spoken and unspoken messages we received from our parents. My parents worried about what I learned in the non-Jewish world, perhaps knowing that world would separate me from them. They did not encourage me to go to college or even to a teachers' institute. Any ambitions I had would be my own. I knew that my parents did not know enough to advise me. If they tried, I would resist them. Schatz, on the other hand, was overwhelmed by prestigious parents and relatives. She would not make decisions without their approval. She trusted them to know what was best for her.

Schatz was shocked by my wish for independence, my threat to leave home and go out into the world to become something. My plans changed from week to week. They were daydreams more than plans and I had no idea of a process, a program that would make them come about. She listened as if she took me seriously, as if I someday could actually become a painter, a singer or, best of all, a writer producing books that could be lined up on shelves like the ones over her desk.

At thirteen, Schatz knew she would become a teacher, but not for long. She expected to marry someone her parents chose for her and to live wherever they lived so she could help them when they became old and infirm as they had helped their parents. She was prepared to have as many children as God gave her and looked forward to being a good Jewish wife, mother and daughter all her life. She wondered whether her husband would have to be a doctor, a merchant, a teacher or a rabbi but knew he would have to be pious and learned to fit into her family. She considered herself lucky to have been born into a "modern" family. She had been taught that it was possible to have accomplishments in the secular world without giving up Jewish traditions and learning. She looked forward to being the helpmate of an educated man.

I, on the other hand, gave no thought to marriage. My dreams were only about what I wanted to do "all by myself." Schatz worried for me. She saw something improper and dangerous in my long-ings. I envied her her secure future but thought of her as a beautiful bird with clipped wings that would never fly and also never fall from some place too high.

Years later I would think of Schatz more as a principle than a real person, as an object of envy that I could not use for a model. If only I could have been born a diminutive Schatz, protected and supported and praised rather than as a big-boned foureyes needing to reach beyond my grasp, torn for life between irreconcilable wishes.

Long after I had forgotten about my friendship with Schatz, the sight of a proper Orthodox family walking to *shul* on Shabbos would invoke the old envy and conflict. I was embarrassed to drive by the fathers and sons in *kippot,* the little girls in white stockings and mothers in modish hats.

On one of my regular pilgrimages to the Jewish neighborhood where I stopped at the kosher butcher, baker and the grocery that kept kasha, matza meal and poppy seeds on the shelves, I met a young woman that brought Schatz to mind again. I first saw the braid swinging down under the small kerchief and then noticed the long sleeves and covered legs not expected in the middle of summer. When she turned around I was taken by the pale skin, the look of innocence that had become so rare. The street was full of young women in jeans or shorts and sandals, bra-less under their tee shirts, wild hair flying in the style of their generation. She asked me the time and then whether I lived in the neighborhood. "Are you Jewish?" she asked, surprising me both by the question and the fact that she couldn't tell by looking at me. She was on her way to a hasidic institute for young women and was unsure of her directions. I asked what she studied and she said, "The laws of kashrut and *taharat hamishpaha,*" blushing as she spoke as Schatz used to. She invited me to come to her class if I had the time. She said visitors were welcome.

I thanked her, said I had studied those laws when I was young, and then our conversation took an unexpected turn and I was admitting to this eighteen-year-old that I did not observe the laws that I knew so well. "How is that possible?" she asked. "What is the point of knowing without doing?" I assured her that I agreed with her.

"Then you must begin," she said with youthful confidence. I shook my head to show it was not likely. "Why not?" she asked. When I told her I rebelled when I was young, she said, "Why did you?"

Uncomfortable with her directness, I admitted that I didn't know. The trolley she was waiting for came in time to save me further embarrassment. She turned as she hopped on and said, "You're old enough to know. With the help of Hashem you will."

The trolley disappeared and I regretted not asking her where she came from. Had she grown up with choices like my own independent children or with the law laid down, firm and immovable? Had she invented herself or was she like my old friend Schatz, the product of an environment too strong to resist?

My circle of questions closed the day I met Schatz herself, the real person, not metaphor or surrogate. The way she turned up fit all my fantasies of how it might happen. That didn't diminish the pleasure or surprise of finding her again.

I was traveling across the country to publicize a book I had written. In every Jewish community I would find it easy to pick out the voices from New York and marvel how far we had all traveled since our childhoods. Schatz found me in a small city where I had never been before. At the end of the lecture, after the questions had all been asked and the little circle of well-wishers had dispersed, she was waiting in the hallway, a sweet-faced grandmother, white-haired, wearing glasses with heavy blue plastic frames. She was still a head shorter than I and half my weight.

"Wasn't your name Chava?" she asked. "And didn't you go to the Talmud Torah of Williamsburg?" When I said yes to both questions, she said, "Then do you remember Esther Frankel?"

"Schatz, the rabbi's daughter?" I said in my confusion.

"Granddaughter," she corrected me, but pleased that I had not forgotten her completely. "I recognized you right away," she said, "but I was expecting it to be you."

She said she had been reading things I had written for nearly thirty years, always wondering if it was her old friend from Williamsburg. "Someone saves your life, you don't forget them."

When I looked confused about my saving her life, she reddened. "Who knows what harm those boys might have done if you were not such a tough fighter?" It seemed funny to me that she thought me brave and tough. I had no such vision of myself.

She wanted me to go home with her, but I had a plane to catch. "Then I'll take you to the airport," she said, and I accepted. We had a little over an hour to cover more than forty years of our lives. We checked off the easy things first. Her husband had been a rabbi but was the director of a yeshiva. I was married to a professor of physics. One of my sons was a mathematician. The other was in medical school. We had no marriages to boast about; no grandchildren to play with. Schatz had four children and twelve grandchildren, with more on the way.

Her life had turned out pretty much as she expected, I thought. I was not eager to talk about our sons. They were mine and yet not mine. They were still looking for ways to separate themselves from us. They had no ties to Jewish life. They felt free beyond my wildest expectations of freedom. In my dark moments I sometimes thought I was reaping as I had sown, getting what I deserved, the punishment for offering more choices than were necessary.

I was not ready to share my fears and doubts with my old friend. There was too much to explain in the time we had available. I was also not ready to hear her say, "I envy you your worldly life, your educated children. I'm glad you succeeded in your work."

"I envy you your children and especially the grandchildren,"

I said. "In this day and age, that's no small accomplishment."

She answered me with a shrug of her shoulder. "They are very *frum;* they have given up on worldly knowledge. They are all in Israel, close to the *rebbe* they've chosen to follow. My great-grand-parents were more modern than my children, who are trying hard not to be *my* children. So forgive me for my envy."

"It is forbidden to envy," I reminded her, as if that would make any difference to either one of us. We exchanged addresses before I boarded the plane. We promised to keep in touch just as we did when I moved away from Williamsburg. The distances had grown from a half hour in a trolley car to three hours in the air. Everything had changed and yet remained the same. It was still hard to live in more than one world at a time. But she was no longer called Schatz and I could no longer remember the last time I was called Foureyes.

The Red Goblets

It was nearly time for the children to arrive. The table was set in the dining room, a proper Passover table with matza and wine, hard-boiled eggs, horseradish and parsley and the Haggadot in a neat pile ready for distribution. The kitchen was temporarily calm. The surfaces were cleared for the confusion to come and all the fragile and dangerous things out of reach. The doors to the bedrooms upstairs were open, and two cribs had been taken down from the attic for sudden sleeping emergencies.

I was, however, still nervously opening and closing closets, rummaging in the back of shelves. "What are you looking for?" my husband called from his study. "Can I help you? Tell me what you're looking for. Maybe I know where it is." I was too distracted to answer him and too embarrassed about my frenzied search for what he would call *"a nekhtiger tog"* [Something useless and unnecessary], to ask for help. Then, just as time was running out, I found what I was looking for. On the top shelf of the linen closet, behind the large wine-stained tablecloths I had not used in years, I felt the rough carved glass under the tissue paper.

"Found it," I called down in a voice that belied my relief that the search was over. My mother at such moments would say: "When is a poor man rich? When he finds something he thought he lost."

Reprinted from *Hadassah*, April 1985, by permission.

One need not be poor to know the pleasure of finding something lost. I unwrapped the package of little goblets as if I were unwrapping the years of doubt and anxiety in which they had been hidden away, the years in which I couldn't bear to look at such strong reminders of unfulfilled expectations and promises.

My husband watched me with a skeptical look as if he were wondering how this meager treasure could be worthy of my wild search. He saw only three little red goblets, coarsely carved, neither beautiful nor valuable. I was not ready to explain what they meant to me. I washed them as carefully as if they were my best crystal and set one at each of the places where our grandchildren would sit. These ordinary gestures released feelings for which I had no words in English. My normally cool, secular style was overwhelmed by the Yiddish aphorisms of my childhood: *"Az men lebt, derlebt men"* [If you live long enough, you live to see a lot], *"Fun gedult, kleibt men royzin"* [With patience, you get roses], and similar sentiments that lost their power when returned to the boundaries of English decorum. I had, however, lived to see the day and was unabashedly grateful.

Then the children arrived. The little ones, carried like first fruits at harvest time, brought all reflection to a halt. Cousins, they toddled together like wound-up dolls, standing, falling, creeping. Their toys spread underfoot. They left a trail of bottles and pacifiers throughout the house. The Seder this year was traditional only in the preparation. Two little girls under the age of two and a boy of five months created an order of their own. They upstaged the Haggada. The blessings were speeded up, and the readings minimized. The little red goblets, however, were a great success. The little girls sat high on their pillows, holding their goblets in fat little hands.

Their noses and chins turned pink with grape juice. They thought they had entered the world of adults, but in fact they had turned us all into children. We babbled and cooed, gave them all our attention. Conversation died in the panicky shrieks for caution about spilling and dropping and the fear of falling. I was sufficiently rational to be pleased that I had not invited any other guests. Only doting parents and grandparents were likely to be able to cope. We were all in the thrall of a new stage of life, perfect examples of the narcissism of what is now called "parenting." Observers from the real world, however, might be less tolerant of the food-smeared little faces, of the grape juice dripping in little rivulets down their bibs, and the matza crumbs piling up under the table.

The Seder began early for the sake of the children and came to an early end because of the children. The youngest nursed his way through *Had Gadya,* and the afikomen was forgotten in the confusion of diaper changes. I had only praise for my daughter and daughter-in-law, who were proving that educated, professional women could also be good mothers. Watching my son with his child on his shoulders, I remembered my father holding him with that same look of pride and pleasure. Other fathers might be uncertain about being a grandfather, but mine had said: "A crown for an old man's head. That's what a grandchild is."

We spent a long time at the door exchanging kisses. Our children apologized for leaving us with such a mess, and we promised each other a less chaotic Seder next year. They drove off, and we were left with the carpet of matza crumbs, the hard-boiled egg that had rolled under the buffet, and the mystery of the *knaidel* our tactile granddaughter had lifted from her soup, squeezed and lost.

Small things. Hardly worth mentioning. We put dishes in the dishwasher and threw the crumbs out the window for the birds. Crawling about on hands and knees to retrieve the food and cutlery the little ones had dropped, I wondered how my mother had managed when my sisters and I came home for Pesah with our assorted broods. I remember only how her face lit up at our arrival and how it fell when it was time for us to leave. I remember her standing at the mirror with one of the children, tiny arms around her neck, saying: "See my new necklace. See my new jewel." If they grew up to be brats and pests who disturbed the order of her house, I had no recollection of hearing her complain.

Tricks of memory. I remember special moments and occasions and forget the rest. I remember going to the Seder at my grandparents' house but little about the confusion. They had five daughters and three sons. There was a long line of grandchildren to kiss them good-by at the end of the evening. I had been taught to say, *"Shluf gezint, shtei auf gezint, un zie gezint."* [Sleep well, get up well and be well.] I can't imagine how we all fit into their small Brooklyn apartment. There was surely no room at the dining room table for children. It's very likely that the women served the meal but did not sit down to eat with their husbands and sons. The Sedarim of my childhood were male adult occasions, which children were not supposed to disturb.

My grandfather was the center of attention. He wore a special white robe and a white, jeweled *yarmulke*. The old leather lounge chair from the kitchen was transformed by pillows and white sheets into what a child might see as a throne. The uncles and grown-up male cousins sang in lusty voices. The neighbors would take out their folding chairs and sit under the windows to enjoy the singing that went on until midnight. Even in Williamsburg in the late 1920's, my grandparents' style was thought exceptional by their more American neighbors.

I was one of their grandchildren, one of the cousins who fought over the *afikomen*, which was hidden and stolen many times in a single night. Tears would flow at the end, when one by one we went to capture the reward, only to find that the matza we had hidden had disappeared.

The night of the red goblets was one on which my grandfather waited for the commotion to die down, for my sisters and cousins to go back to their games in the kitchen, before beckoning to me. He had been watching me, he said, and he was pleased that I had not cried when the *afikomen* I had stolen could not be found where I left it. He folded me into his white robe and surreptitiously handed me a little package. Pretty red goblets— *"sheine royte bekherel"*—to drink from on Passover. He said that I could share them with my sisters, but that they were mine. I was to take them with me when I married a *"sheinem bokher"* some day. I was to be careful not to break or lose them, so that my children and my children's children could drink from them in the years to come. *"Gedenk,"* he said, and I promised I would remember. "And before you drink, you will make the blessing, and you will teach your children to do the same." I promised, was kissed on the head and set free. I was five, surely no more than six.

I didn't take the goblets with me when I married. I left them in my mother's china closet, where my children could find them when I brought them home for Pesah with their grandparents. They were kept with other family mementos until we emptied the china closet after my mother's death. Our children were in college by then, drinking from larger goblets. They were no more ready to come home for Passover than I was ready to confront the little red goblets and the promises of my childhood. Clear as this seems from the safety of hindsight, it was murky and uncomfortable during those foggy, anxious years.

For years we had been celebrating Passover with friends in the same limbo, all of us waiting to see how our families' futures would unfold. Anxiety was the glue that kept us together. We felt it as a low-grade chronic fever that we couldn't shake off. We did not ask each other about our children and sent our messages in looks and sighs. We were old friends who were brought together by our children. We had taken turns chauffering them to Hebrew school and music lessons and chaperoned them at high school dances. We watched them grow up to test themselves in a world we could neither control nor understand.

Our circle was smaller each year, as our friends fled to Florida and Arizona, to city condominiums and exotic resorts where one could escape memories and expectations. Only a few still lived in the houses in which they had raised their children. We were all besieged by real estate agents offering extravagant sums for our modest suburban houses. I understood the temptation to jettison the past and escape to warm places and new faces. There was no point to saving the old cribs in the attic, the sleds and playpens and highchairs. I thought I couldn't bear to part with thousands of books I might never read again and boxes of pictures I might not look at. I watched my neighbors scatter their possessions in yard sales and second-hand furnitures stores, but every offer of a new life made me cling more tenaciously to the vestiges of the old. I settled the issue one day by telling the agent who called to make me yet another offer that I planned to stay until carried out in 25 years or so and not to bother calling until then.

We had lived to see the bedrooms opened and the cribs reassembled. Our children, once they became parents, could come back to visit. The tensions of the years of separation and struggle seemed unreal in this new time of life. I felt, however, as if I'd been swimming for a long time and just made it to the other shore, a shore that was not as substantial as it seemed from afar. I kept some residue of caution. I was wary of expectations and promises and wondered what was going on in my grandfather's head when he gave me the goblets and blessings and exacted my promises. Did he know his power? Or was it his faith in "The One Above" that made him seem so confident? How I envied that aura of confidence.

It was almost eleven when my friend down the street called to tell us that we were missed at her Seder. "How was it with the children?" she asked.

"Thank God," I heard myself say in a voice like my mother's. "Much to be thankful for." What I really meant was: "It was wonderful. The children are incredibly beautiful. This is the happiest I've been in years." But I spoke as if the telephone were bugged by evil eyes, as if there were some danger in tempting fate with moments of joy. Wasn't I imprinted early with "Laughing in the morning leads to crying at night." I kept a low profile. I said, "Sorry to tell you I've had no bad news to report." That was as close to boasting as I dared come with a friend who's still waiting out the future, still troubled about marriages that may not come to pass or are falling to pieces, about the grandchildren that may not materialize, and all the twists and turns of this dangerous life, a lottery in which all do not win.

"I'm so happy for you," said my friend, raising our relationship to a higher level. I read somewhere that the friend who can rejoice in one's good fortune is even closer than the friend who can commiserate in time of trouble. "Thank you for giving me hope," she said. "Maybe my time will come. Everything is possible."

"Remind me," I said in parting, "to tell you about my little red goblets."

Fanny's Children

I knew as soon as I heard my mother's voice that she had bad news to report. Her breathing gives her away. I pick up little sighs and pauses that are never there when she doesn't have anything troublesome to tell.

"So what is it?" I asked impatiently, wanting to be spared the "I'm sorry to have to tell you. . . . There's nothing to worry about, but I'm afraid you must know."

It was Aunt Fanny, my mother's youngest sister. She was in the hospital, felled by a stroke and asking for me. My mother's message caught the vestiges of a lifelong conflict between the sisters, not resolved even at zero hour. She tried to tell me that this was probably the last request my aunt would make of me and that I was morally obligated to honor it, while simultaneously letting me know that she would be very understanding if I couldn't come. Under it all was the scaffolding of 50 years of resentment. My mother had never been able to forgive Aunt Fanny for separating herself from the family, for daring to call herself an artist and, most of all, for deciding not to have any children. How many times had I heard, "If she wanted children to comfort her in her old age, she should have had them when she was young."

I could catch the flash of displeasure, the tightening of my

Reprinted from *Hadassah*, May 1986, by permission.

mother's lips when Aunt Fanny came to borrow a child for a few hours, by the time I was five. My brother usually refused her offers of trips to the park, the circus or the zoo and would not sit still long enough for her to try to do a drawing of him. My sister took her turn reluctantly. I, however, was always ready to go off with her and always sorry to come home. My mother's disapproval took away some of the pleasure of being borrowed, but I never refused. I loved the bus trips to the Cloisters and the strolls through the museums. Fanny took me to free concerts in the park and to Radio City Music Hall on my birthday. When I was 12, her present was a boat trip on the Hudson to Bear Mountain. I was easy to please. I could have a wonderful time going back and forth on the Staten Island ferry. I held her pocketbook while she sketched.

I loved the presents she gave me: little art books, plaster replicas of famous sculptures and fantastic shells from distant places. My sister preferred clothes and would say, "What will you do with that? What's it for?" My father, in a fit of anger, smashed my collection of plastic figurines. "Idols!" he shouted. "What are they doing in this house?"

I never told Aunt Fanny about what had happened to them. I knew, without understanding all the ramifications, that my parents were offended by my affection for Aunt Fanny and feared that I might take her for a model, becoming a free, artistic woman who avoided real life and responsibility.

Fanny, with no support or encouragement from her family, had invented herself as an artist. She spent several hours a day in the back bedroom of my grandparents' apartment, painting pictures of idealized, angelic children and tidy little still lifes of plastic fruit and flowers which she set up on a red velvet cloth draped over the dresser.

She exhibited her work in the annual shows at the public library and was often asked to donate pictures that would be auctioned off for the benefit of good causes. Every now and then a sentimental soul actually bought one of her pale pink and turquoise canvases, and decorators sometimes came with swatches of cloth looking for a picture that would pull a room together. Fanny had a few commissions to illustrate privately printed books of poems and had also done two children's books. This was after she married Mr. Straus and went to live with him in his sprawling West Side apartment.

My best memories of Aunt Fanny, however, are from the years when she still lived with my grandparents, the *alte moid,* the 32-year-old girl who lived in a world of her own, though under the family roof. She was the youngest of eight children, the only one to go beyond elementary school in America, and the only one to speak perfect English. She alone would move into what my father called "the American world." Though there were almost 20 years between us, she treated me as if I were a younger sister or a cousin, rather than a niece. We felt closer to each other than to my mother, who never left her parents' orbit. Their thoughts were still governed by the standards of the Bukovina village from which they had come. My mother remembered her "old home," but Aunt Fanny left when she was four and swore she couldn't remember anything that happened before she got off the boat.

My grandparents were good, warm-hearted people. I knew that from the way they looked at me and talked to me, but I also knew from the way my mother worried about them that they were worn out from the ordeal of emigration and the problems of raising eight children. Fanny, the child of their older years, came too late to get their attention. My mother, as the oldest, mothered her and tried to control her. She encouraged her to go to secretarial school and was dismayed when she enrolled in the Art Students League instead. Mama tried, in vain, to find her a suitable husband. She wept bitterly when Fanny announced her marriage to Mr. Straus.

Mr. Straus was 18 years older than Fanny and had already buried two wives. My father called him "the German," but he was a refugee from Vienna, a hand-kissing Austrian. He was Fanny's professor of art history, but not a starving teacher. He made a fair living by selling insurance and dabbling in real estate. My mother found him loathsome and spoke of him as if he were something edible that turned her stomach. My grandparents saw him only as "a *goy,*" a representative of the forbidden "other." My aunts and uncles mocked him, thought him an imposter, someone freakish and inauthentic—a perfect match for Fanny, who went about with paint under her fingernails and the smell of turpentine rather than perfume in her clothes. Aunt Beckie never got over her sister's willingness to marry a widower who was half a head shorter than she, a "little bedbug of a man," when she had her choice of dashing young businessmen, promising accountants and even a dentist ready to open a practice.

I never spoke up in her behalf, but I was Aunt Fanny's staunchest ally, and the more I heard her mocked, the more dedicated I became. Watching her was an education in resisting public opinion. "You don't have to do as you're told," said Fanny. "You have to figure out for yourself what you need and what's good for you. Never mind what people say. What do they know?"

I found Mr. Straus strange but not ludicrous. I saw him very rarely and sensed that he was not interested in me. I didn't care. I much preferred having Fanny all to myself. I saw enough, however, to be taken by the way he treated her. "He makes me feel like a princess," she said. "He behaves as if I were some treasure to care for, not some nut to scold and embarrass. I have a beautiful life with him, Beverly. Never mind what the biddies have to say."

Fanny began dressing like a lady rather than an artist when she became Mrs. Straus. She sometimes even smelled of perfume. They traveled to Vienna and Paris. She sent me postcards from Florence and Venice. Most important, however, was the studio he set up for her and the generous way he had of praising and encouraging her. It was all balm for her spirit after the hard time she had with her family. Her parents were openly ashamed of her, and her brothers and sisters had shown little sympathy for her efforts to transcend them. Aunt Selma had scandalized my grandmother by showing her Fanny's sketchbook from her life drawing class. All that male and female nakedness had shocked her to the core. The family spoke of Fanny's "shmearing" as a kind of *meshugas* beyond their help.

After all this, it was no wonder that Fanny fell in love with Mr. Straus. He played the ideal father and she, the perfect child, until she buried him at the age of 75. That was almost 20 years ago, so she'd had plenty of time to live her own life as she pleased.

It was all about over. Aunt Fanny, the *bonne vivante* and family artist, was in her 70's. My mother, who'd made it to 87, still thought of her as her crazy little sister, a danger to herself and the people who cared about her. So I dropped everything and took the plane to New York and a cab to Mount Sinai Hospital, where I prepared myself for the worst.

I could have used more time to sort out my feelings and make myself ready for a visit with Aunt Fanny. The truth is that I was thinking only of myself and how quickly the years had flown since I took Fanny's advice and left home. In some place inside myself, I was still a daughter, dutifully calling her mother at candlelighting time on Friday. My mother dropped a few coins in her blue boxes before blessing her candles, and I dropped mine into a telephone, no matter where I was or whether I had anything to tell her. I knew that the price of my freedom and mobility had to be paid in reassurance and reliability.

I dragged my feet from the plane to the cab and was grateful for every red light and traffic jam, but I arrived at Mount Sinai Hospital in spite of myself. I found my way through the hospital labyrinth to Aunt Fanny's bed and held by breath till she gave me one of her old grins. "Darling girl," she said and grabbed my hand and kissed it. Her speech was a little blurred, but I could make it out. "Knew I could count on you," she murmured.

Her left arm was paralyzed, but her right one was all right. She opened and closed her fingers to show me she could do it, and even lifted her hand to her thin, frizzy hair. "I must look terrible," she said so that I'd assure her that she looked pretty good, all things considered.

"Long as I can paint and eat, I'll manage," she insisted. "The left leg isn't all that great, but they say it will come back to me. And I haven't forgotten a thing. My head is all there. It's just my tongue is a little fuzzy." When the nurse came by, however, she introduced me as her daughter. When I reminded her that I was her niece, she became agitated. "If I say you're my daughter, then you are my daughter." The nurse, with a little grimace, let me know Fanny had had a lot of medication.

The next morning when I came back as I'd promised, she was ready and waiting for me. Her hair was combed. Her eyes were bright as a bird's, and she was ready for an orgy of remembering.

I'd forgotten the aspect of Aunt Fanny that drove the family crazy. She had always kept a strict account of her favors, remembered everything she gave and waited for returns on her investments. She did not forgive my siblings and cousins who didn't want to be reminded about her treats and presents of 30 years ago. It turned out that I was the only one to keep in touch, to send birthday greetings and pictures of my children.

When she had finished castigating her delinquent nieces and nephews, she settled back. She needed to tell me that she was disappointed in them because they were American children who had all the advantages and should know how to behave. She assured me that she had forgiven her parents, long dead. "Poor immigrants," she said, "ignorant and superstitious. The stories I could tell you." She had expected nothing from her sisters and brothers. "Undeveloped people, uneducated, uncultured, what can I say? I escaped with my life."

I was worried about tiring her, but she was testing herself. "Lying here, empty-handed, I keep trying to see how far back I can remember. I can remember the first time Mr. Straus came to pick me up at my parents' apartment. I'll remember that to my dying day. I desperately didn't want him to come. I begged him to let me meet him in the lobby of a hotel somewhere, on a street corner— anywhere but the apartment on East Second Street. I couldn't get out of it. You see, he thought I was ashamed of *him* and didn't want to introduce him to *my* family. So what could I do? He was a dignified person and concerned about respectability. And my luck! Of all the nights of the year, it was the night of *shluggen kaporus*. I'd forgotten all about it. You see, he had tickets to Carnegie Hall, and he asked me and I said yes. We'd been meeting after class for a cup of coffee for many weeks, and this was the first, you know, real date.

"Picture my feelings, Beverly, when I realized. There were chickens in the bathtub, live chickens and the smell of a barnyard. And it was my good fortune the bell should ring while your Zeide was twirling the chicken over my head, and your Uncle Benny, instead of waiting until it was over, opened the door. And there was my Mr. Straus. If I live to be a hundred, I won't forget the look on his face when he took in the scene, this *recherche du temps perdu* on the fifth floor on East Second Street. He had such poise. In a second, he put his hat back on, waited till it was all over, told my parents it was a pleasure to meet them, wished them a happy New Year—and away we went to Carnegie Hall.

"He said he'd heard of the ceremony, but never seen it. He took it as an anthropological experience and wanted me to explain what it was about. But what did I know to tell him? All I could do was cry, because I felt so humiliated. But it was all right with him. He had grandparents who came to Vienna from the same part of Europe we came from. He was fascinated by my being from the same generation of assimilation as his mother. He was the one who taught me that you can't choose your parents. You have to accept them, however they are, but your own life you can choose."

Aunt Fanny pitied my mother her narrow life, her inability to separate herself from her parents and her refusal to become American and free. "She could have gone to school at night," she said, "but she didn't have the get-up-and-go. She could have traveled, but she wasn't interested. You know, Beverly, when I came to tell her that Mr. Straus was taking me to Europe, she said 'What for? That's where people come from. It's not a place to go.' So she never saw Paris, never saw Vienna or the beauty of Italy. She missed out on everything. She spent whole afternoons sitting at the window waiting for something to happen. I was never bored. Beverly— never in my life. I had lots of pleasures and I have no regrets.'

"Neither does my mom," I said quietly. "She had me and Bobby and Evelyn. She had lots of people to take care of. She likes taking care of people. She's crazy about her grandchildren."

"But how did she do it?" asked Fanny. "How? Remember when you came to me crying. You thought you were going to die. And what did she have to say to you? Did she explain anything?"

The things she remembered. She remembered the day I began menstruating in the era of innocence when it was possible to be 13 years old without knowing anything about the process. It was Aunt Fanny who allayed my fear that I was afflicted with some terrible disease. It was she who welcomed me into the world of women.

"Just wanted you to know I was there when you needed me," she said, like a good politician. "I had a good life. I'd just like a little more of it." Then she apologized for being too tired. "I'm going to have to close my eyes a little."

I sat by her bedside as she slept for a little while. Asleep, she looked like a worn-out 70-year-old woman, not the tough lady she made herself out to be. When the nurse stopped and said that she might not wake for several hours, I left a note, blew her a kiss and went down to wait for a cab to take me to the airport.

Weeks went by. I sent little notes so she'd know she wasn't forgotten. My mother told me when she left the hospital for a recuperation center, and then some months later, I heard that Fanny was back in her apartment. "I worry about her," my mother said. "She has a woman staying with her, but not a soul crosses her threshold." My mother lived too far away to be of help to her. My sister and brother refused to visit her because she subjected them to such tongue-lashings and complaints.

I thought of coming to see her, but my life was sufficiently complicated that I kept putting it off, until Fanny called me. Shaky-voiced, tense, she said it was an emergency. She had to see me immediately and would not take no for an answer. So I canceled all my appointments, apologized to my family, and went off to New York.

It has been years since I'd been to the apartment that had looked so elegant to me when I was a child. It had turned dark and musty, cluttered with what they call "collectibles." The sunny rooms I remembered had been made gloomy by new houses that shut out the light and covered the view. Fanny, caged in her walker, came to the foyer to meet me. This time I was not her darling girl. "So you finally got here," she greeted me. "How long did you think I'd sit around waiting for you?"

I was overwhelmed by the sight of my spindly Aunt Fanny, surrounded by her pictures. Every bit of wall space from the ceiling to the floor was covered, and there were stacks of pictures in the hallway, lined up like books. As if she knew what I was thinking, she said: "My children—all mine. And now the questions is what to do with them. Never minded when they didn't sell. Hated to part with them and, anyway, didn't need the money. Mr. Straus was a good provider. But now, Beverly, I have a big problem, and you're the only one who can help me. Sit down. We'll get right down to business."

Her blue eyes seemed overbright, manic. I took off my coat and sat down at the edge of the chair. "Aren't you going to offer me a cup of tea?" I asked, hoping to ease the tension for a bit.

"You want tea, you can take some. Do you think you're in your mother's house? Barely in the door and she's feeding you. Whenever she did that, I'd think to myself, that's the difference between an artist and an ordinary woman. The woman gives and gives. The artist takes and enjoys. Never understood why you wouldn't let me teach you to draw. Had the feeling you had some talent. So you had a thrilling life as a social worker?"

"I'm a psychotherapist, Aunt Fanny, with a doctor's degree," I said, hoping to calm her. "It's not so bad."

"How it could it be good to be listening to people's troubles all day? I never envied you."

She followed me to the kitchen and watched me put the kettle on, but she didn't want to be slowed down or put off. "I've made up my mind," she said. "I'm going to leave all my paintings to you. That's what I've decided."

It took me a few seconds to figure out what to say to her—and to find the right tone of voice so I could hide my dismay. "Aunt Fanny, that's not sensible," I finally said. "I have no place to hang them. They should go to a public place where lots of people would enjoy them—maybe a hospital or a nursing home. I'd be happy to take a few for remembrance, but you have hundreds of pictures and I couldn't do justice to all of them."

"I can't just give them to strangers. My whole life is in these pictures, Beverly. All my feelings. All my moods and memories. All the places we visited. Everything. I painted if I was happy, and I painted if I was sad. If I was angry at someone, I worked it out on a canvas and didn't take my troubles to any therapist."

I let the little dig go by and said: "You were very lucky to have been able to do that, but you still have to part with the pictures and let other people benefit from them. I can't be responsible for all of them."

I sipped my tea. Fanny stood in the doorway and watched me. Then I realized that tears were silently running down her cheeks. "Nobody wants them, Beverly. I have been trying everywhere. Can't find a home for my children. After all these years."

I assured her that she would, that some place would be happy to have them. What could I say?

I struggled for weeks to get the image of my old aunt and her pictures out of my mind. The van pulled up just when I had begun to succeed. I was relaxed enough to think that the driver was lost and looking for directions. But he had a note for me that let me know that I was the one who was lost. It read: "Dearest Beverly, There's nothing else for me to do. Be a good daughter and take care of the children for me."

The crates filled the back of the garage and spilled into the garden shed and the laundry. I kept dialing her number as they carried them in, though I hadn't figured out what to say to her beyond "How could you do this to me?" I was both dismayed and relieved not to get an answer. At 8:00 that night my mother called to say that Fanny wouldn't be troubling me any more. She said that she'd sent all her pictures away and gone to sleep forever.

Months went by before I found the time and strength to open the crates. I was relieved to find a few pictures that my husband and I liked well enough to hang in the den. Then I got the idea of turning the guest room into a mini-museum for Aunt Fanny. I covered the walls with her angelic children, her still lifes and pale landscapes—and found the effect quite pleasant, the whole somewhat greater than the sum of the parts. I brought a car full of pictures to the Hadassah thrift shop and carried off the rest to neighborhood yard sales.

Watching the garage empty lifted some stones from my heart. When I could get to the washing machine without cracking my shins on the sharp edges of the crates, I began to feel as if I had, in spite of myself, fulfilled my responsibility to Aunt Fanny. A pity that I just happened to come out of the door at the moment my neighbor began slashing the pictures she had bought with garden shears.

"What are you doing?' I shrieked, out of control. She looked at me curiously, as if I were the one at fault.

"I only bought them for the frames," she said. "The pictures are pretty bad." As an afterthought, she added, "I hope they're not yours. Sorry if I hurt your feelings."

I assured her they were not mine. She offered to take the other canvases out more carefully and give them to me if I wanted them. I explained that I had too many already. What I could not explain was the pang of remorse or guilt that passed through me. I was finally ready to mourn for Aunt Fanny. I was ready to stop worrying about her children. That was how it was in the real world— the one I lived in, the one that my Aunt Fanny avoided all her life.

Glossary

Afikomen (Heb.)	Pieces of matzah, hidden during the *seder* to be eaten at the end of the meal
Aveirot (Heb.)	Sins
Baal Teshuva (Heb.)	Jewish convert to Judaism
Birkas Hamazon (Heb.)	Grace after meals
Bocher (Yid.)	Young man
Brindze (brinze) (Yid.)	Goat's milk cheese
Bris (Heb.)	Circumcision
Challeh (Yid.)	Braided loaf of bread eaten on Sabbaths and holidays
Davens, davening (Yid.)	Prays, praying
"David, Melekh Yisroel" (Heb.)	"David, King of Israel," a song
Davkenik (Yid.)	One who does things for spite
Dayenu (Heb.)	"It would be enough," from a song in the Passover *Haggadah*
Eidele mentshen (Yid.)	Gentle, refined people
Fluden (Yid.)	Fruit tart
Frum (Yid.)	Pious
Gedenk (Yid.)	Remember
Goy, goyim (Heb.)	Gentile, gentiles
Gruss Gott (Ger.)	Hello, (literally, "Greeting to God")
Had Gadya (Heb.)	Song from the *Haggadah,* ("One Only Kid")
Haggadah, Haggadot (plu.) (Heb. and Aramaic)	Collection of stories, blessings, prayers, and songs read at the Passover *seder*
Halakha (Heb.)	Legal portion of the Talmud

Hamantashen (Yid.)	Three-cornered pastry eaten at Purim
Haroset (Heb.)	Mixture of apples, nuts, ginger, and wine
Hashem (Heb.)	God, literally "The Name"
Hazak (Heb.)	"The strong one"
Hometz (Heb.)	Bread and other foods with leavening forbidden on Passover
Huppa (Heb.)	Wedding canopy
Hutzpah (Yid.)	Nerve
Kaddish (Heb.)	Prayer said for the dead
Kashe (Yid.)	Groats
Kashrut (Heb.)	Dietary laws
Kazatska (Yid.)	Russian dance
Kest (Yid.)	Support of a young bridegroom by the bride's parents
Kiddush (Heb.)	Sanctification, the blessing for wine
Kipa, kippot (Heb.)	Skullcap, caps
Knaidel, Knaidlakh (Yid.)	Dumpling, dumplings
Kosher (Heb.)	Acceptable according to the dietary laws
Lekach (Yid.)	Honey cake
Maariv (Heb.)	Evening prayer
Mamele (Yid.)	Little mother, term of endearment
Mamelige (Yid.)	Corn meal boiled to a firm consistency
Matzah, (matza) (Heb.)	Unleavened bread
Mazel, mazeldik (Heb. and Yid.)	Lucky
Mentsh (Yid.)	A mature person
Meshugas (Yid.)	Madness
Mikveh (mikve) (Heb.)	Ritual bath
Minha (Heb.)	Afternoon prayer
Mitzvah (mitzva), mitzvot, mitzvos (Heb.)	Good deed, good deeds
Moshav Zikanim (Heb.)	Home for the aged
Nahes, shepping nahes, nahes fun kinder (Yid.)	Pleasure, getting pleasure, parental joy in the well-being of their children
Nudnik (Yid.)	A bore, a pest
Pid yon haben (Heb.)	Redempton ceremony for first born son
Rebbe (Yid.)	Teacher
Seder (Heb.)	Passover dinner with reading of Haggadah
Shabbos (Heb.)	Sabbath
Shahris (Heb.)	Morning prayer
Shema (Heb.)	A prayer that begins, "Hear Oh Israel"
Shlugen Kaporus (Heb.)	An atonement ceremony before Yom Kippur, the Day of Atonement
Shtreimel (Yid.)	Large fur hat worn by some Hassidic rabbis

Shul (Yid.)	Synagogue
Strudel	Fruit-filled pastry
Succah (Heb.)	A temporary booth built for the Festival of Tabernacles
Taharat hamishpaha (Heb.)	Rituals to maintain family purity
Taiglakh (Yid.)	Balls of dough coated with honey
Tallis, talleisim (Heb.)	Prayer shawl, prayer shawls
Tehillim (Heb.)	Psalms
Treif (Heb.)	Unacceptable according to dietary laws
Tsepel	Braid
Yarmulke (Yid.)	Skullcap
Yeshiva (Heb.)	Jewish religious school
Yichus (Yid.)	Lineage
Yiddishkeit (Heb.)	Cultural Jewishness
Yorzeit (yortzeit) (Yid.)	Anniversary of death
Zeide (zaydeh) (Yid.)	Grandfather
Zemiros (Heb.)	Songs, song after eating at the table

Sylvia Rothchild is a writer who has published numerous short stories and articles and several books. She is a columnist for the *Jewish Advocate*, a contributing editor to *Present Tense*, and a teacher at Hebrew College. Her books include *Keys to a Magic Door: The Life and Time of I. L. Peretz, Sunshine and Salt, Voices from the Holocaust*, and *A Special Legacy: An Oral History of Soviet Emigres in the United States*. Rothchild won the Jewish Book Award for *Keys to a Magic Door*. Her stories and articles have appeared in *Commentary, Conservative Judaism, Midstream, The Writer, Moment*, and *Hadassah Magazine*.

The typeface for the text is ITC Garamond Book. The display face is ITC Garamond Light Condensed. The book is printed on 55-lb. Glatfelter text paper and is bound in

Manufactured in the United States of America.